CHASING CELESTE

COVEN OF CRYSTALS BOOK ONE

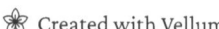 Created with Vellum

To all the women who are told they're 'too much' or 'too loud'.
Keep it up.

CONTENT WARNING

This book contains adult subject matter, such as sexual situations, graphic language and drug use. Please see the author's website for specific triggers.

www.savvyroseauthor.com

PROLOGUE

"We gotta leave...now! She knows about us–she knows everything. If you wanna be with me... leave with me, now."

"She will find us. You know exactly what she is capable of, Anise."

"Then we leave, in the middle of the night...move somewhere far away from here. She will not be able to hex us if she cannot find us."

"Fine. Tonight, we leave."

"Not without my crystal...it's been passed down for generations."

The girl thinks she is clever, but there is none cleverer than I. I have foreseen this day but still chose to marry the man I loved. Love cannot be explained and often isn't ours to keep forever.

I gathered the hair, the blood of her menses, and a jar. Placing the black salt, lemon, and cayenne inside, I glanced around the room that glowed with candlelight, a tiny flicker of a flame letting me know a presence was near—drawing a line of blood with a dagger across my palm, the pain and intention raising my vibration.

The altar that stood before me was covered in offerings to my Iwa, Papa Legba. Cigars, rum, long sashes of red and black. Candle wax dripped down the pewter tapers handed down from my grandmother. I lit the tallest red candle and began the chant that would call him to me.

"I call a hex upon my betrayer and her family–" I take my blood and write her name on parchment, folding it three times and placing it inside the jar, "pain, death, and misfortune will follow you like a shadow, chasing your kin. I call upon him"–I take the small skull covered in sigils from the top shelf and hold it to me. I held them in my mind for a while, watching them together–"Papa Legba...a giving and loyal Iwa,"

The candles around the room danced, and a rough wind stirred my tightly wound hair. A loud crash came from behind me, and the mirror passed down for centuries fractured into thin, black lines. I watched the mirror as black smoke seeped from inside, permeating the air around it and causing me to take a cautious step back.

It was done.

I saw Death himself when I was just a child. His skin a deep dark black, and his face painted white. Large teeth that protruded from a wide grin that terrified me; a laugh that squeezed my insides until I could no longer breathe. The strong scent of cigars soon followed.

When I told my mother that I had seen Death, she dismissed me with a wave of her hand, '*such silly and imaginative things you say, my little Starseed. We are special women, do not worry.*'

She would kiss me in the middle of my forehead each time, gently touching the crystal I always wore around my neck.

The following day, she began to cover all of our mirrors.

Her behavior puzzled me but also interested me.

It didn't help that the neighbors whispered about her odd behaviors, and the rumors soon began.

Her voice was more of an echo now. I can't remember exactly the tone or inflection, but I do remember that she always made me happy. Laughter rang in my head; there was always laughter when I was with her.

*

I surveyed the run-down strip mall in front of me, with few choices for clothes shopping—compared to the other towns that had more than just one grocery store and two gas stations.

The small strip we had in Bakersfield, CA, wasn't anything like the strip in Vegas. The place Jane, my child-hood best friend, and I would spend hours dreaming about out loud together.

Jane went missing a little over two years ago. My brother, Logan, said he thinks she's dead because she wasn't found in the first forty-eight hours or whatever.

I think she just found an opportunity and didn't look back.

Money was hard to come by around here unless you wanted to work for corporate America. Rigorous routine wasn't something I was exactly excited about getting into.

Jane and I were both adopted by our aunts, who we equally hated, and laughed maniacally about seeing their faces if we told them we became strippers in Vegas.

I was on the curvier side, filled out in all the right places, but always a little too big for the 'hot guys'. Jane, on the other hand, had the perfect body for stripping, and I wouldn't put it past her to actually *do it*.

I once worked at *The Gap* but was fired on the spot for telling a middle-aged woman that her nose job looked fake.

I was good at explaining my way out of situations, but not that time. Most people didn't like hearing the truth, but a job would never keep me from telling it–I couldn't do fake.

I pulled into a parking spot near my favorite clothing store called, *Wrecked*.

I needed a new eyebrow ring before the seventy-five-dollar piercing closed up. I had absolutely no business spending that kind of money on a piercing, but I was drunk and trying to impress a girl when I did it.

Unfortunately, the girl was gone in the morning, but the piercing remained.

Pausing at the glass door, I looked at my reflection. Touching thighs, rounded hips, and muscular calves, red hair that touched my waist, ample cleavage with a purple crystal nestled between. Brushing my hair back over my shoulder, I fingered the jewel and remembered my mother's words, '*As long as you wear this, Death will never touch you. He may visit you, but he will never be able to take you*'.

"Hello? Are you going inside or are you just going to stare at your reflection all day?" the woman's voice was full of attitude, hand on her slender hip.

"Maybe I am going to stare at my reflection all day... but please, by all means," I stepped back, presenting my arms towards the door, "don't let me *ruin* your day."

Rolling her eyes, she whipped open the door, leaving me standing outside the shop with half a mind to turn around and leave.

"Awe, you look lost,"

I turned, surprised that I didn't see the man approaching me from the glass's reflection.

"I'm not lost. Who the hell are you?" I shoved my hands into my pockets, waiting for the one-liner that was sure to leave his lips. Why else would a stranger approach a woman?

"Taj, nice to meet you...?" he stretched out his long hand to me, and I stared at his glittered-fake nails for a moment, confused. Taking it, we shook, and I backed up a bit so I could take in this tall man's perfect, dark complexion. He wore a pair of futuristic-looking sunglasses, that wrapped around his face reflecting my face back at me. His head was covered with a deep purple hood attached to a soft looking long-sleeved shirt.

"Celeste," I answered with a smile, enthralled by his high cheekbones and plump lips. His charm clouded my judgement.

Dammit! Why did I give him my real name?

"I'm so very pleased you shared your name with me, Celeste. Did you know that there is a rare crystal called Celestite? Named from the Latin word coelestis, meaning *heavenly or celestial.* Here," His voice was calming, melodic. He handed me a small stone, "a green stone to match your eyes and your name."

Before I even knew what was happening, he was ushering me inside a door covered with silks, jewels, and bells.

"What is this place? I've never seen this place here before, and I am always next d—" Taj holds up a hand to me.

A lava lamp sat behind his chair on a small, hexagon table. The floating lumps of red and pink swirled around one another, reminding me of fire. The space was small and very dimly lit, and the one large window at the front was completely blacked out.

"Come, come. Sit and let us do a card spread for you, Spirit insists. Past, present, and future," he led me to a round table, and I sat in awe at the different colored and textured crystals that lined the wall behind the table.

When he said the word *future*, it was as if he had already seen it, a small smirk playing on his lips.

I didn't want to know anything about my future, not now. Not ever.

"I've gotta go," Turning to the door behind me, I heard him shuffle a deck of cards and...*thunk.* I turned to see his face smiling down over the fallen card.

"One card has simply *jumped* from this deck for you— did you hear it? Let us have a look. *Sit,"* He continued his shuffling, and–*thunk, thunk–* two more cards fell.

I didn't know which was more shocking, the fact that I was scared or that I had considered seeing a reader this morning. My fingers tingled, and I felt my chest grow tight. This was no coincidence; I could feel something prickle at the back of my neck, a whisper.

Do not fear....

I sat down, my curiosity overtaking any sense of dread I had left for today.

Picking up the deck 'jumpers,' he spread the three cards before me, and I gasped.

Our eyes met, and as he flipped over the final card, I noticed it was upside down.

The first card that dropped from the pile was DEATH: a goddess with a horned-skull face and a dark robe.

"Ah, do not fear, the death card can represent a great many things, such as transformation. Or... because this was the card pulled for the past...great suffering and tragedy," His eyes caught mine, and I only nodded slightly, rarely speechless, but stared at the spread of mystery cards in front of me. Three little cards telling a full story about my life, without saying a word.

"Present: The Tower," Dramatically, he covered his

mouth with his hand, sitting back in the chair. His purple and blue shirt shimmered in the dim light as he moved.

"What? What is it?" I leaned forward on the table, eager to know everything about what he saw.

I knew a little about Tarot, but I didn't remember in detail. That was kind of Jane's thing.

I resisted the urge to slam my palm on the table to make him talk.

Calm down, bitch. This could be exactly what you're looking for, answers.

"You have a lot to learn, child. This card can be a bitch, but if you do what you need to, great rewards will follow."

I sit back and cross my arms over my chest, huffing, "I've learned plenty already. I've had enough trauma to fill THREE people's young adult lives."

Continuing to study the cards, he spoke in his melodic tone again, "Do you know anyone who would wish you," he leaned in close to me and whispered, "*ill will?*"

I swallowed.

Memories of my parents fighting trilled inside my ears. Each time they would fight, it would be her name etched into my brain when they were finished.

I shook my head, mostly so he would continue the reading.

He touched the face of the last card upside down. It wasn't until he removed his sunglasses that I realized his eyes were a dark blue. Fake eyelashes and a baby-blue eyeshadow gave his face an ethereal glow, making him appear magical, I stared.

"Future: Six of Swords, reversed,"

I don't know why it was at that moment, Taj's blue

eyes or that stupid card in reverse, but I remembered. I remembered it all.

Stop teaching her to practice magic! You are only making it stronger...

"Unfinished business," I said, staring into an invisible space beside where Taj sat.

He nodded, crooking an eyebrow over me, waiting. "Does this resonate with you? Who comes to mind?"

"No one really... but there were fights over infidelities and...over *witchcraft.*"

"Well, if anyone can help you with unfinished business, it's my friend Moxie." Taj ran his eyes over me, studying me. He stood, walking over to a tall black shelf, opening a wooden box.

"Here. Tell them Taj sent you, they will give you a nice room to stay in," he said, handing me a silver, shimmering card that just said **Alvarez inc.** and had an address on the back.

I turned the cheesy-looking business cards over in my hands, noticing my bare, chipped nails.

I looked up from the card, and Taj was gone, the beads hanging on the back wall moving with little clacks, marking his exit.

There are signs everywhere.

Another saying that Jane frequented, and I only laughed it off.

Never in my twenty-two years had any stroke of luck come knocking on my door, and this little card could be a sign. What was the worst that could happen? Perhaps this was the motivation I needed to get into my car and drive to my mother's hometown.

I might even find Jane; the address is in Vegas.

I could wriggle my way out of any situation by adapting. I was a survivor...bad luck or not.

Quickly leaving the little shop behind, I plugged the address into the cracked screen of my Blackberry. The keys stuck as I typed, but I furiously checked to see how long the trip would be.

Four hours? That's a few tanks of gas.

I needed to get to Aunt Nancy's to see what was left of my parent's life insurance policy.

Fuck it—I was going to New Orleans, but first to Vegas to find Moxie.

CHAPTER

TWO

"You saw a Tarot reader?" Logan asked.

Logan was the only person I had in my hometown, and I damned sure wouldn't let anyone other than blood know my secrets. My brother was there the night of the fire, also the only other survivor. He still accepted me; I knew it was because he had my protection that night.

"Yeah, he just came out of nowhere...like a sign or something" I repeated the words that made me think of Jane, cocking an eyebrow.

He knew just what I meant by the look in my eye. We weren't exactly raised in an open-minded environment. That is probably the reason why we were both so fucked up. Well, that and the fact that our parents died when we were just kids.

"A sign? Damn, sis. I guess you really are starting to change," He said, bumping my shoulder. "You only believed in that stuff when Jane was around, and I like hearing you say that, honestly."

Logan still lived in the reconstruction of our old

house. Insurance covered a good portion of the damages, but the house was half the size it used to be.

He let me spend the night when I needed a place to crash, but that rarely happened after what happened the last time I stayed.

"Come on, Est. I know it's only been two years since Jane went missing, but you two were all about that shit. Astrology, and all of that," We sat outside on the front stoop of the house together. Logan was rolling a joint, and I was trying to work up the nerve to ask my uptight aunt for my savings.

I eyed the rolled paper, licking my lips at the thought of the spark, the pull, and the high once it hit my bloodstream.

Just hearing Jane's name brought feelings back to me that made my head spin–ghostly fingertips fumbling with my bra straps, brushing my nipples. I missed my friend and the benefits that came along with it.

"Maybe you're right. For once," I shoved him playfully with my shoulder, snickering in his direction, a smile pulling at the corners of his mouth. I scrubbed his rough, close shaved head. He reminded me of *Eminem*, a skinny-white boy with a sordid, dark past.

Taking a slow drag, he offered the joint to me, holding out his hand, and I take it eagerly. Bringing it to my lips, I pull and let the smoke fill my lungs and the high prickle my senses. I exhale, eyeing my black car as if it was an old friend.

The day Logan handed me the keys to Moe, he gave me a freedom I never knew I needed. He could have kept the car for himself, but he gave it to me instead. I think he knew I needed it more.

We've seen a lot of things together, Moe and I.

Moe is a 1978 black Lincoln Continental and the only constant in my life besides my brother.

Growing up in California had done little for me, except give me a thick skin and resourceful attitude, but I planned to get as far away from this flattened town as I could. There was just one thing holding me back.

Money.

That was something I hated about money; it had total control over everything you did in your life. Plus, people with money usually held the most power.

I stood from the steps of our childhood home, although it looked much different to me now. This place was a standing tomb, a rude reminder of the tortured deaths served to my parents.

"I'm headed inside for a nap and a shower, then I'm hitting up the food store. You coming with?" I flicked my cigarette butt to the ground beside my boots, kicking up gravel towards Logan's faded, classic Adidas sneakers.

Squinting up at me, he said, "Come on, Celeste. You know I don't ever leave this house."

Turning off the engine of my purring machine, I hopped out into the sweltering heat of the August sun. A white and blue house sat before me on a charming cul-de-sac, straight out of Good Home Magazine.

Gag.

My denim cut-offs felt tight and unbearable. I hitched

my thumbs inside the waist and tugged causing the soft curve of my belly to poke out slightly over the top. These shorts fit like a second skin and hugged every curve in all the right places.

I held my hand up to the green door with the peeling paint and American flag hanging awkwardly off a wreath hook. I knocked gingerly, almost hoping for no one to answer.

Alas, if there were no answer, there would be no money.

"Celeste! Come in. It's hot as Hades out there today," My Aunt Nancy stood in the doorway, waving me inside before I could even say hello.

Nancy graciously took in my brother and me when our parents died. She moved to California from her hometown of New Orleans alongside my mother and her new husband before I was born.

My tattoo sleeve and black eyeliner didn't exactly go with Nancy's country décor. Her 'country chic' theme, with his and her scarecrow-straw dolls, was purposefully placed atop a weathered bench.

The generic quotes that hung on her walls made my skin crawl.

Fake flowers end to end, just as I remembered it.

"Well, at least it looks like you're eating well," Nancy smirked and pinched the small fold above my hip.

I rolled my eyes.

"I'm doing just fine, Nancy. I've been couch surfing for a few months, but I think it's finally time for me to hit the road," I said, plunging my hands into my jean pockets and raising my eyebrows.

Nancy reached out a wrinkled hand that smelled like Crab Tree and Evelyn and stroked my wild red hair.

"Hit the road? And what road would this be?" she pulled and poked at my hair and my tank top as she spoke.

"For now, to find Jane,…but, the goal would be Mom's hometown," The words slid from my mouth, knowing the repercussions that would follow.

Nancy stopped, her eyes growing wide. She stepped back from me, her short, red hair curling around her ears, mocking a sixties hairstyle. She placed her hands on her hips, "Oh, really? And what business do you have down there?"

"I don't know, just crossing one off the bucket list," I lied, too easily.

She stood there for a moment, observing me.

"You've always looked just like Anise, and wanted to be just like your mother. Copying everything she told you to, with excitement. Ethereal and wild, just like the women from our past. If only she just stopped all that hocus pocus nonsense when she was a teen, she could have had an easy life, like mine." She pursed her lips.

"She didn't *want* an easy life. She *told me* about our bloodline, Nancy. Why would anyone turn their back on their own heritage?"

Nancy's eyes narrowed on me, and I knew there was no way I could tolerate another rant about my mother abandoning their religion to go live with a voo-doo practitioner. Every time I saw her, it was tears and regrets all over my mother and 'the life she chose'.

Her justification for the horrific way her sister died.

If she only knew the fire was because of me, then she'd really have a reason to hate me.

My stomach knotted at the thought; I swallowed, pushing it deep down once again.

17

I guess I'm not much for emotions or sentiments. I barely remembered my father, but I do remember them fighting.

I was twelve when it happened. Logan was almost nine, so I guess it had a greater effect on him. His emotional instability sent him straight to drugs. I, on the other hand, learned to cope with things a little differently. I just pretended they weren't even there.

When your parents aren't the ones who raise you, love and affection felt like a foreign language–unfamiliar and strange.

As a teen, I spent most of my time in my room, listening to music and fantasizing about when I could leave this town and have my own adventure. It wasn't long before my insomnia-fueled Google searches led me into a world of Astrology.

My conversations with friends and relatives dipped into that of Astrology, witchcraft, and moon phases. In other words, people said I was strange, and conversations dwindled before they could even begin.

Twelve-year-old girls were mean and turned me into a hateful and defensive little thing. I was always the one left out, whispered about, and avoided.

Eventually, I gave up.

I decided I would save myself the trouble and never give anyone a chance to get that close to me.

Girls would whisper and boys wouldn't look my way. You couple that with having a Right-Winger Evangelical caretaker and I was downright evil, to most.

I shuttered away the hurtful memory, bringing myself back to the reality of Nancy and her *Lilly of the Valley* perfume.

"I need the debit card from the safe. Like, now," My

bluntness often shocked my aunt, leaving my face stinging after a smack from her palm.

Nancy wasn't shocked by my sharp tongue at all today, she was well versed in my sarcasm by now. I didn't live with her anymore, so she couldn't smack me around.

The grandfather clock in the room's corner chimed.

One-*gong,* two-*gong,* three-*gong,* four-*gong*

After the chiming ceased, Nancy's recollection returned, and she looked down at the baby-blue carpeting.

"Yes, the money. Well, I'm not sure what's left. Your brother needed to pay off some... tickets, I think. You know how great he's been doing lately," She looked me over as she said the words.

Logan was predictable, and I...

Well, I was the wild card.

She wouldn't have given him anything if she knew what he liked to spend his money on. My aunt always complained about the junkies that littered the sidewalks downtown; little did she know that her nephew was among them, just not in plain sight.

But hey, ignorance was bliss.

I followed Nancy through the foyer that smelled like stale pot-pourri, to the formal dining room with a picture-perfect barn table, complete with a vase full of daisies.

Nancy rummaged through her leather purse, which looked older than me.

"Here you are, dear. Please be careful with this money. You know this is the last of the savings your father had," Nancy said, handing me the silver and blue bank card I swore I would never need.

I turned it over in my hands, and on the back was the

same white sticker with the four-digit pin. My aunt must have guarded it with her life.

"How much?" I blurted, surprised at my impatience.

I wanted a cigarette badly and drummed my fingers on my arm. I wanted to get the fuck out of her flower-laden black hole.

"Pardon?" Nancy blinked.

"How much?" I repeated, hand on my hip now.

This old bitch had always been thick-headed.

"Well, I'm not sure. Find an ATM, young lady. I don't have all the answers," Nancy's reply was flustered and annoyed.

I needed to leave before I made a scene. I wouldn't want dear old Nancy in tears.

I started toward the front door, shoving the bank card in my back pocket.

I hoped there was at least some cash to get me gas, a hotel room, and a burger.

Shit, I really wanted a burger.

I could feel Nancy at my heels as I opened the heavy door.

"Where do you plan to go? Where will you stay? Please, call me when you get settled," Nancy chased after me in a panic.

I stopped and turned to her.

"Fuck if I know. I barely use my cellphone," I smirked as I walked down the steps to my car.

THREE

I opened the squeaky car door, sunk into the sticky leather seats, and lit a butt.

Taking a deep inhale of my American Spirit light, I looked at the card as if it would give me the answer.

How much??

I had no choice but to drive to the bank in town, next to a *Jack in the Box*.

Slipping on my Aviators, I started the engine, surveying the cookie-cutter houses and children that littered the small driveways.

I pulled away from the tucked-away neighborhood, watching it disappear behind me in the review mirror.

The purple, jeweled skull that hung from it swayed back and forth, a grim reminder that life was, in fact, short.

No regrets.

Droplets of sweat dotted my chest, and I added another cigarette butt to the full ashtray. The wind felt glorious, lapping away the moisture that covered my skin.

The freedom I felt at the wheel was unexplainable, yet it was what I lived for. Even as a teen, I couldn't wait to get behind the wheel. If I got to drive, a quick trip to the grocery store always felt like a small celebration.

My stomach growled. I had about five dollars left to my name, and I wanted to eat first. After that uncomfortable reunion, I deserved to enjoy some air conditioning and greasy french fries.

I safely tucked Moe away into a faraway parking space and sprinted across the fast-food parking lot, eager to enjoy some greasy red meat.

Every situation had an adventure if you could find a way to make it fun. That's what I hated about most people. They were dull and lacked imagination.

I was determined to live my life to the fullest, no questions asked, no regrets behind me.

I opened the glass door, and an icy breeze brushed my face. The young guy behind the counter stared as I walked inside, I smiled but didn't show my teeth.

The magical powers of youth and big tits, something I would never let go to waste. They say fortune favors the young, but I never felt that way. My life felt like a ticking clock, counting down to the next life lost. I still couldn't explain the death of my boyfriend, and the rumors began that I had killed him.

Witch.

I knew the power was there; mother had told me it was within me, passed down from generation to generation. Yet, she warned me to use it carefully after I nearly set my cake on fire when I was just a child.

I almost ruined my seventh birthday, which ended in

another lecture from my father. That was when the fighting started to get out of control.

I became obsessed with the media and absorbed myself into the TV screen until one day I met a kind girl who made me forget who I was.

Jane.

I blinked the memory from my thoughts, focusing on the present moment and the cute attendant behind the counter.

I ordered a soda and a burger and flashed a white smile after he recited the total. I didn't move toward my bag, I simply leaned forward on my elbows. "I just realized I left my wallet at home. I'm all the way across town," I took the soda and bit the straw, looking up at him through my eyelashes. He smiled and blushed slightly. He couldn't have been older than eighteen. "Don't worry about it."

I grabbed the bag, winking at him and swaying my hips to the exit, with just dollar bills left to my name.

I sat in my car silently, but the bank next door taunted me. I inhaled my food, licking my fingertips.

I ran through a bunch of the worst-case scenarios.

One: the money was pitiful, and I was SOL. Two:

there was a small amount to get me a few towns over. Three: there was a shit ton of money and I would have to watch myself to not blow it all in a matter of days.

Either way, it was time to face the music.

Moe hadn't failed me yet and I hoped it would stay that way. After my brother fixed the old Lincoln up, I had never had a problem.

I gently patted the steering wheel, feeling silly at the sentiment.

I rolled down the window and gingerly slid the card into the ATM slot. The machine pinged and beeped as I entered the pin number quickly, preparing myself.

Option number two is not a total disappointment.

What did I really expect? Dad was a mechanic, and Mom never worked a day in her life. She was too busy harvesting her gardens and making moon water. She always had an excuse.

"I have to be here in our home for Logan and Celeste, J. We don't want some stranger raising these precious minds, now do we?"

Her voice was high and lilting, and when she sang to me before bed my eyes would light up. She was everything a Libra encompassed–beauty, high art, and diplomacy.

I took out the maximum amount it would allow, crisp twenties sliding into the cache.

I was resourceful. I would figure out what to do once I got there. I was a Sagittarius, and surely my ruling planet would bring me gifts, abundance, and luck.

I had no address for New Orleans, just the city from the picture I still had of my mother and Etienna, the woman my mother always spoke so fondly of, yet, the person I was told not to ask questions about.

I would just have to start with the address I had in Vegas.

I had a better chance of finding Jane than Etienna at this point.

"GET OUTTA THE WAY!" comes from behind me. Loud honking and angry shouts brought me back to reality and the realization that my mother was no longer here.

I shifted Moe into drive and pulled onto the highway.

System of a Down played through the custom system my dad had put in, and I turned up the volume as far as it would go and screamed along.

Fuck cellphones, fuck mediocre, and fuck these scared people. I was going to live every damn day like it was my last.

If not for me, for Jane. She didn't deserve to die—if she were dead, I would make up for it by doing everything we promised we'd do together.

The grim cloud that followed me would have to catch me first.

I lit another cigarette and floored it, eagerly leaving the small town behind me.

I reached over to the bag on the seat, wrapping my fingers around the small wooden box with the intricate heart pattern scrawled on its side.

It was time to start my journey.

Ashes to ashes, dust to dust, I said to myself as I threw an opened salt packet over my left shoulder.

CHAPTER
FOUR

The sun burned down on the black hood of dependable Moe, reflecting harsh rays of light straight into my emerald, green eyes. My eyes began to ache, and sunglasses could only protect me from so much. I still didn't know why I had migraines that tormented me; the only two remedies I had found were orgasms and weed. The throb would start behind my eyes and work its way out, blurring my line of sight. I leaned forward in my seat and gripped the steering wheel, and blinked a few times, seeing a run-down building on the side of the road. If doctors and *Advil* couldn't help me, the weed could. I felt it would be easy to find if I used my fine tools of persuasion.

The sign in front of me read, "Welcome to Death Valley,"

Pfft.

How perfect.

Running my hand through my tangled hair, I pulled Moe over to the side of the road and into the first parking lot I could find. The sticky heat mixed with my pounding head made the sky blur in front of me.

I put the Lincoln into park and struggled to get the door open. I gave it a heavy shove open with my shoulder and the heavy leather upholstery sticking to my skin. Gripping the edge of the window, I narrowed my eyes to focus on the wide building in front of me.

I never had trouble finding a decent strain of Purple Kush anywhere in Cali. Now that it's legal, walking into a dispensary and sharing what kind of high you were looking for was all it took.

Shielding my eyes from the sun, I struggled to read the gigantic sign.

"PJs Auto" was scrawled in red, and a picture of an antique tow truck was painted next to it.

Probably not the ideal place to find herb, Celeste.

The road had stretched on for miles without one building in sight, but I knew I was somewhere near Utah.

The building looked abandoned, and there was hardly any noise coming from inside when suddenly, a loud piece of machinery blasted just beyond a half-open garage door.

Just as I started asking myself where the hell the entrance to this dump was, a broad-shouldered guy clad in a mechanic's uniform emerged from the garage.

"Can I help you?" His voice boomed, taking me a little by surprise, considering his distance.

"Possibly," I trilled back, hand on my hip and flicking the cigarette butt onto the ground. I marched toward him until I could clearly see his bold, blue eyes and dark blonde hair.

He took me in, pausing at my thighs but quickly redirecting his stare to my face.

"You need some work done on that car?" He called.

"Nah, I'm not here for that."

He smiled, a cheeky crescent dimple appearing to one side of his perfectly high cheekbones. He had nice teeth but his lips were cracked..

I read the name tag sewn onto the filthy, blue uniform.

"Paul" was stitched onto the crooked, white square patch.

I dragged my eyes back up to his face to meet his eyes, leaving mine, and walked slowly down to my cleavage.

I let a smirk touch my glossy lips.

Heat simmered inside my veins, and a pressure low in my belly tightened. I was excited at the thought of a release even with a greasy mechanic.

"Join me in the office," he said, the smile still teetering on the edges of his lips.

The place reeked of gas and oil, making my head pound even harder. My cheeks felt flushed, and I looked around for a vending machine for something to drink.

Paul walked around to the inside of the faded countertop and rested his forearms on top, leaning in close to where I stood on the opposite side.

"What brings a pretty-little-thing like you to a place like this?" he asked, low and gravelly.

The wrinkles at the corners of his eyes showed his age, his skin deeply tanned from living in the middle of a desert.

"And where exactly are we?" I teased, narrowing my green eyes at him, but I smiled. I can be cheeky, too.

"Oh, I see, you're lost. Must be my lucky day," he said, voice lowered as if someone might hear.

Yawn.

He reached over to grab a folded-up map, and I noticed the gold wedding band around his finger.

I raised my eyebrow but let him continue. Maybe this was why Paul was giving me slime ball vibes.

"You're here. Furnace Creek, or Death Valley, as the tourists like to say. You won't find much around here, besides train museums and hotels," he drawled, standing up straight and letting his wandering eyes trace the outline of my hip, biting his lip.

Perhaps Paul was long overdue for attention from a female, regardless of being married. My father accused my mother of cheating daily, but everyone knows the accuser is usually the guilty party. It was the thing they fought about the most, besides our magic.

I reached into my back pocket, pulled out a twenty, and slapped it down onto the counter.

"What's that for? Sex or some body work?" he laughed, amused by his joke.

"Sex? Honey, women don't pay for sex. I'm here for some weed, and if you don't have any, I'm sure you know *someone* who does," I said, hand still on the bill.

He took a deep breath and let it out in a long puff, looking around his desk. He stood and looked outside, past my shoulder, then rested his hand on top of mine.

Instinctively, my other hand reached around into my back pocket, wrapping my fingers around the steel cat ears my brother had made for me.

I glanced down at the feel of warm skin on mine, and a powerful urge to elbow him in his face burned through me, but I resisted.

29

Wrapping his fingers around mine tightly, he pulled my hand toward him. He led me around the countertop and through a doorway to the back of the garage. He looked over my shoulder once again, surveying the parking lot through the opened garage, and turned the doorknob.

I expected him to lead me to a waiting area complete with a water cooler and cheap plastic chairs, but I was wrong.

The room could only be described as a glorified bedroom with an oversized desk in the middle, and a hot plate was in the corner.

I ran my eyes over the disheveled, unmade bed that was tucked into the corner under a dusty window and almost laughed out loud.

Mr. Sophistication took a seat behind his big-boy desk and opened an unseen drawer ever so slowly, as though he was about to grace me with the golden chalice.

Looking up at me under hooded lids, he smirked with a sideways smile. Pulling out a one-hitter as if he was a naughty schoolboy.

"I really appreciate this, but is that it? I'm not about to give you that," I pointed to the folded bill beside him, "for that," I walked over to him and fingered the small pipe with the tip of my nail.

I stood up and crossed my arms over my chest but just slightly under my tits, pushing them up and watching as his eyes darted to them.

Already impatient with this transaction, I rolled my eyes. It wasn't happening as fast as I would like who were confused by tits were as weak as they come.

"You're a feisty one, huh? Where you from?" the mechanic man asked, leaning back into his chair.

I'm ready to blow this popsicle stand, but my head throbbed and I was dizzy. I needed to smoke.

"Pack it up, boss," I said, waiting for a lighter.

He handed me the bowl and a lighter covered in scratches, "How much are you looking for, exactly?" he questioned.

"As much as possible,"

"So, not just a pretty face. What's your name?" he asked, packing the pitiful pipe.

What is with all the questions?

"Tara," I lied.

"I know a guy in Vegas. I travel that way sometimes with the guys, ya know, have some good clean fun," he said, bringing the small glass piece to his mouth and lighting the end, causing it to glow a deep red with the pull of smoke.

Good clean, fun? You mean sniffing strippers and praying for one to go home with you?

Releasing the hit, a puff of smoke rolled my way, and he coughed uncontrollably.

Once he gets his cough under control, he passed the one-hitter to me.

Finally.

I lit the end and took my own long, luxurious deep breath in, pulling the smoky mixture into my lungs and closing my eyes as I held it.

He suddenly interrupted my thoughts by asking me if I liked the taste.

"Yeah, it's... great. Where can I find this Vegas guy?" I asked in between gluttonous inhales.

"He owns a strip club, but I can't remember the name," I passed back the pipe, and Paul looked at the now empty bowl.

"Cool, I'm already headed that way," I said, feeling my body hum with the THC that was now swimming through my bloodstream.

Now, here is where I am different from most people—seeing Death at such a tender age had hardened me, jilted me, darkened my soul.

Whatever you want to call it, masochistic or psychotic, doesn't matter. Doctors said I teetered on the edge of both, only I didn't like meds.

I sat on top of his desk, his face going white as the center of me covered his hand. He didn't pull it away, so I rocked on it a little, feeling the crease of my shorts biting at my slit.

He stood, pulling his hand out from under me aggressively, and grabbed me by the throat with the other. He slammed me onto my back, ripped off my shorts, and threw them on the floor.

He was on me faster than a ravenous and bloodthirsty bear.

He kissed sloppy and haphazardly, devouring my face as if he hadn't had a woman in his life.

I could smell that hunger from a mile away.

I didn't stop him, and I didn't say no. His rough fingers were inside me, and I gasped, closing my eyes and hating myself for enjoying the pleasure it brought me. I pushed against him with my hips, and he thrust back harder, slamming my ass back onto the wooden desk. He fumbled for his zipper, and I couldn't help but cringe.

I looked at the photos that sat on the windowsill behind him as he grabbed a condom out of the desk drawer, little smiling faces of three children, no older than ten.

I felt bile rise in my throat.

It had been too long since I came, and these headaches were getting worse.

I really want to come...

I clutched the sides of the desk and arched my back, trying to ignore the images of him with his children, but the sounds of fighting when my dad would disappear for days filled my ears. Memories of my mother screaming at him about his disappearances began to crawl over my skin—arguments over religion and the past.

This is why you can't let her practice this...it's witchcraft! It's why we fight; this is all because of HER.

Their fights only worsened until my brother and I hid inside closets and cupboards.

The memories itched like a mosquito bite, and I couldn't stand his touch anymore.

He flipped me over onto my belly and pulled my curvy frame toward him, off the edge of the weathered desk. Eagerly, he nudged my legs apart.

I reached behind me, grabbing his hands, "Stop. Fucking stop!"

Only he didn't.

Time seemed to slow, a thick blanket of thoughts suffocated me and I squeezed my eyes shut.

My body stiffened, and I bit back tears that stung my eyes—bitter memories of the nights my brother's friends would get fucked up and dare each other to try and fuck me.

Who can fuck her first? Do you think she'll fight back...or do you think she'll beg for more?

I would never let another man treat me like a prize at a fair. This body wasn't a toy–it was a sacred temple. It didn't matter that I wanted it at first. I had changed my mind, and he wasn't fucking listening.

I reeled back, catching him in the face with my elbow. I heard a crack as he grabbed his face and cursed.

I reached for my cut-offs, slid them on, and grabbed my bag.

"Fuck you." I spit.

The anger inside me built, angry at myself for what I did and angry for the kids who deserved a better father than that piece of shit.

If I had it my way, my mother would have walked away from my father and his searing words—I couldn't count the times I had begged her to leave him.

We can leave when he's at work, momma. We will pack up our special things and disappear.

It was always the same question she gave me each time—

But where would we go?

I didn't look back when I heard the explosion.

I didn't hear the firetrucks until the burning building was in my rear-view mirror.

They say God doesn't give you anything you can't handle, and maybe that's the reason I didn't believe in God.

It was nighttime when I finally made it to Vegas, the place Jane and I always talked about fleeing to together. Only here I was, all alone. Pulling into the city of lights made me feel like a little girl on Christmas Eve.

My mother had always thrown extravagant and over-the-top Christmas parties, forcing my brother and me to dress up in our best clothes. She liked to keep up appearances in our small town and did so by decorating our entire house with the best lights. People would fawn over me in my white and gold party dress, always commenting on my wavy red hair and green eyes. It taught me to accept compliments as love. Those Christmas parties held core memories for me, all the guests pouring their admiration all over me and our lavishly decorated home.

My eyes roamed over the bright Vegas lights that twinkled and flashed, crossing over my pale skin like a kaleidoscope. Vegas felt like just the place to make all my dreams come true, I smiled to myself, and leaned back against Moe's black trunk, lighting up another cigarette and taking a generous inhale. I squinted my eyes a little against the black and red scorpion hanging above the grey-stoned building before me. The lights moved between two different neon tails.

This was the address on the card, a goddamned strip joint.

My entire life, I strived to prove that I didn't need one single person to survive. My wits and good looks had catapulted me into a life less ordinary. Structure and discipline were not words that I was familiar with; chaos and adventure seemed to be the main theme. I was born under an Aries moon and have lived up to those characteristics daily. My personality imitates a finicky fire full of different colors, unpredictable as to where the furls would go.

I had been driving for hours, rarely stopping for anything other than beef jerky and black coffee. My tense body desperately needed a hot shower and a warm bed.

A sleek white limo pulled up to the strip club's entrance, the red and purple lights passing over the hood, then the roof. It created a masterpiece of colorful swirls and stars until the vehicle stopped and the driver exited.

He was tall, broad-shouldered with a shaved head, pretty standard bodyguard type. It made me curious about who would exit on the other side. I watched intently.

A tan, very well-dressed man stepped out and buttoned the bottom of his pin-straight blazer, not a wrinkle in sight. His neck was covered in tattoos, a large scorpion scaling much of the left side. His profile turned my way just for a moment, and his features were soft and feminine yet strongly defined like a sharp knife. Perfect black spirals passed his shoulders, and he turned to smile at his driver. My breath caught. When he smiled tingles shot down to my toes. I swung my ass in the air, leaning over the trunk of my car, and watched.

His teeth were perfect, a diamond grill lining the bottom row. The way he walked—he had that swagger, the kind that made girls forget how to talk.

Can't blame a girl for having a type.

After Mr. Caliente entered the club, I decided there was no better time than now to find Moxie. This may be easier than I thought; as I imagined myself sidling up to the dripping hot playboy I just watched walk into the club, I had the perfect excuse to talk to him.

I leaned into the driver's side mirror and swiped my Tarte lipstick in *Choker Purple*. The dark brown color made my lips pop and my skin look even paler.

Pushing up my tits so they looked as perky as possible, I made my way to the front door of the club.

The bouncer at the door smiled at me with a wide grin. Smiling back, I gave him a wink, and he lets me by without question. I'm sure attractive female customers are scarce in these places.

As expected, the air inside is stale and cloudy with smoke, sweat, and cheap cologne.

I found pleasure in the depravity of dark things. Things that hurt your eyes to look at but had a hard time tearing them away from.

The place was already full of middle-aged suits and young-hungries here to live it up. I took a seat at the stage and ordered myself a Sprite.

The surrounding whispers had already begun. The white, bald guy to my left was elbowing his skinny friend and nodding his head in my direction. I ignored them both and kept my eyes on the stage, the lights suddenly dimmed, and a new tempo filled the club. The beat pumped Rihanna's "Pour it Up" from the speakers in every corner of the large space. My attention was fixed on the stage, and a shadowed silhouette stalked up to the pole in the center, her face hidden until she stepped into the flashing lights, grasping it and hitching her long, lean leg around it.

She had stunning, wide features, from the curve of her eyes to her plump lips. I couldn't force my eyes away even for a second, and I watched her caress and wind her way down the gleaming pole. Her brown eyes remained unfocused until they finally settled on mine. We exchanged gentle grins, and I let my eyes drop to her waist as she spun upside down and sunk to the floor.

"Not an alcohol drinker, I see," The spicy smell of pepper and musk filled my nose, and I turned to the presence now seated beside me.

"Who wants to know?" I asked, not moving my eyes from the Goddess on the stage.

His chuckle was low and condescending.

He sipped his stiff drink, and with a long pause, he finally nodded towards the stage, "You like her?"

"Why, is she your girlfriend?" I finally turned to face him, and it was Mr. Caliente in the flesh. A well defined jaw and dark eyes.

Goddamn.

I would let this guy ruin my life.

Another chuckle, only this time he seemed slightly entertained.

"Do you always answer a question with a question, *baby girl?*" His eyes locked with mine, and I felt my cheeks burn for a moment. Then, I remembered who the fuck I was.

"Baby girl? I would have expected a fresher approach from you, considering that suit looks like it cost more than my car," Cocking an eyebrow, I traveled my eyes up and down the length of his pressed black suit.

"An observant one, I see," A smirk touched the edge of his bowed mouth, a chin dimple appearing as a smile formed. His eyes left mine and briefly assessed my lips, his tongue emerging to wet his bottom lip, meeting my eyes once again.

Oh, this guy is too much. He has got to be the owner, big dick energy left and right.

The large bouncer I had seen at the door earlier walked up to Mr. Caliente and whispered something into his ear that I couldn't quite make out.

With a slight nod, he got up from the squat chair and reached out to take my hand, "Nice chatting with you, miss...,"

"Celeste. You too. Although, I didn't catch your name," he leaned down, my small hand inside his perfectly manicured one, and kissed it.

"I'm Alex. Nice to meet you,"

In an instant, he was gone, and he left me wondering what he so hastily needed to attend to.

I still needed to find Moxie.

I heard a glass break and a waitress cursed, holding her bloody hand. The raven-haired beauty on stage stopped, her chest puffing out and her fists clenched at her sides, staring at the waitress with wide eyes.

Leaping off the stage, she crashed on top of the waitress, screams filling the club. I slapped my hand over my mouth as I watched her being dragged off the waitress by two bouncers, disappearing into the back.

The fuck?

What a shame I didn't get to see the goods, even if it was only a brief glimpse of her juicy peach wrapped in a black G-string.

Deep down, I'd hoped that she would appear again, and perhaps she would kindly offer me a place to stay tonight, I would prefer to sleep between her thighs. Maybe it was for the best, she was obviously unhinged and possibly on drugs.

I headed to the bathroom, maybe if I just splashed some water on my face and brushed my hair, I would feel refreshed enough to drive another few miles to find a hotel room.

My funds were decent, but would it be enough to get me to New Orleans? I pushed the thought aside, unsure at this point what I would do if that was the case.

The bathroom was impressive, considering. There were no flickering lights or graffiti to see in here. In fact, it was tastefully decorated. Vintage boudoir photos of Marilyn and Dita Von Teese hung along the deep red walls. Dressing room lights ran up and down the sides of silver gilded mirrors. Even the bathroom stalls were a gleaming chrome.

I leaned over the sink and filled my hands with cool water, splashing my face until my mascara ran down my cheeks. I cleaned my face with the stowed away makeup wipes and looked in the mirror at my reflection.

Most would say I am even more striking without make-up, but I prefer to hide behind the mask of black paints, eyelashes, and lipstick. My bag was loaded with all the needs of a wandering heart.

Jane was the only one I allowed to see my bed-head and make-up-free face.

Logan told me I obsessed over her too much. He said I liked to think too much about a dead girl.

There was a foot sticking out from under the stall door in the reflection on the mirror, a black stiletto awkwardly bent.

I walked over and knocked loudly on it, "Are you okay in there?" I called into the small crack along the hinges.

A muffled groan was what I got in response. .

Years of living with an addict and alcoholic had taught me all the signs of anyone in danger after substance abuse.

"Do you need help? Can I help you?" I tried to see inside the stall door, but I could only make out dark waves that was plastered to her sweaty face.

I heard her heels scrape against the floor as she dragged her body to the door.

It squeaked open, and I was presented with exactly what I asked for, the stage goddess before my eyes—only she's covered in her own vomit.

"Shit, girl you're hella sauced," My voice is a little above a whisper, but her eyes fluttered open before returning a grunt in response.

I would like to think I'm in pretty good shape. I used to escape my brother's drug benders by going to the gym and lifting. She was dead weight as I lifted her arm around my shoulder and tried helping her up off the floor. I shuffled her over to the sink, the water still running, and grabbed one of the black towels that was stacked in the corner. Trying my best to clean her face and brush her hair back, she looked up at me and smiled, "I like that lip color."

I smiled back, brushing the remaining hair back from her face.

She was even more breathtaking up close; her brown eyes were flecked with gold.

I whispered, "Thank you,"

"MARISELA!! MARISELA!" a loud man with light, curly hair busted in through the bathroom door, stopping quickly as he took us in, both crouched over the sink.

"What is going on? What's happened? Who are you?" His words rolled off his tongue quickly in a Spanish rhythm.

"Vete a la mierda, Xavier! Pestering me just like my cocky twin brother. Dos guisantes en una vaina!" She shouted at him, next to my now ringing ear.

I stepped back as Marisela regained her balance, pushing the stocky dude with the wide mouth to the side and stumbling past him and out the door.

Both of us stood in silence, his face softening as he brought his hands to cover his face with a sigh.

"It's bad enough *I'm the one* who needs to make sure this place doesn't go under with its financial dalliances. I also have to babysit you! Lío borracho," shaking his head as if speaking to the walls, he raised his eyes to the ceiling, saying a prayer in Spanish.

"I was just trying to help her out, I don't even know her name," I packed up my bag, swiping on some mascara and lipstick before I turned to leave.

"Please, let me thank you somehow. Where are you staying? I will have a gift sent to your hotel room," His eyes were soft, and his demeanor had changed.

"Oh, thanks. I haven't found a hotel yet, I just got into town," I walked past him, but he reached out and grabbed me by my elbow.

"Even better, let me get you a room at our hotel a block over," his eyes locked with mine, but he let go of my elbow, muttering an apology, "I'm sorry, things are just... stressful around here lately,"

"Maybe you *can* help me. I'm looking for someone named Moxie."

He raised both his eyebrows, looking a little surprised.

"Moxie? How do you know Moxie...?"

"I don't. I was given this..." I reached into my back pocket, pulling out the business card that Taj had given me.

He took the card from me, turned it over, and then looked back at me.

"I know Moxie, she runs our families' businesses."

"Family business?" I asked, curious.

"Sí, this place"–he opened the door, motioning for me to exit– "obviously, and quite a lot of others." He followed me into the main room, and I stopped, turning to him as I adjusted my bag.

"Can I meet her? I need a job." I said bluntly.

One corner of his mouth perked up, and he nodded.

This was too easy...I wonder what kind of job Moxie had for me. But hey, beggars can't be choosers.

"I'll see if I can set up a meeting with..." he tilted his head towards me, and I stuck my hand out to shake his.

"Celeste."

"Celeste, so nice to meet you."

"If I need to come back here to meet Moxie, I would love to take you up on that hotel room offer." I said, giving him a bright, toothy smile.

"Right next door, I can even have Casper escort you." He motioned to where a bodyguard watched at the door, but the shaved head dude didn't move, only kept chewing his gum loudly.

"Perfect," I said, rubbing the back of my throbbing neck.

Finally, a hot shower and a change of clothes. Maybe even some room service and wine.

SIX

I followed Xavier into the front parlor, where the empty stage stood. Without the lights and music, it just looked... lonely.

"I better get back to work, I'm the only one who hustles for this family, but someone's got to do it," He gently placed a hand on my back and winked, warming the spot he touched.

I desperately wanted to dig out my robe and athletic shorts, tattered as they were. Whether a hundred miles away from home or at a neighbor's house—I could always rely on my robe, my favorite sleepy-time tea, and chick flicks for comfort.

Comfort is what I need right now.

I looked around the room, assuming Xavier would direct me where to go. The thought of staying in a hotel room after driving for so long was all too exciting.

The familiar pain that began at the bottom of my neck started making its way up to the top of my head. I closed my eyes and took a deep breath in as I followed behind Xavier.

A voice filled with rage caused me to turn around, but only enough to witness the altercation with my peripheral.

"No touching. It's that fucking simple," His voice was stern and controlled.

I bit my lip and kept my ear perked toward the altercation.

"That's strike three, Bobby boy. You know how this works, don't come back,"

The gravelly voice held a skinny, older man with a heavy brown beard by his plaid collared shirt, inches from his face. The dude looked like he was about to piss his pants. His face beat red.

"Okay, Casper, okay. I got it; I know. You know me, man! It won't happen again!" he held up his hands in front of his face as if he was expecting a blow.

"Get. The fuck. Out," His words were low, level. A chill ran through me.

Uncurling his fist from the tiny man's shirt very slowly, he returned to his full standing height, and I blinked my eyes about five times.

He was fucking tall. The kind of tallness that terrified women to get into bed with a man of that stature. Which immediately made me think of how big his cock must be.. I snapped my eyes to his face, only to find his gaze on me.

His shoulders were wide and rounded, his chest spreading his shirt tightly across his chest.

Xavier waved him over to us, closing the space between us in seconds.

"Celeste, Casper. Casper, Celeste. Take her to Indigo for a room," Xavier said, clapping his hand onto Casper's back and quickly making an exit.

The air was heavy between us, an awkward silence he

tried to ignore. My heartbeat slowed, and I silently wished I could see how sexy he looked when he smiled, but no such luck; his face was emotionless.

"What did *he* do?" I asked as his cologne hit my nose in a heady cocktail of heat and musk.

I squeezed my legs together.

"I don't know what you're talking about." He quipped, his brown eyes flicking to the front door, watching the skinny dude leave.

"Um, the guy you're staring at," I laughed a little but stopped myself when his face turned back to mine, his face stern yet handsome.

I didn't exactly get a friendly vibe from this guy, but at least he was easy on the eyes. His stare was heavy, making me very aware of my body, and I sized him up in return. He tried not to lose his focus on my eyes but faltered and landed on my lips...but only for a brief second. Jerking his eyes back to mine, he squinted, "I'm not sure how that's *your* business."

I wasn't used to seeing men this good-looking or fit. The guys from home were wiry boys with big dreams of living in Lake Tahoe with their snowboards. Not the kind of guy I would throw myself at.

Walking into The Scorpion's Stinger was like entering a movie set with paid actors. I had watched the movie *La Bamba* on repeat—noting the way Ritchie Valens moved and loved his woman... it awakened every tight coil of desire inside my curious teenaged body. There was a certain swagger to the men I'd met here tonight, a kind of swagger that can't be faked.

My shorts felt uncomfortably tight at that moment, and I shifted my feet, feeling *nervous.*

Nervous? Why is this guy making me nervous?

I cleared my throat and straightened my posture, "I'm a guest at *your* hotel. You shouldn't be rude to a hotel guest, *Casper.*"

I strode to the heavy front doors and pulled them open, met by the setting sun behind the Vegas horizon.

The night had come fast, and I had no plans to make this a permanent situation. If I were going to take up space anywhere, it would be with Etienna, not these hustlers.

I grabbed my keys from my pocket and unlocked my car door, grabbing my bag and pack of cigs. I lit one up and inhaled, hoping the nicotine would curb a little of my frustration.

The cigarette was yanked from my lips, my hand mid-air, "Hey! What the f—"

Casper's tall frame blocked the sunlight, shocking me as I stood straighter against the car.

"I don't have all night. Let's go."

I watched as his muscular back turned on me, and he broke out into a jog to the hotel across the street. His joggers did little to conceal his muscular thighs rubbing together. I watched his shoulders work as he made it to the other side.

I followed behind him, slightly surprised at the comfort of him ordering me around. I didn't like that. He acted like he hated me and didn't even know me.

At least give a girl a chance...

It was hard for me to keep my curiosities to myself; I liked asking questions, and I had a lot of questions for this dude...a very good-looking dude.

I looked in the direction where he walked along the sidewalk, the cars whipping past and bright lights glowing around each building. The city's sky was lined with bright signs and tall hotels. There was small comfort in the constant activity of cars, businesses, and people.

Life.

A white car blasted its bass as they flew by me, the passengers dancing and singing. I smiled, the flash of a happy memory of Jane and me when she first got her license.

As the dark of night descended on the city, the lights and music pulsed all around. Vegas was coming alive, and the feeling of celebration was infectious.

I could get used to this.

The walk was short, and within minutes we were standing in front of a modern hotel with gold accents and old-fashioned filigrees around the doors and windows.

"So...*Casper*—how did you even get a name like that? Is that even your *real* name?" I asked, running a hand through my long hair, catching up to him once we were inside the hotel.

He didn't answer, and I just assumed he didn't hear me.

The girl behind the reception desk couldn't have been older than eighteen. Her black hair was smoothed into a low bun, and her cheekbones were high. I read her name tag, *Bianca.*

Not taking any notice of me standing directly in front of her, she slanted her head slightly and stared at Casper as he stepped up to the desk.

"Hey Cas," She sang, looking up at him from underneath her lashes. He merely nodded in her direction and handed her a black and gold key card. Bianca swiped the card, punching in a few beeps on a pin pad. Handing it back to Casper, she winked.

Confused by their familiar exchange, I wondered if he'd fucked her.

I mean, it *wasn't* my business, but the thought of those two getting it on was *hot*.

I followed behind him, but not before I stole another quick glance back at Bianca, who's now blatantly staring at his ass.

Instead of taking me to the hotel room, he continued walking down the deep crimson hallway and to the hotel restaurant called "Snake Bite,"

I followed him inside, unable to do much else without my room key.

I didn't expect to be going on a date tonight. Especially not with this fine as hell man with a body that looked like a weapon of mass destruction.

"Best burgers around. The tequila Sunrises are tasty, too," He didn't open a menu or hail a waiter, but minutes later, two stacked burgers with every topping imaginable appeared before us. Two tequila sunrises right after.

This must be what it feels like to be wealthy and powerful.

"You can have mine," I said, pushing the drink toward him.

I don't drink, but I don't want to ruin everyone else's fun.

Part of me was irritated with the fact that he had simply made my plans for me. I was ready for a hot shower and some tea. Hopefully, a decent night's sleep.

Clearly, he had other plans.

Never having my father around to put me in my place created a brat inside of me that reared its head from time to time. I refused to let anyone tell me what to do.

And when a man *does* take charge...my panties get all knotted up.

"I'm going to try and say this a nicely as possible...and

I'm only going to tell you once. You're going to go pack up your shit and get as far away from here as possible. You don't want to get mixed up with this family." He didn't look at me when he said the words. Casper didn't touch his food, but I took two large bites, the smell of cayenne working up my hunger again.

"I wasn't planning to stay, so no worries, pal. Not that I need your fucking input," I wiped ketchup from my mouth and stood from the chair, grabbing my hoodie and bag.

He stood as well, his eyes tracing my body as though he was just seeing me for the first time now.

"I'm just trying to do the right thing. You should be warned," He said, throwing down a stack of twenties on the table.

I followed behind him once again, irritated that he wouldn't just give me my fucking room key.

"Can you show me where I'm staying, beefcake? I'd like a shower and some time *alone*," I huffed as he punched the up arrow on the elevator. The doors were gold-framed mirrors, and I stared at our reflections side by side.

Now that's a hot couple.

"What's your *role* here, anyway? A bodyguard with *connections*? Or maybe just a spy or something?" I asked, quirking an eyebrow at him.

I tilted my head slightly, staring into space, imagining what it would feel like to have his thick arm wrapped around my waist—tightly gripping my hip.

"You ask a lot of questions. It's irritating," He mumbled, punching the P button.

"You know what's irritating?" I quipped back, "when someone is rude for no good reason."

51

He tried to stifle a snicker but failed, "*You* are assuming I'm being rude. This is just...how I am."

I snorted, bursting with laughter at his ridiculously vague explanation.

"*Riiiight,*" I said, pulling back my hair into a low bun.

He didn't respond and slid on a pair of sunglasses.

Whatever, I would probably never see this guy again.

I raised my eyebrows at the thought of staying in a penthouse.

Alone.

The awkward silence between us hung in the air, and I let my eyes roam down his long legs and impressive feet. Adidas trainers that looked as white as they did when they came out of the box.

"*Alone* time, huh? I doubt that."

I blushed, my dirty thoughts glowing my cheeks with guilt.

The doors opened into a massive room, a complete apartment on the other side.

"Enjoy your stay. Don't say I didn't warn you," Casper handed me the keys, and from the elevator, his eyes watched mine until the doors closed, and I was finally alone.

❦

The penthouse boasted a jacuzzi tub, wet bar, and fully stocked kitchen.

Fruits of every kind, fresh vegetables, and sushi rolls

in glass containers. The bedding was thick and lush, and I ran my hand down the soft black and grey duvet as I explored the space.

I found vintage and gothic adornment throughout, two skull-hand wine glasses atop a mirrored tray lined with red crystals on the edges. Black candles completed the motif, already burning in the low-lit room.

I marveled at the rich décor.

A note penned with 'We hope we satisfy all your desires. Enjoy your stay,' lay next to an expensive bottle of champagne and rose-shaped dark chocolates.

This was the swankiest place I'd ever stayed in my life.

When I was couch-surfing, the couch usually came with a caring family who wanted to help, but barely enough food and beds for their own, let alone anyone else.

I set down my bag, kicking off my slides and unbuttoning my shorts. Walking to the bathroom, I turned on the water, grabbing a dark purple bath bomb from a glass vase filled with assorted colors. The glass etching said, *Relax.* I tossed it into the tub, reaching over to turn on the jets, and watched it fill.

I couldn't wait to sink into the warm water-- if only there were a way to request someone to join me, maybe Alex or Marisela from the club.

I grinned to myself, trying to imagine what Alex would look like completely nude. Ripped to shreds, I was sure. The glory of wealth ensuring he was in tip-top shape.

I bet he was devilish with that mouth and that tongue...

I slid into the tub, the streams of water tickling my feet, emoting a small "ooh" from me.

I stretched out my legs and sunk beneath the water, immersing my head. When I came back up for air, I wiped my face with my hands and looked around.

The bathroom was bigger than my childhood bedroom. Our family was comfortable in the middle-class rat race; my mother seemed thankful for what we had. I always assumed she grew up poor because she grew up in the south. I also assumed that was why she left.

My thoughts were interrupted by a loud knock at the door. I gasped, startled, reaching for a towel that hung on a hook beside me.

My heart pounded in my chest, I wasn't expecting anyone, and there was no way anyone knew I was staying here.

Wrapping a towel around me and grabbing my cat knuckles, I crept to the door, "Who is it?"

"Alex."

I bit my lip, smiling to myself, and opened the door.

Alex and Marisela, dressed head to toe in formal designer wear, stood before me. Alex smirked a cocky grin, and Marisela's eyes shot me with daggers.

My wet hair dripped onto the carpet.

Well, shit, all my dreams are coming true.

CHAPTER
SEVEN

"Baby girl," The diamond grill that lined his bottom teeth gleamed. He smiled, displaying the row of shining molars. I liked how he looked at me and spoke like he already knew me.

"Come on in, it's your hotel, after all," I stepped aside, and Alex didn't hesitate to enter the door with a cocky authority.

Marisela lingered outside for a moment, but I gave her a shy smile, and she reciprocated.

Alex quickly made his way to the bar, familiar with the room. He poured himself a glass of champagne and sipped, stalking my way.

"You are quite the girl. You stole everyone's eyes away from my stunning sister tonight," he gestured towards Marisela with his glass.

I sat on the bed, neck, and head aching, leaning back on my palms, "She's definitely checks all my boxes," I darted my eyes to her soft brown ones.

I let my focus drift over her face and took my time

trailing down her perfect form and over the tight black dress she wore.

Marisela bit her lip, returning her stare to my long, bare legs.

I casually sat on the bed, leg crossed, my hair brushing over my shoulder and one feathery tendril falling into my left eye. It didn't matter that I only wore a towel; I knew I still looked good.

"Are you just visiting The City of Sin, or are you looking for a more... permanent arrangement?" Alex took a seat beside me, his suit brushing my arm.

Boy, this guy was bold.

Marisela acted uncomfortable; her body language told me she was hiding something. She nervously shuffled her feet.

"Not sure. What you got?" I turned my face away from Marisela and looked at Alex. He was so close I could smell his expensive moisturizer.

A small patch of freckles sprinkled along his nose, his lips full and mauve.

He had one large freckle just below his right eyebrow, giving him a boyish quality.

His phone rang loudly between us, and he abruptly stood from the bed to answer.

"Yeah?" His voice was loud and irritated, and he exited the room in one fluid motion.

Marisela's beauty was that of Selma Hayek mixed with Bridget Bardot. A classic and rare beauty that most people wouldn't even know what to do within its presence.

Alex seemed smart and put together, but there was something off about these two.

Why else would she get so drunk that she choked on

56

her own vomit?

I looked at her again, nervous and chewing on her lip. I patted the bed beside me and smirked, catching her long-lashed eyes.

Marisela sat next to me, she smelled freshly showered- like lilies and vanilla. My belly flip-flopped.

"What's your sign?" She asked bluntly.

Part of me wanted to act coy; I'd never had anyone ask me that before. I was overly cautious when I talked about Astrology to anyone new.

"Sagittarius. You?" Something about her made me want to share, to connect.

"No wonder I like you. I'm a Leo. Fuego mamas," she put her fist out.

I laughed, bumping my fist to hers.

"You sobered up a bit?" I raised my eyebrow and tilted my head, a gesture that often-made people feel empathy.

"Sobered up? Ha! I live a life of... *peligrosa,*" She kicked off her heels and rubbed the soles.

"Criminal?" I asked, knowing a little bit of Spanish, and interested now.

"It's too late for me, I signed a deal with El Diablo," She transitions between Spanish and English; I'd learned to speak a little from my brother's friend, Rodrigo.

I wasn't sure if she meant Alex or someone else.

Just then, Alex swiped a key card, regaining entrance to the room.

That's comforting.

"Come on in, knocking is overrated anyway," making sure the sarcasm in my voice was thick.

I heard Marisela snort.

"Marisela, I think you should thank this beautiful woman for saving your *pathetic* life," Alex stood in front of

57

us and clasped his hands together in front of him. His gold rings flashed with the movement.

Marisela rolled her eyes and looked at me, a warm caramel–light on the outer rim but deepening in color around her pupil.

I licked my lips.

"Thank you. You had... perfect timing," Our eyes stayed locked together for a lingering moment. I thought I saw water well up over her bottom lashes, but she turned too quickly. She looked down at her hands but quickly regained her tough resolve.

It was an act. I could feel it; I had always been good at reading people, a gift and a curse.

What was she hiding?

I slowly inched my hand over to hers, in between our bodies.

Impulsively, I grabbed it and squeezed.

She gently squeezed back.

"Gucci. Now let's talk business. Would you be interested in a job? More accurately, *joining our little family business,"* his smile bordered on psychotic. It was too wide, too calculated.

Marisela suddenly pulled away from my grasp and began rubbing her palm with her thumb.

"Family business? Sounds to me like it won't work. I'm not family," I leaned forward, propping my chin on my hands.

Alex rubbed his hands together like a fat guy ready to devour a prime rib.

"Well, I don't give job offers to just *anyone*. We only collect the rarest crystals. And when we find those crystals? We keep them forever," His psychotic smile was back again, and when he ran a hand thru his corkscrew curls, my belly dropped.

I already knew what he was going to offer me, and I had already decided I wasn't going to stay... this would only be temporary.

After what Casper said, I doubted taking a job with them was a good idea, but...why was he warning me? He didn't know me and told me to pack up shit and go. What kind of *business* was this?

My curiosity was already starting to get the best of me...

What can I say? I liked to go against the grain.

Only, I didn't want something permanent. There was no such thing.

Plus, I couldn't dance for shit.

Who knows what depravity was required to be one of his 'crystals', anyways?

I glanced at Marisela again, but she didn't look at me this time.

"We don't need to talk business right now, you should probably get some rest and eat some food, but come talk to me tomorrow." He adjusted his collar, reached into his pocket, and pulled out a brand-new iPhone still in the box.

"Here. A little gift. Call it a down payment," The box arcs through the air and lands behind Marisela and I on the bed.

I thought about my cracked Blackberry that hadn't been turned on for two days at the bottom of my bag.

I didn't like phones. It made people way too accessible.

Exactly why he was setting me up with this gift.

Alex opened the door and held out his hand to Marisela.

I watched her hesitate.

"Noches, candente," She kissed both of my cheeks, and then they were gone, leaving the sweet smell of flowers and musk behind them.

CHAPTER
EIGHT

The next day, I decided to look inside the operation known as The Scorpion's Stinger.

Alex had invited me anyway, might as well.

There was something more going on in this place; I could feel it in every one of my five senses.

From the first time I entered their heavy doors, the feel of lurking stares and hidden faces not seen with the naked eye gave me chills.

Even today, as I brushed passed the stacked bouncer, every hair on my arm stood at attention.

My skin became electrified, and my fight or flight senses triggered.

With my wits and senses at full strength, I could handle whatever came my way.

I was sure of that.

I had a lot of questions to ask, and Alex wasn't the one I wanted to talk to.

It was time to find Moxie.

Even in the afternoon, the club was packed and smelled like sweat and cheap perfume.

Everything from the bathrooms to the shiny, dark cherrywood stage looked expensive.

A monstrous and elegant chandelier dripping with crystals hung above the tables and illuminated the hand-made Turkish rug that sprawled throughout the room.

I had spent enough time at the San Francisco Art Institute to learn a thing or two about Vintage Décor to see that everything in this place was hand-picked.

Too bad I dropped out before I could even have bragging rights.

No way this was all paid for by bad tippers and drink orders.

I did feel slightly under-dressed, the only clothing I packed being a mixture of band T-shirts and wife beaters.

And jeans, always jeans.

I made a mental note to ask Marisela where I could go shopping for some upgrades.

I sidled up to the bar and ordered myself a whiskey straight.

I needed a bit of liquid courage if I wanted to get any information out of Xavier, and I targeted him since he knew where I could find Moxie.

Still devoid of herb, I drank a lot more than usual.

Maybe it's because my new hangout is a fucking strip club.

The bartender looked younger than me, with a silver hoop in her nose and rainbow hair shaved on the sides.

"Is Xavier here?" I asked, swirling my finger around the rim of my drink.

Rainbow girl's eyes followed my finger, then grabbed a towel and started cleaning a glass, "Who wants to know?" she asked, letting her eyes travel down to my cleavage.

"Celeste. The chick who kept Marisela from choking on her own vomit last night," I said, smiling.

She slammed the cup down on the counter and started pouring in ingredients for what I guessed was an old-fashioned, and said, "In the back, past the bathrooms. I'm guessing you know where those are."

After a tall waitress covered in entirely too much glitter from head to toe grabbed the drink the bartender had poured, rainbow bright picked up a towel and started drying the glasses piled in front of her, still staring at me.

"Thank you," I tipped back the glass and downed the tawny liquid.

It burned all the way down and filled my belly with fire.

I strode to the back of the room, past the bathrooms, and came to a set of black doors labeled '*Private*' at the end of the long hallway.

And Casper was standing in front of it.

Ugh, this cocky asshole again.

Unfazed, I strode up to him with confidence.

"I need to speak with Xavier," I said, fluttering my eyelashes just a little.

He tucked away his phone and crossed his burly arms in front of him. He stood up straighter. He had to be two feet taller than I was...my traitorous nipples tightened under my tank.

I swallowed, but he continued to stare at my frame until I cleared my throat.

His face blank, he said, "I told you to go home."

He had a baby face, dimples, and soft brown eyes with curls that barely brushed his shoulders.

But damn, his body was lean.

I watched his face as he ground his teeth, causing the firm muscles of his jaw to work around his rigid jawline.

Damn, why was that so damn hot?

"Glutton for punishment, I see," he shifted slightly and cocked his eyebrow.

"Guess so. I'm also not a very good listener," I shrugged my shoulders just for good measure, hoping to push him a little more.

"I can tell," He said, his eyes giving me a brief once-over before he turned, cracking the door.

I heard him murmur a few words into the room, but he returned to face me and gave me a small nod.

"Thanks," I tried to squeeze in between him and the doorframe, but his broad chest blocked most of it, and he stood there, unmoving.

Fucking dick.

I squeezed my body past his. I wasn't about to let this guy intimidate me.

Our bodies pressed together as I wiggle my ass against his crotch to get by. I think I heard him growl, but before I could look back at him his eyes, the door shut behind me.

"Hello Celeste. I've heard so much about you already," a scantily dressed middle-aged woman sat at the over-sized office desk.

Confused, I looked around the room, "I'm sorry- I thought this was Xavier's office,"

"Xavier?" she asked, "Xavier is *one* of my sons. I'm Moxie," She placed her hand on the desktop, clicking her red fingernails a few times.

"Oh- I just assumed a man—"

She laughed and dismissed my comment before I

64

could even finish, with a wave of her hand, "It's fine, I understand. I don't answer to *any* man, darling."

"This place is...dope. You own any others?" I asked, plopping down into the over-stuffed leather chair in front of the desk.

The room was lined with glass shelves containing spirits of every kind. The lighting was expertly woven through each unit, and flat tv screens stretched out on the top of each shelf. Each one was a security camera for the private rooms and parking lots.

The antique desk she sat at dominated the room. It housed three computer monitors and multiple ledgers, and a pen laid abandoned on top of one of them.

"Curious creature, aren't you? I knew you were different the minute you stepped into this place," she leaned back in the winged back chair, referring to one of the screens atop the desk. She wore a red silk robe, which opened slightly to reveal a black lace lingerie set, nothing else. Strands of pearls dripped down her cleavage, and gems of all kinds laced her wrists.

I laughed awkwardly and shrugged my shoulders, "I'm not from here, if that's what you mean."

"We own a few different places. But what I'd give to see what kind of money you would bring here," she grinned, reminding me of Alex and his panty-melting smile.

We.

"I don't know about that...but I would like to meet these 'crystals' as Alex calls them before I accept any position. *If, I do.*" I reclined a bit and propped my foot against the edge of the desk.

Moxie eyed the intrusion but chooses to ignore it.

"Ah, you've heard about the ladies. There are only

three right now. Unfortunately, one went missing," She steepled her hands and fixed her eyes on me.

Keep her talking...

"Missing? Why would anyone want to take a stripper?" my voice teased.

"They are not just *strippers*. And unless you plan to take Alex up on his offer... that's all the information you get currently, sweetheart." Now she was smiling.

Moxie seemed calm and grounded–an earth sign, I was sure of it. But the way she spoke was calculated and manipulative.

I had studied birth charts since I was old enough to read. The fact that our birth was reflected in the sky by the planets and constellations was the most fascinating information I had ever encountered. After my mother and father passed, I was hungry for explanations. Learning about my own chart gave me clarity about why I behaved the way I did, and it was the very reason for what little self-confidence I had gained.

You could tell a little from their sun sign but much more if you had the complete map of planets in the sky at the time of a person's birth.

"I get it—business comes first, then pleasure. Alex on the other hand, I get the feeling he does a lot of thinking with his cock," my face remained serious, and Moxie didn't look shocked. Then, she burst out with a laugh, coughing at the end.

"Not a bad observation, cariño. I would say that was a correct assumption," she straightened her pearls and grabbed a pen.

"What can I say, I'm extremely observant," I smiled, crossing my legs.

Moxie dragged her eyes down my body and back up to my face.

Smiling but never leaving my eyes, she said, "We have already had some...*inquiries.*"

"Inquiries?" I dragged my thumb along the cat knuckles in my pocket, a habit I had after the first time I'd used it.

"Mm, girls probably take one look at those tits and hate you instantly. And when you lay back on a bed, all curved hips and round ass—aye, that nipped waist. All of it falling into its perfect place, laid out like a feast," her fingers trailed over her lips, and she took in my body once again as though I was purposely on display for her eyes.

Goosebumps bloomed over my skin as her sultry gaze lingered.

"What do you say, Celeste?" she already held out a packet of papers and a pen, smiling at me as if I wasn't about to make a deal with the devil.

"How's the money?" I asked, more than intrigued now. If I wanted to bolt, I would. What were they going to do? Send Casper after me?

"You wouldn't know what to do with it all," she smiled, stretching the pen out further.

I grinned, taking the papers and pen from her and quickly looking it over, paying no attention to the fine print.

She busied herself with a mirror and touched up her makeup, combing her fingers through her short, black bob, acting as if my answer didn't mean shit to her.

This family inflamed my curiosity; I wanted to know more.

What was it about secrets that I liked so much? It was

altogether exciting, illicit, and...fun. Deep down, having this black secret inside of me; was exhilarating.

I've killed people, and I'm betting they have too. Maybe this is my chance to fit in somewhere...

There were bad people all over this world. Perhaps by killing one, I had saved more.

For the sake of research, I lied. I wanted to talk to these girls myself. "I think we can negotiate something,"

NON-DISCLOSURE AGREEMENT was printed across the top of the packet.

Not giving it a second thought, I signed with excitement.

"Beautiful, now we can talk."

She handed me my copy of the agreement, but I folded it up and tucked it into my bag, knowing I would never look at it again.

Bring on the secrets.

"Follow me," Moxie stood up from the leather desk chair, leading me up a flight of stairs discreetly placed behind a curtain to the left of the office.

As we ascended the seemingly never-ending staircase, I noticed sconces with lit candles lining the slanted walls all the way to the top. The walls were a crimson red, and the lilting voice of Grace Potter greeted my ears.

As I stepped onto the landing, the room opened in front of me, with not a wall in sight. It must have covered the entire top floor of The Stinger. My nostrils filled with the familiar scent of Dragon's Blood incense, and I almost gasped as I took in the ethereal décor.

Tapestries and silk fabrics of jewel tones covered the walls and ceilings, draping down and creating a tent-like effect. Large pillows littered the floor, and rugs covered the lacquered hardwood in every shape and size.

Plants hung along the windows, and fountains of all sizes hid in every corner.

The far side of the loft had floor-to-ceiling windows overlooking the strip. A raised jacuzzi tub was almost directly in front of them, plush chaise lounge chairs surrounding the tiled dream.

"Those windows open up collectively, it's like taking a bath in the fresh air," A female's voice snapped my eyes away from the tub. Looking in the direction of the voice, I noticed a thin blonde with waist-length hair trailing her.

"Damn Mox, give us a little-heads up next time, huh? We could have been eating ice cream in our underwear," another voice came from behind me, walking down a small hallway in just an oversized T-shirt and knee-high fishnets.

Each girl was more stunning than the next, with perfect skin and shiny hair.

"This is Celeste, she is thinking about being our fourth," Moxie shoved her hands in her robe pockets, her brows raised as she looked at each girl.

Fourth?

Just as the thought came and went, another girl stood from the large U-shaped couch in the corner of the room.

"Already? Way to give someone time to grieve their dead fucking friend," The girl was light-skinned and had eyes that were lined with black. She stared at me as she approached us. She held a bowl and stabbed a piece of chicken, bringing it to her mouth, and chewed it slowly.

"I can go if this is a bad time. I hate being interrupted when I'm eating," I held up my hands and then shoved them in my back pockets.

Maybe this wasn't such a good idea...

"It's all good. I like your arm cuff," she walked by me slowly and eyed me as she passed. Placing her bowl into the kitchen sink, she made her way back to us again, returning to the couch and tucking her legs under herself.

The other two girls joined her. To show my comradery, I did as well.

"I've got to get back to the house. Grab Celeste water. All good, ladies?" Moxie's eagerness to leave made me feel like I was being left to the wolves.

"We're good," The three said in unison.

Tight crew.

"Dragon's Blood. That's a great cleansing tool," my voice wavered. I wondered if they would even know what I was talking about.

I was never nervous around people, and it seemed like I was a tight ball of nerves since I got here.

"Right...everyone knows that Hun," The girl with the fishnets sloshed around some water in a mason jar and drank, keeping her eyes on me.

"That's Jade," she pointed at mason-jar-chick, "Sapph," she nods in the direction of the blonde girl with opaque, grey eyes, "and I'm Ruby. But you can call me Queen," she laughed while holding eye contact with me.

She was joking, right?

I nearly spit out my water at her bold declaration; it dribbled down my chin as I snorted loudly. I wiped my mouth and responded, "Queen? You've got to be a Leo. It's practically written all over that silk pajama set," I leaned forward in my seat, resting my arms on my knees.

Her face remained motionless; her black hair looked silky and smooth. She almost looked like a Bratz doll if I squinted hard enough.

"All water, sweetie," She twisted out, giving me a once over and then taking in a breath. "And you look like a fire sign. Loose and careless,"

71

Jade laughed out loud, almost spitting out her water.

"That's funny. Alex said the same thing about you," I sat back and pulled out my cigarettes, lighting the end and taking a pull.

"He didn't say that. He wouldn't say a word about me to a *stranger*," she maintained her controlled demeanor, but her eyes shot daggers at me.

"He would, and he did. I knew all your names before I came here tonight."

"Alex told you about us? That guy's got a mouth on him. I swear, that he could make dental surgery sound sexy. If he wasn't such a player, I would totally hit that," Sapph made a feeble attempt at breaking the tension that was crackling between Ruby and me.

They all chuckled at this, but I stifled mine.

"So, what did he say?" Ruby interjected, and it was then that I noticed her multiple piercings.

Ruby was intimidating.

"Not a lot, but it's safe to say I'm very curious what your jobs are. Did he say anything about me?" I asked, helping myself to the popcorn on the glass coffee table in front of us.

"Just that you were 'that hot chick with the red hair and bangin' body'" Jade said, but I could sense the passive aggression in her voice.

"Oh." I said, smiling inside, "So what do you guys *do?*"

They each looked to one another, acting like they were unsure if anyone should speak up. Ruby was all too eager to fill me in, though.

"We're escorts. High-end escorts. All cleverly hidden under a rare-crystal front. Most businessmen wouldn't want to explain a bill for a hooker to their wives. That's

72

where Moxie comes in," Ruby picked a piece of popcorn from the same bowl and sat back.

"Damn. I thought that was illegal?" I squirmed at the thought of all the dead bodies I would leave behind...

"We don't *all* sleep with our clients," Jade lounged lazily, dropping a piece of popcorn into her mouth. She chewed and looked over at Ruby, eyebrows raised.

"Yeah, some of us try to marry them," Sapph lilted and jumped up from the couch, flitting off to light a few candles on the fireplace mantle. She reminded me of a fairy with the way she walked, light steps on her tiptoes.

"Not illegal in Nevada. And this isn't some street corner, red. You need to be a paying member, sign papers."

"See a doctor," One of them snorts, but I can't tell which one.

They laughed together, and I felt the energy in the room shift. Ruby's eyes remained on me, most likely waiting for my reaction.

My inner morbid demons stirred. Not only did it sound taboo and dark, but it sounded *exclusive.*

A phone rang, and Ruby pulled a thin iPhone from her pajama pants.

I tried not to listen, but hey, survival, right?

"It's not a big deal; I can be there by the morning If I take the Jet.

Yeah. It's fine, Moxie, really. It will give me an excuse to chill with Alex. Okay, perfect," She clicked the off button, "Time to make that paper," Ruby called and nodded to the others, stalking down the hallway and disappearing.

I wanted to press further and ask more questions, but my pride wouldn't let me.

I felt there was more to this story than what I had witnessed thus far. It was as though I had fallen into the cavity of a giant machine, witnessing the gears behind the operation firsthand- yet involuntarily.

I needed to know more but I decided to wait until later when I gained someone's trust.

I didn't sleep well that night. I tossed and turned for what felt like hours. Something would stir me from sleep, and my body would jerk. Every time I nodded off, my mother would appear behind my lids. Her smiling face and sing-song voice floated through my ears. But then a wide, dark face with stark contrasted white eyes came closer to my view, laughing all the while, joyful but incredulous laughter.

Death. He would never let me be.

I was drenched in sweat; this had happened two nights in a row.

If I were smart, I would steer clear of Alex and his kissable lips. It never ended the way I wanted it to, and I needed to start believing that.

I powered up the cell phone he had given me, too excited to have a fancy phone to think of the tracking smartphones had now.

There was already a text message waiting.

ALEX: *you ready, baby girl? Welcome to the family.*

I rolled my eyes and tossed the phone onto the bed.

I needed to get out of this room and figure out a way to make some fast cash and then slip out unnoticed.

I rifled through my bag but came up short, nothing but cutoffs and tees.

I needed a killer dress.

I grabbed the *Iphone* and sent a quick text to Alex, asking him for Marisela's number. He must always have his phone in his hands because he responded almost instantly. I grinned, thinking that maybe he'd been waiting for my text.

I sent Marisela a text asking if she was up for some shopping and gossip. Clothing and cocktails were two guaranteed ways to a woman's heart.

I wandered through the suite, touching the fabrics of the furniture and pillows, imagining this was my home. As much as I wanted my travels to be endless, I also desired something–anything that I could keep forever.

Nothing lasted very long in my life, and my cursed luck or astounding self-sabotaging skills were to blame.

I pushed the thought aside and sat, feeling the silence take hold and threaten to suffocate my breathing. Stillness and quiet terrified me; it was the killer of youth and adventure. If I kept moving, Death couldn't catch me.

That's what I told myself anyways.

I fingered the only photo I had of my mother. It was stained and faded; she looked to be about my age–beaming and full of happiness. I turned it over and re-read the same words I had memorized since I was a child, *Me and Etienna- New Orleans, 1982.*

It was all I had left of her. Aunt Nancy didn't keep anything; she got rid of it all. She didn't believe in keeping things from the deceased. It was all nothing but bitter memories. Nancy's cold demeanor was disturbing

CHASING CELESTE

at times, but it was the only way she knew how to cope, along with everything needing to be spotless. Nancy and my mother were both raised catholic, but my mother ran away after years of strict beliefs.

I often wondered what life would have been like if she was still here, still my mom. When I thought of her, I thought of wind chimes, flowers woven through my hair, and laughing at the shapes of clouds in the sky—the smell of lavender and her calm embrace.

The phone chimed, bringing me back to my current reality.

It was Marisela, overly excited by my invite.

I looked down at the text:

MARISELA: Shopping? How about a road trip instead?

Marisela clearly had plans of her own, in true Leo the lion fashion. Loud and proud of who she was.

I loved that about her.

CHAPTER
ELEVEN

The walk to The Scorpion's Stingers was quick, and when I got to the parking lot, Marisela was standing beside an Escalade, the girls from the loft lined up beside her.

"Noches, amor," Marisela greeted me with two deft kisses on each of my cheeks. J'adore perfume filled my nostrils, and I smiled, romanced by her flowery smells.

She looked and acted much better tonight, but her cheeks looked hallowed and her skin a little discolored.

"I love that perfume. My friend used to wear it," I took in her tall, taut body. She wore high-waisted distressed jeans, a gold chain around her belly, and a crop top with "Lioness" on it.

I knew exactly what she had planned for the evening just by her outfit.

"So...this is what you're wearing?" She looked me over from head to toe, pausing at my ripped Def Leopard T-shirt.

"I was just about to ask if you have something I can wear. Dressing up isn't exactly my strength. Make-up and hair though- I gotchu," I tucked a strand of hair behind my ear, the rare feeling of nervousness that she and her cocky, handsome brother seemed to pull out of me.

"Hmm, I can try and think of something…Sapph, do you have anything that Celeste can wear? I know you carry an extra wardrobe around with you in your bag," She elbowed Sapph, and she nodded,

pushing her waist length hair behind her and swung the long strap of her boho bag around to the front, rifling around the inside.

"Here, this was just an extra dress I packed in case Marisela puked all over herself again." Sapph handed me a shimmering black dress with a lace halter. It was stunning.

"This is way too small; it will never fit me," I said, handing it back to her.

"It's not *mine*. It's one of those one size fits most kind of dresses," she tugged on the fabric, "see, stretchy, hugs you in all the right places."

"Sorry about the vomit joke, Mar." Sapph laughed, a light inside her eyes that warmed me.

Marisela narrowed her brows at Sapph and elbowed her gently, causing Saphh to grab my arm so she wouldn't topple over.

"Ohmygosh, I'm so sorry," She placed two hands on both of my forearms, steadying herself, but her eyes locked with mine. At first, she simply looked shocked. But time seemed to stop when she grabbed me, her fall happening in slow motion.

Crashing to the ground, she landed at my feet on her hands and knees. For a full minute, she stayed there like that, all the others looking at her, horrified.

I bent down to help her stand again, but she shoved

me off, looking deeply into my eyes, each pupil darting to the other.

"How? How do you carry that pain around all the time?" She steadied herself as she stood, the two other girls wrapping their arms around her and murmuring questions into her ears.

With the dress in my hands, I turned and headed back to the hotel room to change.

The murmurs continued behind me, but I didn't give a shit what they were saying. I would be gone soon, and I wouldn't have to deal with them.

How did she know?

"Where are you going, Candente? Just change in the car! I want to leave!" Marisela called behind me, and I stopped.

Seriously?

"Are you too shy?" she pushed.

"No." I quipped.

I walked to the Escalade, its black rims and lift kit made it look slightly intimidating. Casper sat in the driver's seat, the length of his arm stretching out of the window.

"Let's go ladies. I don't want any trouble from anyone of you tonight. I'm serious," he pointed at Marisela, and she simply shrugged.

"I don't know what you're talking about, but tonight...tonight I finally get to show them all! Everyone who said I couldn't make it as a singer,"

Sapph playfully shoved Marisela towards the SUV, and Marisela emphatically raised her hands in the air and started to belt out *I Could Fall in Love.*

"The next Selena! Ow, ow!" Jade hooted.

They both piled into the SUV one after another. Marisela and Sapph, followed quietly by Jade.

.

I let my eyes flicker to Casper for only a moment; his hand rested on the rearview mirror, tapping to an invisible beat.

I quickly climbed into the back, disrobing while keeping my eyes on Casper with his shades on.

"Don't look." I said as I pulled the dress on over my head.

"Wouldn't dream of it." He said, low.

The traitorous pulse between my legs began to thrum- the excitement of a night out mixing with these attractive people. Once I had liquor in my system, I would loosen up.

I deserved to let loose.

Finally changed, I was surprised at the way the stretchy-silk fabric of the black dress hugged my body. My legs bare to the thigh, no panties.

"All set?" Mar asked, letting her eyes roam over my new outfit.

I nodded while the others buckled in.

"You look like you're on another planet," Ruby waved her hand in front of my face, looking irritated that she had to put in the extra effort to talk to me.

"Lots on my mind, that's all," I watched her push a lollipop into her mouth, her full lips wrapping around it. She popped it out and licked her lips, pointing the pink pop toward Casper. "I see you stealing looks at him," she took another long suck, "Careful, the last girl he was crushing on ended up missing."

She turned her back to me, chatting with Marisela, leaving me squished uncomfortably against the door.

It was odd the way half of this crew wanted me here, and the other half warned me to stay away.

I didn't know what the fuck Ruby's issue with me was, but my temper had its limits.

About one hour and two bottles of champagne later, we pulled into a crowded parking lot with a blazing white neon sign that read, 'Venom'. It was directly off the highway, with flashing signs that offered dollar drinks and a 'females only' disclaimer.

A safe place to get shit-faced with your friends. Sounds like genius marketing.

As we entered the club's upper floor, we were stopped by two muscled bouncers with black suits and silver ties.

"Females only, bro," the shorter of the two stepped in front of Casper.

Marisela's perfume filled my nose as she confidently stepped up to him. "He's with me, Kev. Don't be a prick,"

She almost stood as tall as him in her shiny heels, but he shook his head in response.

"Listen, *bro,* I don't want to be here, could give a fuck less about who's in there. Consider it an extra pair of eyes to watch out for predators" His voice was low and firm.

"Fellas, fellas. Please, let Casper and Marisela pass. We should be most grateful for her mere presence here. Come."

The voice came from a slender, broad-shouldered man who looked overly preened. Close shaved silver beard and perfect matching crew cut. A large chunk of his ear was missing, leaving me wondering what had caused such a wound.

His suit was a deep green, and the laser lights on the dance floor below illuminated the sharp features of his face.

"Marisela, you look stunning, as always. Are you ready for your performance?" He wrapped his lithe fingers around her slender waist, and I caught Casper eyeing his hand.

"Domenico, always such a gentleman," She purred into his neck.

"There is a VIP area there," He motioned to a curtained-off section at the bottom of the circular stairs with a pale hand.

His eyes trailed me as we walked, and the music beat softly, the club loud and crowded.

As advertised, it was all females. Marisela began to dance to the beat of *Waves by Mr. Probz* and followed Domenico down the staircase.

Each girl perched themselves above the dance floor on the balcony, looking over the gyrating bodies below.

They collectively emitted confidence in themselves that could only come with age, knowledge, and experience.

I had a feeling each one had seen some things. It just made me wonder how long each one had lived here. I could only imagine the things they had seen growing up in Las Vegas. I didn't grow up in the city, but more in a suburban neighborhood. City life moved faster, and it made my head spin at the thought.

My childhood had been filled with fields and meadows, fireflies and gardens...nothing like it was here.

My mother had fussed over plants, moon phases, and the chemicals in boxed foods, a whole different world from this one.

I leaned in next to Sapph, her light complexion looking other-worldly against the silver glittered highlighter she wore on her cheeks.

"Did you grow up here?" I asked her, watching as two short-haired women kissed and groped each other at the bottom of the stairs.

"Yeah, I was adopted when I was six. The foster system sucks, but I was thankful to stay in the same place. My mother was from here, my father was a bookie on the run. I'm not even sure who the guy is," She picked at her nail polish as she spoke.

I already liked Sapph. She was chill, calm. She seemed like the reasonable one. The friend you call when you're going through a rough patch.

"You?"

"My parents died when I was young. A freak accident. My stick-in-the-mud aunt raised me. So, I feel you there. It's like sometimes I can remember something simple about them, but other times it's like I barely knew them at all."

Casper loomed closely behind us, his veined hands clenching and unclenching, on the offensive.

Ruby led the way down the stairs to the lower floor. Like a row of ducklings, each girl followed behind the next.

I did as well, taking my place behind Sapph.

The VIP area was a small alcove, surrounded by candles and sheer-white curtains. As soon as we sat, a server appeared dressed head to toe in black and silver. She wore gloves with jewels on her fingers. Popping a bottle of tequila, she poured a tray of shots, asking if we wanted any food tonight.

Jade stretched out the length of her body along the circle of seating and pulled out her phone. Sapph and Ruby did a couple of shots, Ruby offering one to me. I shook my head no but asked the waitress for an Irish whiskey on the rocks.

Casper stood outside the room on watch, arms crossed. I got the feeling he did this often. Following The Crystals around and protecting them at all costs.

Why though? It didn't seem as though these girls were in any danger.

It made me wonder if they had also signed contracts, and if they had, were they all required to agree to the same things?

Secrets tended to solidify relationships, so perhaps they knew more about the Alvarez family and their skeletons.

Closeted skeletons were something everyone had. It just took someone with the courage to bring them into the light.

"Hey Cas, can you grab my sweater from the SUV? It's freezing in here," Sapph poked her head through the curtains and wrapped her hand around his forearm.

The way Casper catered to these girls and how they seemed to trust him—pulled at my heart strings.

I wanted to belong, to be protected.

Was I really considering staying and getting involved with this crew?

I didn't sound like myself; I didn't want to stay here and work for this family that I knew nothing about.

One thing I did know for sure was that I was running out of money.

Fast.

"Shot?" Ruby held a thin glass to my face again with a wide grin, only this time I took it, feeling the weight of my decision pressing down on me.

I grabbed it and clinked the glass against hers. Her eyes never left mine, and when she sat back in her seat, she asked, "What's your deal, anyways? You just show up to Vegas all by yourself? Sounds sus to me," She poured herself another shot and adjusted her fur coat.

A little dramatic for summer in the desert.

"I like the *thrill,*" I sneered.

She laughed at this, and I noticed Casper listening as he returned with Sapph's sweater.

"What's your sign again, Ruby?"

This question usually ushered a defensive response from most people- one, for not knowing, or two, they believed astrology to be nonsense, witchcraft. I doubted the latter. It always gave me insight into someone instantly.

"Scorpio. Spare me your stories and theories about Scorpios; I've heard them all. That's what happens when your boss is an Astrologist," She sipped her shot instead of tossing it back.

"Mysterious, observant, transformative–deep water. Sounds like admirable qualities to me," I said, smiling.

She offered me a weak grin in return, "Truth."

She poured us both two more shots and raised her in

the air.

"Moxie is an Astrologist? Damn, that's cool. I know a bit about birth charts but not Tarot, although I'd love to learn more."

I watched as Casper handed Sapph her sweater, his dimple appearing as he gave her a sweet smile. I felt a small tug at the bottom of my stomach. He caught my eye, and the smile was wiped from his face. Taking his post by the door once again, I imagined what it would feel like to be the one responsible for his smile.

"Tarot?" She laughed, incredulous and mocking.

"What's wrong with Tarot?" I asked, watching her eyes scan the room as if she was looking for someone.

"Nothing. I had a housekeeper back in New York when I lived with my father, who taught me all about that—along with Santeria." She said, adjusting her nose ring.

"Santeria? What's that?"

We were interrupted by Sapph announcing that Marisela would be taking the stage.

"Holy shit, Mar is performing?" I got up from my seat, ready to rush the stage and support my new friend, but Sapph sat back down beside Ruby.

"I hate crowds, the bodies bumping into me and the loud music. I'm going to stay here and watch," Sapph wrapped her sweater around her shoulders and tucked her legs underneath her.

The VIP area held a small view of the modest stage; it was in our eye line but on the other side of the dance floor.

In the short time I had known Mar, I knew this was her dream—and I couldn't wait to watch the show.

CHAPTER
TWELVE

Marisela belted out the songs like a champion, and the entire club clapped and cheered. Suddenly she doubled over, clutching her stomach at the end of her set.

I watched, horrified, as she vomited, sweat sticking to her pale face.

Her red lipstick was smudged as she was helped off the stage, and when we made our way over to her, I grabbed her hand and brushed my thumb over her bottom lip, wiping away the smeared lipstick.

My thoughts veered back to the first night I had seen her on stage and how she was carried off in a fit of rage.

Maybe the girl has a drug problem, and she's trying to clean up her act.

She smiled, but she looked sick.

"What's the matter?" I whispered

She shook her head, her hand over her mouth.

"You did great—don't worry about it, you were just nervous," I walked her back to the VIP area, her chest heaving while she motioned to Casper for water.

I couldn't help but think back to the night I first met her and how sick she was then after attacking the waitress.

We sat together while the other girls were occupied by two very tastefully dressed businessmen, both wearing the same black and silver attire as the waitresses.

Casper handed Marisela a water bottle, sitting down beside us and leaning back, "I already knew you needed water, sis," He winked, and Marisela thanked him.

"I thought they didn't allow men here?" I whispered into Marisela's ear.

"They don't. Those are Domenico's business partners. This club is *extremely exclusive,*" She whispered back, watching as Domenico approached us.

"Marisela, *bella*, come join me for dinner...alone?" He eyed Marisela, then me. She took his hand, her smile spread wide crossed her face, following him out.

"Mar—" Casper stood, reaching for her.

"You have to stop worrying, amor. I am fine," Marisela looked back at Casper, and something passed between their eyes that I couldn't read.

Casper sat back down, grabbing one of the abandoned beers on the table.

"Why don't you like having any fun? Marisela does. She's your sister, after all,"

"Half,"

"Oh, half," I rolled my eyes and wriggled my butt up close to his body so that our hips touched.

"My sister is reckless. Kind of like you," I felt his body tense at my touch, and he stood abruptly, walking out of the small alcove and onto the dance floor.

What was it with this guy?

Usually, men couldn't keep their hands off me, and he

acted like I was just some random. I guess if I looked like any one of these girls, maybe he would, they were all thinner than I was.

I sidled up to his unmoving body, leaning against an empty high-top table.

"You know, the dance floor is for dancing," I circle the table, rolling my body to the beat of the bass that pumped through the speakers. I backed myself up to his body, gyrating my ass into his crotch, and I felt his body tense at the contact.

I tried to keep myself from laughing; it was hard for me to keep a serious face sometimes.

"I don't dance, pumpkin."

"Ohhh, I see. You don't like thicker girls. I get it," I continued to assault his lap with my ass; I never backed down from a challenge.

The music was loud, and the bass made my heart pound even faster.

"It's called self-control. Even if your curvy little body makes my dick hard, I can ignore it," His lips close to me as he said the words, I felt the heat stroking the inside of my ear, and I shivered.

I grabbed another drink from the passing waiter, twirling as I took it.

I might be a little drunk.

"I thought you said you didn't drink?" He motioned his head toward the glass, which I was promptly sucking down with a straw.

I stopped sipping and looked down at the glass, trying to remember when I would have told him that.

If he heard that conversation, he must have been trying hard to listen.

"I don't. Usually. Not that that's any of *your business,*"

I turned his own words on him. A neat little trick I learned in psych class.

A rush of adrenaline and bravery surged through me; maybe it was just the alcohol, but I kept my body pressed to his and swayed to the music.

He was the only guy here. It was almost comical.

Although Venom boasted a haven for women some were looking for a sexy man to bite into by the look of their insatiable stares. I sipped my drink and moved next to him, following his eye line.

A petite blonde with prominently flared hips grinned in his direction. I watched his eyes flick to the floor but then back to the curves of her body. Noticing this, she bit her lip and looked back at him over her shoulder.

Jealousy bristled behind my eyes, and it took every fiber of my being to remain where I stood and not mark my territory. Not that he was my territory.

Blondie sashayed her way to Casper, acting as if I wasn't standing there, "Hi. I thought men weren't allowed here...what makes you so special, *papi*?" she leaned against the high-top table, blocking me completely from his view.

Casper surveyed her stance, nodding toward me at her back. She turned side-eyeing me, standing about six inches taller than her. I hold my hand and wave, smiling enthusiastically. She rolled her eyes, returning her gaze to Casper.

"Oh, I get it. You're like a bodyguard. Is she famous or something?" she backed away from the table a little, hand on hips in an offensive posture. When a female put her hands on her hips, she was either ready for a discussion or already pissed off. I could spot that shit from a mile away.

Casper stood still, arms crossed, still watching the dance floor. She waited for his response, but I knew she wouldn't get one.

Why couldn't she just take the hint and walk away?

"Hello?" she waved her hand in front of Casper's face, stumbling a little as she did it. She was drunk.

At least now I know I'm not the only one he ignores.

"Listen, let's get you some water at the bar," I moved to grab her wrist, but she jerked her arm back, shoving me away from her.

"I'm good weird bitch," She shoved by me, nearly knocking my drink from my hand. It all happened so quickly; I didn't have time to see Ruby grabbing the girl by her hair, "rude bitch."

The girl screamed as Ruby's fist came down over her face repeatedly. Casper was on them both, cursing as she ignored him in a fury. My hand was clamped over my mouth the entire time but backing away so I would be out of the way of any flying fists. I considered jumping in but figured it would be broken up before I could even get to the girl.

Casper had Ruby in a hold, hands behind her back. One of his muscled arms wrapped around her waist while she fought futilely against his solid body. I watched as his jaw worked, mouthing something into her lucky little ears. She stopped fighting, and I wondered was he said to her to make her stop.

I watched as Casper waved over the girls in one simple movement; the girls circled us and followed him up the staircase to the exit.

I did the same, not wanting to get separated from them. The crowd parted, allowing the line of beautiful women to pass. Each girl carried herself with pride, head held high; it made me do the same.

We passed by the exit and into a dimly lit hallway with a red door at the end. The way the light cast over the intricate patterns beneath the paint, the door looked ancient.

With one hard knock, it was opened for us all to enter.

Ruby snapped her wrists from Casper's grasp.

"Don't make me tell Alex to come get his girl..." he growled.

Ruby scoffed at this, but Casper's comment cleared up the mystery of her attitude towards me.

Her dress was bunched up from the struggle, and she yanked it down before sitting on a chaise in the corner of the room.

"Are we done here? I've had my fill of problems for the night," Casper said dryly.

Marisela strode to the back of the room and to the large desk Domenico sat behind. She eased onto his lap with a grin as he wrapped his arm around her cinched waist.

"You can take a girl out of New York, but you can't take the New York out of the girl," Jade said, snickering.

I continued to sip my drink, smiling to myself as I watched everything unfold. Sapph and Jade adjusted themselves to sit on the chaise beside Ruby.

This must be Domenico's office. I looked at each girl, and they all looked comfortable.

I eyed the books that lined the walls, old, dusty. The entire room made me feel as though I was transported to another era, much like taking a sip of an aged whiskey.

The lights were dim, I noticed how prominent Domenico's bone structure was for the first time. Hard, almost statue-like. I stepped in closer to Casper, a shiver running through me; I did not like to be cold, and it was cold as fuck in here.

Marisela adjusted herself, she pressed her back to Domenico's chest, his long, pale fingertips stroking her waist. From the corner of my eyes, I saw Casper slightly narrow his eyes at them.

"Problems? I see no problems," Domenico smiled, unbothered by Casper's complaint.

Marisela had only briefly mentioned Domenico on the car ride over. That he was giving her opportunities she'd never had before. That, being a performer, I assumed. And not the kind that gets naked on the stage for once.

"There wasn't much of a problem until you started inviting her here," Casper said, pointing to Mar.

"I'm unsure where this irritation for me has stemmed from, *Cas*. Your mother and I have been business partners for years–free of any problems. A *pleasurable* partnership if you will," He turned his head to Marisela, who looked at him over her shoulder, meeting his eyes with a toothy grin, "or is it because your mother...*how do you say*...isn't your *birth* mother?" Domenico sneered as Mar craned her neck around to place a kiss on his lips.

It was when I noticed a pair of two perfect, bloodied circles just below her jugular.

No fucking way.

I darted my eyes to the white, antique chaise that Ruby lounged on, sipping red wine. She lazily smiled at me over her glass, clearly gaining satisfaction from the reaction of my realization.

I swallowed.

Suddenly, I felt very out of place. Each one of these

girls knew what he was, and I was just standing in the middle of the room like a goat delivered to T. Rex.

Was this some weird sacrificial situation?

"You're a fucking vampire," I blurted. Jade snorted loudly after the room went silent at my outburst.

"Jesus, Celeste. Why don't you just scream it from the parking lot?" Ruby spat, downing the rest of the wine in her glass.

"Is that wine, Ruby? Or are you a vampire too?" I spat back, darting my eyes around the room, looking for more evidence of each person.

Were they all vampires?

I always knew there were things beyond our comprehension in this world. It was one of the biggest reasons I was bullied. It was also why my aunt never made me feel accepted. If you didn't accept their religion, then you were a sinner, a soul damned to hell.

"No one's a vampire except Domenico, and I'm sure he would greatly appreciate it if you kept your fucking mouth shut," Ruby snapped, grabbing an open wine bottle from behind her chair.

"Ladies...please. I assumed that Celeste was aware, considering she just signed a contract for Moxie..." Domenico's voice was hard as stone yet smooth enough not to notice the clipped tone.

A contract I didn't read...

"I haven't signed any contract...yet," I lied, standing with my empty drink in one hand, the other on my hip. I was suddenly very aware of the blood pumping through my body.

"Ah, I see," Domenico patted Marisela's thigh, signaling her to get up, "you must understand how *rare* of an opportunity this is. What was your childhood like,

Celeste?" He stood from his chair once Marisela took a seat between Jade and Sapph. His eyes scanned my body a little too slowly, in my opinion, and I remembered I didn't have my cat knuckles on me, not that I had any place to tuck them in this mini dress.

"My...my childhood? What does that have to do with signing a contract?" I shifted uncomfortably in my heels, like I always did when anyone asked me to talk about my past.

I looked over to Sapph, the only one that's been kind to me besides Marisela. We met eyes, and she raised her eyebrows, nodding carefully. I felt a sudden wave of warmth and confidence. As if a hand was caressing my back, words in my ears reassuring me.

"I...I... didn't have my parents around. I was raised by my aunt..." I looked down at my chipped nails and the dress that wasn't mine. I'd never had much, and it never mattered to me but suddenly, at this moment, it did.

"Mmm, I am so sorry you went through that, *belle*. This...this life would give you wealth and freedom you have never known before..." Domenico said, rounding his desk and unbuttoning the grey blazer he wore. He sat on the edge, his foggy eyes never leaving mine.

There was no way this guy could know what I wanted. I just met him, vampire, or not.

"Come sit, Candente," Marisela's thick voice broke my thoughts, and I looked over at her as she patted her lap.

For once in my life, I chose silence. I did as I was told, robotically walking to her and sitting on her lap. I needed time to process this. Was I the only one that was shocked by this revelation? Clearly, everyone knew but me, and I began to understand why Casper didn't like this dude; I wasn't sure if I did either.

"I do hope you make the right choice, *Candente,*" He drawled, mimicking Mar and holding my eyes... his stare was murderous.

Look what you've gotten yourself into now.

My aunt's voice echoed through my head, but I squeezed my eyes shut, refusing to let her control me from hundreds of miles away.

Casper shoved his hands in his leather jacket, jerking his head toward the door, "Let's go ladies, it's late."

Striding to leave without acknowledging Domenico seemed dangerous to me, but everyone did as they were told without question and followed Casper out.

Marisela blew kisses at Domenico, and I looked back as he continued to watch me.

While he stayed silent, his gaze on my back was heavy.

"Will you stay with me, tonight?" I whispered to Marisela.

THIRTEEN

"Girl, we need to order a pizza or something. I am fucking starving," Marisela sat on the perfectly made bed in my hotel room, kicking off her red bottom stilettos and rubbing her feet.

"Go for it, I doubt I'll be getting any sleep tonight," I said, peeling off the too-tight black dress over my head.

I padded into the large bathroom and turned the shower to the steam setting. I moved to the bamboo seat in the corner of the stall that looked straight out of a spa.

I had always wished for a life outside of my fucked-up situation. That's all I'd ever wanted.

A fresh start.

My brother was the only loyal family member I had left. My aunt didn't accept me, or my mother for that matter. She always favored my brother and overlooked any mistake he made.

Not me; she watched me like a hawk and never missed an opportunity to chastise me for my bad decisions. Maybe it was her trying to protect me from suffering the same fate as her sister.

Jane and I always spoke of running away to Vegas together, and now here I was, running headfirst into a rare job offer. I should probably read that contract at some point...

The shower door opened, the steam ushering out in coils. Marisela poked her head in with a meat-covered pizza slice in her hand. She chewed and smiled, surveying my nude form.

I never had many girls I would consider friends growing up besides Jane. But it did award me a much higher level of self-confidence that I didn't often see in other females. No one complained to me about their fat rolls or cellulite. I just learned to love myself over the years with not much to compare it to.

"Beautiful girl..." Marisela purred, making me smirk.

My breasts were heavy but perky. Pink tipped nipples that turned slightly up and out. I liked them, and I didn't mind showing them off.

I cocked my head to the side and smiled at her, pulling my long hair up into a messy bun, "And you, as well."

"I think my brother likes you...but I like you, so I feel I need to tell you something..." she took another bite of the pizza, the smell making my stomach growl, "Alex is like a wild stallion, and I have yet to see a woman tame him."

I cocked my eyebrow, half surprised at her admonishment and half interested in taming a wild man.

I shrugged, "I'm not sure what I'm doing, Mar. I will probably be gone by tomorrow. I would love to get used to all of this..." I raised my palms, "but after what I saw tonight, I'm scared...and not much scares me.'

She threw a towel at me, startling me, but I caught it, "Finish up, let's chat."

She winked, turning on her heel and exiting the bathroom.

I turned off the spray, toweling off my neck and hairline.

Another Alvarez family member is trying to talk me into something...I'm seeing a trend here.

I changed into a pajama set that was far more comfortable than that dress; I sat beside Marisela on the oversized king bed. She had already discarded her *Selena-esq* outfit and wore one of my oversized *Meatloaf* T's.

"That was my Dad's T-shirt. You better give it back," I said, combing out my hair with my fingers.

"I promise I will," she smiled, her heavy lashed eyes sparkling as she met mine.

It felt as if Marisela and I already knew one another. It was bizarre how familiar she was and how we instantly connected. She was the reason that I hadn't already blown this popsicle stand.

"So...Alex seems...interesting." I side-eyed her, eager for her to spill the tea on him.

She rolled her eyes, "He's dramatic. It keeps most people from starting shit at his club, his reputation preceding him. People call him Alex 'the whip' for his gun beating methods of brawling.

Gun beating? Ew.

"A guy who's dramatic? That sounds awful." I laughed, but I chewed on my nails, giving away my nervousness about the entire situation.

"Do not fear Domenico..." she began, tracing lines on the feather-down comforter, "he is not a monster...but more of a...powerful anomaly," She smiled.

I wasn't sure what she expected me to say. *Oh, ok! Phew! I'm so glad you cleared that up.*

"He's a vampire, Mar. He literally survives off blood. Does he even eat food or drink drinks?" I moved closer to the pillows, grabbing one and hugging it.

"Yes...well, he doesn't *need* food, but he likes it. He enjoys a meal from time to time. And all vampires drink alcohol. It almost makes them seem human," she said, raising her brows and giving me that big phony smile again.

"Vampires? Plural? So, there's more of them. Fantastic. I feel like I'm in the movie *From Dusk till Dawn* and the bloodshed dance party is right around the corner," I said, pretending to play a guitar with the air.

"Candente...they will not harm you. You can see those very words right in the contract my mother gave you. You read it, yes?" she asked, scooting up higher on the bed beside me. Her legs were long and well-toned; if she weren't with Domenico, I would run my tongue up those legs until I reached her...

"Celeste? Did you read the contract?" she snapped her fingers in front of my face.

"Oh...sorry...yeah, um I doubt I will. I doubt I will

stay...I'm sorry Mar," I said, fingering the edge of the pillow.

Casper did warn me and told me to pack up and leave as soon as possible. Was it only Marisela that kept me here?

The money, the freedom, the power...

Turning back to Marisela, I shook out of my thoughts, "Where would I even live? The whole point of this trip was for me to get to New Orleans. I need to find the woman who raised my mother. I need to find out why I am the way I am—where I came from."

Marisela took my hand in hers, "You can still do that... even if you sign the contract. My mother is controlling but not so much so that she will keep you from an important matter like that, besides, do you have enough money to get to New Orleans? That's far away."

She was right; I didn't have enough gas to make it all the way there. Not to mention, I wasn't sure if that antique car of mine could make it there.

Oh yeah...

Knowing that Moxie wasn't controlling did comfort me, but I still made a mental note to look up how to kill a vampire. I did have that new fancy phone from Alex. I could learn how to exist besides these creatures. I was a master at adapting...

"I'll think about it, but you're right. I need the money." I rolled my eyes.

"You know, Domenico has a high-garden mansion in New Orleans. I bet he would let you stay there." She side-eyed me as she said it.

Fuck.

"Mar! I said I would think about it! Now, tell me more about Casper's hard on for the missing girl," I said, leaning in closer to her and grabbing a slice of pizza from the box at the end of the bed. She laughed, but her eyes looked heavy, and her skin was a bit pale. "It's okay, we can go to bed," I glanced at the clock; it was near four AM. Dawn was quickly approaching.

She nodded, wordless, and climbed under the covers.

I turned off the bed lamp and put the pizza box on the floor.

Who would have thought that I would be staying at a penthouse in Vegas a week ago.

I wish Jane could see me now.

CHAPTER
FOURTEEN

L ast night was the first time I didn't have a dream about the white-faced man in over a month.

The curtains were drawn tight, and very little light made its way into the room. Marisela was flat on her back, motionless, and I stretched my body, swinging my legs over the side of the bed.

My head throbbed, and I rubbed it, closing my eyes. Standing, I stretched again and walked to my bag on the floor beside the black-leather loveseat.

Grabbing my hoodie and the phone Alex gave me, I powered it up again. I set up the required information that I had skipped over last night–exactly the kind of thing I *hated* doing but must to be a functioning person in society.

The phone pinged, and it was a text from

Alex: Welcome to life on the edge, baby girl.

I rolled my eyes and turned off the screen. It seemed this family was set on having me join them, and I wondered if they would even take no for an answer.

I turned back to the bed, and Marisela was gone, the bathroom water running.

Sneaky.

"Morning, Mar! How'd you sleep?" I called to the bathroom, yawning, not expecting a reply. She appeared, looking fresh as a daisy.

"Like the dead," She trilled, smiling her pearly white, perfect teeth. She still wore my dad's band shirt, but she grabbed a pair of sunglasses and a blanket, wrapping it around her head and shoulders, "you can open the curtains now...if you want."

I found the sunglasses strange, but I'd seen the cast of *Love Island* wear them in the morning after a night of partying. Maybe she was just hungover.

I grabbed the remote and pushed the arrow on the top. The heavy black curtains pulled to the sides on their own, revealing the bustling Vegas strip below us.

"What's your plans for today? Vampire sex party?" I called to Marisela on the couch, bundled up like an Eskimo in a snowstorm.

She didn't respond, and for a moment, I thought she was sleeping again

"That's not funny, Celeste," her tone was leveled and serious. It only made me want to pick further.

"Why not? It is if you think about it... you work at a strip club-there's vampires lurking about...c'mon it's funny!" I threw a pillow at her head, irritated that she wasn't playing along. That was one thing I loved about her.

"I have a set tonight," She said, unmoving, "but why does that matter, you're leaving."

I see; she was upset about our conversation last night. My stomach did flip-flops just thinking about being on the road again alone. I liked to be alone, but I also liked having friends.

"Aw Mar, I'll come see your set tonight before I leave, okay?" I plopped down on the couch beside her, putting my head on her shoulder.

"Fine," she said, placing her head on mine.

"How sweet. Look at you two bonding." Alex must have let himself in, as he suddenly appeared in the entrance just to the left of the bed, a full step below where we sat atop plush covers.

Instead of walking over to the bed where we lounged, he walked to the sprawling balcony window.

The bright lights burned through the glass, and he stood there silently.

Marisela looked at me and raised her eyebrows, and mouthed, "Loco."

Marisela liked to gossip, even about her family.

Here comes the drama...

*He walked toward the bed w*ith his hands deep inside his black *Gucci* suit. He took a champagne glass from the wet bar and filled it, bringing the bottle of Veuve Clicquot with him. Topping off both mine and

Marisela's glasses, he raised his, "Time to talk business,"

I sighed and tossed back the flute, sticking it out towards him.

"I'm not staying, Alex." I nodded at the glass and met his eyes, more curious about what he would say when he heard the word no.

Calling my bluff, he refilled it.

"Sure you are. Marisela tells me that you're looking for herb. Quite a bit of it," He took a sip of the champagne and licked his lips. "Only, that's not what I do. We call that a party favor. Now, if you want something stronger than that, we can talk."

I rolled my eyes at his disregard for me.

"Herb has always been a small business for me. It was a way for me to make money on my own terms. I learned how to hustle from my brother," I looked from him to Marisela and took a drink of the champagne, already feeling light-headed.

Alex chuckled, flashing the bottom row of his grill again.

My skin prickled.

"Marisela, why don't you head back to the house. You have a set tonight, you should get ready," Alex stood before the two of us, power rolling off his body. His large hand dwarfed the glass in his hand, and it was all I could do not to imagine taking a thick finger into my mouth and sucking...

Marisela rolled her eyes and made a dramatic exit, slamming the door behind her without even grabbing her bag. I stared at the door.

Alex turned to me, toothpick half out of his mouth, and grinned.

I remained seated on the bed but shifted back on my arms. My heavy chest splayed proudly.

Marisela had convinced me to change into a long-sleeved-lace black top she had brought with her. The collar came high up around my neck, but the fabric stretched around my curves like a second skin.

Alex removed the tailored blazer he wore and folded it neatly over the back of the antique desk chair behind him.

I rubbed at the back of my head, feeling a migraine erupting from the base of my neck.

"What's wrong, baby girl?" he plopped down on the bed next to me, all legs and arms.

A tree I would certainly like to climb.

He took my hand and held it, confusing me.

He placed a small, light blue jewelry box into my palm. I raised my eyebrow, meeting his eyes.

He looked down and chuckled, his body shaking in dramatic emphasis.

"I think it's a little too soon for that, but that's just me," My voice thick with sarcasm.

"Open it," He motioned to the box, keeping his eyes on my face.

I took the top off it and five generous nuggs of purple kush lay on the tiny velvet cushion.

I laughed and snorted a little at the same time.

"Marisela told me about the headaches. I get it now. But I also want to find a way to *make sure*, you stay," He trailed his long finger up the length of my legging-clad thigh.

"Thanks," was all I gave, keeping my eyes on that succulent finger.

"You know what?" his voice was hushed but still heavy with bass, and he leaned toward me.

His lips brushed my ear, and he whispered, "I think you like me,"

I craned my neck around to his face, and his gaze slowly traveled up my chest to my neck, then my lips.

He bit his lower lip and released it, sliding his eyes home and straight into my dilated pupils.

"Oh really? Well, you know what?" I bent my head close to his, our noses almost touching, our eyes still locked.

"What's that?" he whispered.

"I think you like me too...but what about Ruby?"

He blinked a few times, most likely shocked that I didn't start humping him right then. I didn't care; I knew Ruby and him had a history. It was obvious. I would never smash my friend's exes.

I abruptly stood from the bed, his hand sliding off my thigh and onto the empty spot.

I walked to the glass table and its alcohol accruements, mixing and pouring myself a dirty martini.

I heard Alex spark a lighter and listened as he inhaled. He already had a fresh joint ready to go. I turned and sat beside him on the bed again, his hand outstretched to me.

He really knew the way to a girl's heart.

Instead of giving the joint to me, he gently placed his lips on mine and exhaled the smoke into my mouth. My ears began to buzz, and I hungrily inhaled.

"Don't worry about her. We go pretty far back." He cocked an eyebrow at me and grinned.

I couldn't tell if he was doing this out of his desire or if it was a ploy to get me to stay.

Or Moxie put him up to it.

Either way, he was sexy as hell, and I wondered if I should go there with Alex, no matter the consequence.

That consequence most likely was Ruby's fist to my face.

I didn't have time for any of this, so for now, I'd rather just stay away. My end goal had always been Etienna; I needed to know more about where my mother grew up. She had the answers I wanted so badly.

I had to believe that.

My mother had said she was protected with her, I had guessed it was from secular religion.

Or maybe she would just tell me the fates doomed me.

"You always thinking, huh? That's what I like about you. You could really make this kind of life work for you," he reached out and brushed his thumb across my lower lip, leaving it tingling. The touch was intoxicating, leaving me wanting more, a sharp prick of need landing at the ends of my nipples.

Goddamn it.

I felt the blood rush to the bottom of my belly, building into a tiny ball of tension. I rocked my hips a little to alleviate the throbbing there.

Alex picked up on the motion, brought his hand to my hip, and I jerk slightly at his touch. His hand nearly encompassed the entire curve of my waist. The warmth spread from that tiny ball in my belly and moved swiftly down, deep inside my hips and between my legs. The ache deepened as I arched my body toward his.

Almost instinctively, he glided his hand around my thigh to cup my ass and squeezed. Our bodies pressed together now. I softly groaned and closed my eyes.

He ran the backs of his fingertips down along my forearm and stopped at the tip of the inked arrow with a Sagittarius sigil.

"You're a Sag?" his face was serious, and I looked up into his glazed eyes.

"Yeah, you?" My heart quickened at the excitement of getting this information.

"Me too," He continued to trail his fingers up to my shoulder and down around the nape of my neck, his thumb pressing just under my ear lobe.

He gently pulled my head towards his and opened my mouth with his treacherous tongue. Our mouths crashed together over and over in a wave of need. His lips glided between mine. He smelled so good that I wanted to inhale him and grind his body into the bed.

He pulled back suddenly and gave me his wide, joker smile. Biting his lower lip again, running his hand over my breast, playing with the buttons.

A wild horse...

"What's your moon sign?" I challenged, pulling back.

I couldn't let this go any further; this guy was trouble, and he reeked of it.

"My *moon* sign? You think I don't know it? Baby girl, my momma is deep into that. I'm a Gemini moon," He laughed, moving his hand back to my breast again.

"Why is that so funny?" I asked, feigning that I had no idea what he could have been laughing at.

"I know all about what people say about Geminis. I already know what you're gonna say," he sat back on his elbows. He shook out his watch, returning it to his wrist, and my eyes traveled to the noise.

"Let's hear it," I said, waiting.

"Liars, manipulators, cheaters, crazy," He said in defeat, looking down at his legs a few times.

"Their also intelligent, adaptive, and great communicators," I countered. Grabbing my jaw between his forefingers and thumb, he kissed me gently...slowly.

"You?" he whispered onto my lips.

"Aries," I kissed him again, but I felt every alarm bell going off in my head, telling me to stay away from this one.

"Damn, the God of war.... Casper is an Aries," He pulled away from my lips, kissing and nibbling down my neck. The world stops moving at the mention of his name. I can no longer focus on the man in front of me, and I realize that it's Casper's mystery that's kept me here, the need to know what's behind those soft brown eyes and hard exterior.

I let him continue the kisses down the collar of my shirt, and I reached down to bring his face back to mine.

"I can't stay."

"You can...just come to this rich asshole's party with me and you can see how all of this works. *Trust me,* you don't want to miss out on this bankroll," he was about two inches from my face, and his breath felt hot on my mouth.

I can't lie; I wanted to know what kind of money we were talking about.

His smell took me over, salty and sweet at the same time. The way he licked his lips left only the thought of his kiss.

His mouth captured mine again, and our tongues tangled together.

Rolling me onto my back in one swift motion, his body is pressed to mine in its entirety, my legs falling apart in defeat. I grind up against him, feeling his hard length in the crease of my thigh. I sucked and bit at his tongue until he moaned into my mouth.

It felt good to surrender, to feel the rush of desire burn through me again. If only I could stop thinking about Ruby and Casper.

"I'd love to see that curvy little body writhing under me. Is that something you want too?" The bass in his voice sent a tremble through my body, and all I could manage was a small, "I'm not sure."

He pulled back, his face shocked.

My phone pinged loudly behind my head, bringing me back to reality. I reached under the pillow and grabbed it.

Saved by the bell...

Alex sighed, brushing out the lines in his slacks, looking irritated.

I bit the end of my thumb as I looked down at the screen, "It's Marisela, I'm going to answer it," I hit the answer button as Alex sat back on the edge of the bed, annoyed.

"Hey. What's up?" I turned away from him, knowing I may not get another shot.

Oh well.

"Okay, cool. I'll see you then," I ended the call and turned back to Alex, still seated on the bed.

"Are you not into men?" He stood a few inches taller than me, but he wore a grin that said he was just fucking with me.

I couldn't help but laugh, a question I was continually asked throughout my life.

I walked up close to him and outstretched my hands

towards his firm torso, running them down to his belt, "Can't I like both?"

"You're sexy but I've gotta get going," He winked, picking his jacket up off the back of the chair.

Staring at the closed door after he left, I can't help but wonder what it would feel like to be on his arm. No one would fuck with me, and I would drive around in a brand new blacked-out Cadillac, with black rims too. I doubted I would ever go without weed.

Was Alex a vampire? Did I need to start checking everyone's pulses? My head felt dizzy, and I forced myself to find my center. I would be fine; I could figure out anything.

I liked Marisela enough to make me sad about leaving her, and no one had caught my attention the way Casper had. Was it because he wasn't laying it on me? Was I just looking for a challenge? His quiet ways and level head drove me crazy, and I wanted to take a deep dive inside of it.

I knew something that the rest of the world didn't, but would that also come with a price?

Having this information while the rest of the world continued, excited me. Power through knowledge itself.

There were vampires.

Which only meant that everything I have ever connected to in witchcraft could be real. Curses, spells, and fortunes. Energy and object manipulation. Ghosts.

I sat down on the bed, overwhelmed by the info dump I induced onto myself.

This knowledge made the Tarot reading more believable, the fact that I was a Sagittarius, and how it created someone as fiery as I was.

Always looking for an adventure, living large, and chasing paper.

My fuck it attitude came back, and I grabbed the contract from my bag.

I flipped through the pages, making it to the back page of the thick document.

'If an escort establishes a safe word, the vampire must discontinue to feed from them if used during intimacy.'

Feed?

I kept reading, eager to know what this party would require of me.

Could I really let a vampire feed off me? What would I feel like? Would it hurt?

There was a small clause about consensual sex, about aftercare, and the biggest portion—an agreement not to share the existence of vampires with anyone. The punishment: death.

CHAPTER
FIFTEEN

The music boomed on the outside of The Scorpion's Stinger. I looked both ways before crossing the street, my high ponytail bobbing behind me as I ran. I put on a little extra makeup tonight with silver glitter liner. I wore the only pair of pumps I owned, and they were cute strappy sling-backs, but scuffed.

My *Paris Hilton* perfume filled my nostrils as I took a deep breath before opening the club's heavy front door. With my contract in hand, I marched past the bar and straight to the back like I owned the place. I knew exactly where Moxie's office was.

I knocked loudly on the door marked *private*, and I thought it odd that there wasn't any burly bodyguard watching the door. Just as I was about to knock a second time, I was greeted by Xavier with a cross look on his face.

"What?" he snapped.

He looked handsome under this lighting, all curly hair like the Alvarez brothers, only it was a light blonde.

"Where's Moxie?" I asked, shifting in my uncomfortable shoes.

He didn't answer but instead leaned against the doorway and smiled.

"Ah, Celeste. Come in."

The office looked different to me; the desk was in the corner now, next to a stack of textbooks on the floor. A small couch sat opposite the dark green walls, and it looked like someone had been sleeping there. I pushed the soft blankets and pillows to the side and sat.

"Now, what is so pressing that you need to speak with Moxie?" He took a seat behind the desk, put on a small pair of wire-framed glasses, and shifted through some papers on the desk.

I assumed Xavier ran the financial portion of things; although he looked a little like Alex and Casper, he was much lighter in tone and stature.

"I want to know more about this contract, can I *please* see her?" I said, putting on the most charming smile I could, even though I was fired up inside.

He stopped shuffling papers and looked at me over the rim of his spectacles.

Man, if I were into nerds, this guy would be it.

"No," he said, flatly, continuing to look through a stack of papers.

I wanted to argue, to demand. Something told me it wasn't going to work on him.

"Ah, here. This has your name on it, I'm assuming this is for you," He handed me a thick folder with a stamped Scorpion on the bottom. The title at the top just said, *The Crystal Shop* with my name written on the line beside it.

I opened the folder, and my senior photo was clipped to the front page, along with a copy of my license.

Marisela...or maybe Alex. Fuck.

An address and event scheduled for tonight were highlighted at the top, and the bottom listed the payment amount.

I had never seen that many zeros on any paycheck, including my inheritance.

With this money, I could finally get to New Orleans and visit the place where my mother grew up. A small piece of the puzzle was sliding into place right in front of my eyes, and my chest felt full.

The Universe is directing me, and I need to start listening. Mom always told me that the Universe would always provide.

While I could easily fake confidence, I couldn't fake the truth anymore. It was no longer working in my favor, and now that I sought the truth, the solutions for my problems were popping up left and right.

I could get used to this lifestyle—I could get used to working next to monsters.

I guessed there was no backing out now, and my desire to be a part of the Crystal Coven grew steadily.

I smiled awkwardly at him, but he was too busy typing on his laptop to notice. He stopped for a moment, looking at me again over the rims of his glasses, "is there anything else?"

I shook my head no, closing the folder and getting up from the couch, "Um, no I think I'm good, but," I crossed my arms at the wrists, holding on to the file loosely, "do I drive there myself?"

With a smile, Xavier took his hands off the laptop and placed them in his lap, "Absolutely not. You need protection. Casper or Malcolm will escort you."

He continued with his work, ignoring me.

I let myself out.

The Crystal Shop? Is that what they call this? A shop? This entire situation confused me by the look of the file, it was a lot of reading- and I hated reading. Fiction was fine, but not directions.

It was late, well after dinner, and Marisela's set was about to start.

I needed to talk to someone about the stipulations of this contract, *now*. Escorting was one thing- but voluntarily becoming a blood bag for vampires to feed from? I had questions. A lot of them.

The club was packed tonight, being a Friday night. I watched each face intently, trying to pick out which ones were dead and which were alive.

"Are you ready for your first time?" a husky voice whispered in my ear, and I could smell his peppery scent.

Alex.

I turned, grinning, "With you?"

He laughed, "Nah, your first job is tonight, remember?"

I looked down at the folder and envelope I still held in my hands.

"Yeah...I know. Will you be there, too?" I asked, hoping he would say yes.

I had no idea what I was in for; stripping was looking really good to me right now.

"Everyone is going. It's a zodiac party one of our patron's throws every year during Leo season," He watched the stage as he spoke, and I turned my head toward Marisela, who sauntered onto the stage.

Tove Lo's Habits began to play, the strobe lights flickering with each word. I watched the Leo queen's silhouette again, enthralled with each curve and dip of her hips and thighs.

"Sounds exactly like something a Leo would do," I said, running my fingers through the end of my red ponytail draped over my shoulder.

Alex lifted his hand to my face, stroking it with his thumb, "So beautiful, and so dangerous at the same time. I think you're going to like it here."

He leaned into me, brushing his lips lightly over mine, but only teased me with the tip of his tongue and pulled away. He turned from the stage, gone in an instant. It amazed me how this family moved under the radar, making me wonder how far of a reach they had.

Marisela swung around the pole as the song climaxed, her long hair whipping around her curves.

I looked over my shoulder to find Ruby watching me from the bar.

Shit, she saw me with Alex.

I thought about walking over to her and trying to strike up a light conversation, but instead, I decided to ignore her stink-face and have a cigarette in the parking lot.

"Those will kill you, you know," A soft voice said from my left as I inhaled my cigarette. The throbbing in my head began again, and I forgot to bring my weed. I guess I could always go back to the hotel...

Sapph appeared beside me, puffing on a small black cartridge that smelled like cotton candy.

"What is that?" I asked her, tossing my cig on the ground and stamping it out.

"This? It's a vape. You can buy almost any flavor you want. It's better this way, ya know, classier," She giggled, so childlike and infectious that I joined her.

"Can I try?" I asked, reaching out.

"Sure," She handed it to me.

I inhaled deep, the taste hitting my nose first. This was way better than a smelly cigarette.

"Is this where we wait...for a ride to the party?" I asked, handing the small pen back to her.

"Yeah...did you read the precautionary clause before you came? I would say that was the most important part of this experience..." she whispered.

Instead of getting upset about that clause, I pretended not to know in hopes that she would continue, "I...I...didn't...but I read the rest of it. What was in that section again..." I cleared my throat, trying to hide any trace of a lie.

"You must stay hydrated, and most clients prefer it if you don't eat meat. Makes the blood taste too salty. Have you picked out a safe word yet?" she asked, standing close enough to me that no one would hear us.

My stomach tightened. Every fear I had about this situation was confirmed. I was about to be a fruity cocktail served to a vampire on a warm platter.

"Oh. Do we have to sleep with them?" I asked, chewing on my cuticle.

She laughed but then narrowed her eyebrows, "You didn't read it, did you?"

"What? Ha! Of course, I did! No, I skimmed it, and stopped when I reached the horrifying section that said I would be bitten by one of these things," I rifled through my crossover bag, grabbing another cig.

The rest of the crew exited the club about fifteen minutes later, looking like a damn mafia squad.

"Pick a safe word, Celeste." She raised her eyebrows, taking one last drag off the pen, and walked toward the limo.

I squished between Alex and Marisela, obliged to make physical contact with them both.

I turned my head to Marisela and smiled, letting my eyes slip down her frame–she smelled like vanilla and cayenne pepper. All wrapped up in a tight black dress. Her familiarity calmed me.

The limo pulled away from the curb, and my tits jiggled at the motion, Alex's eyes darting to them, but Ruby's dark eyes were on me, and I blushed.

Alex was model-handsome, his perfect smile holding a toothpick to the side, rolling it back and forth between his teeth with his tongue.

Alex watched Ruby as she eyed me, "What's good, ma'? *You* look *good*," He grinned, cocking his head to the side, but she rolled her eyes and ignored him.

"You gotta relax, Ru. Let your demons out to play sometimes. I know all about your demons more than anyone else," Alex's voice was thick with cockiness, enough to turn my stomach a little.

"All my demons came straight from you, Alex," she said, taking the glass of tequila from his hand and knocking it back. She gave him a weak smile.

"You *loved* my demons, remember?" He pulled a glock out from the back of his belt and held it up to the side, gripping it tight. "You know why they call me 'the whip'... tell 'em," He kissed the barrel and looked back at me.

"You're such an arrogant prick," Ruby groaned, grabbing the tequila bottle.

"I don't need brass knuckles when I have my glock. It always makes them remember Alex 'the whip'."

I heard someone snicker across the seat from me and was surprised to see Casper with a wide smile and raised eyebrows.

He didn't look like he was trying to hide his laugh very hard, it made me want to laugh as well.

One side of my mouth perked up; a bright smile looked good on him. It changed the way his face was shaped, and his eyes sparkled.

These two men were *very* different.

"The fuck you laughin' at, *Casper*," Alex pointed the gun at Casper and looked down the barrel, squinting one eye.

"No one's scared of you and your beautiful long hair, bro," Casper reclined, putting his hands behind his head.

I noticed the long line from his pecs to his belt, stretching the fabric of his shirt so that it untucked slightly.

"Oh yeah, Military boy? Let's hear what you got," Alex leaned back and refilled his glass with more Don Julio.

"Let's see, two years in Iraq. Sleeping on the ground

and watching innocents die...*not much*," Casper said calmly while Malcolm patted him on the back.

"Yeah okay, we all know you did what pops wanted you to do. His favorite son," Alex sipped his drink.

"You two are quite different, considering you're brothers," I said, my voice sounding small amongst the masculine energy that filled the space.

"Half-brothers," Casper corrected me.

Casper reached over and fluffed the ends of Alex's hair, emitting laughs from them both.

Casper was much leaner in size than Alex, the only noticeable resemblance being their olive skin and deep brown curls.

I politely declined Alex's drink but instead grabbed myself a champagne glass and the bottle of Dom. If I was going to make it through this party, I would need some liquid courage.

"Yeah, and you're a momma's boy," Casper retorted and ran a hand through his hair.

Alex kicked the snickering beefcake, and I found myself enjoying their dynamic.

Alex reached into his perfectly ironed suit jacket and pulled out a blunt.

"Puff-puff pass," Alex announced, lighting the tip of it and puffing on it a few times until the herb caught.

I was in my own 'pot-head' world most nights of my life growing up, and this crew's banter and comfortability with each other had me longing to be a part of a group— or family—just like this.

When I first smoked weed, I was thirteen and never looked back, it was much like an old friend. My aunt would come to collect dirty laundry and reprimand me for my messiness, smelling the potent blend, and scrunching up her nose.

Drugs will only ruin your life.

I could never understand how a little green plant could upset the older generation so much; it brought me calm in my world full of chaos.

The day my aunt found my stash and flushed it down the toilet proved the seriousness of it–two hundred bucks, literally down the drain.

I hated that crusty bitch.

I took the burning, brown paper from him and placed my lips to the end, inhaling long and hard until I felt the smoke fill my lungs. I held it for a moment as I passed it to Marisela. She shook her head and held up her hand, so I skipped her and handed it to Jade.

The tension at the base of my neck immediately eased.

"So, is it true? Have you killed someone?" she asked me the questions between puffs on the joint, squinting her eyes as the smoke wafted around her head.

I nearly spit out my champagne, but the way she asked me, almost as if it was something common.

"Um, yeah. In self-defense," I responded when I could finally swallow my spit again.

"Dope," Jade said, taking a hit and passing it to Sapph. "No thanks, I don't need to see *extra* spirits tonight. Gotta keep that shield tight. She swiped her hand up and over her crown and laughed. Jade laughed along with her and nodded her head in agreement.

Whatever this crew was, they were different.

Vampires though?

I didn't think so, but I felt the excitement bubble up in my stomach at the thought.

If curiosity did, in fact, kill the cat, I would already be dead.

Alex brought his face to my neck and whispered, "I see those wheels spinning, and you ain't seen nothing yet."

I closed my eyes, letting the chills unfurl through me.

I breathed him in, and my pussy clenched, neglected. He gave my leg a squeeze, and his large hand covered my thick, exposed thigh.

I wrapped my arm around his and snuggled into his shoulder, inhaling his scent of smoke and leather.

I felt Casper's eyes on me.

The warning from Casper and the jabs from Ruby just made me want to dig in my heels and stay. Prove my worthiness.

I forbade myself from looking anywhere in Casper's direction, although I wanted to. Maybe he was jealous, or maybe he just couldn't stand me.

No sooner did I have that one simple thought of him, his sultry voice came raining down on me.

"Look at you. Always after it," Casper leaned in from the seat across, eyeing Alex's hand.

I smiled at him and let my eyes fall to his belt buckle, straining at his thick hips, then returned them to his eyes again.

He leaned back in the leather seat and shook his head. *Why did he even care?*

Not that he could have any idea what I was thinking about, but I imagined what it would feel like with my legs draped over the sides of Casper's hard body.

I looked at Casper, his eyes meeting mine and holding my gaze. I felt my cheeks redden, and he shook his head again. Only this time, he was smirking.

I squirmed and pushed myself deeper into the seat. His gaze felt heavy on my skin.

"Nice, kitty," His eyes shot down to my crotch, and he smiled, wide and beautiful.

Shock pinged through my body and straight to my nipples.

I felt my cheeks burn, surely noticeable against my pale skin.

I looked down, my cat knuckles strapped to my bag, like always.

When I realized he was teasing me, I furrowed my brow and backhanded his heavy bicep from across the seat.

"Ow! You're small but damn, that stung," He rubbed his arm, teasing at my height.

"These have saved my ass quite a few times, *asshole.*" I spat.

He stopped smiling and turned to look out the window.

There, how's it feel?

"We're here. Let the fun begin," Casper said under his breath, almost foreboding.

I grabbed the knuckles, brushing my fingers along the razor-sharp ears–the memory of blood and the smell of weed.

That night wasn't the first time I had to defend myself against my brother's druggie friends. I could feel his hot breath on my neck and up to my face, his rotting teeth hovering above me. It always seemed to amaze me how young these junkies started their journeys into heroine. It's a vicious drug that will suck you dry until it takes your life.

He reaches between my thighs and puts his hand inside

*the leg of my shorts. He whispers, 'I know you want it, baby.'
And I roll my eyes and push him off.*

*But he doesn't stop; he keeps pushing and pushing until
he's covering my mouth with his filthy hands. 'I heard your
momma's a witch. Whatchu gonna do now, Samantha?' His
mockery of witches sends me over the edge, my temper
bursting into flying flames.*

*I grit my teeth and reach down for my knuckles, sliding
my four fingers around the loops. I pull back and roar in an
upward motion, puncturing the thin skin of his throat. I don't
hesitate. I don't even scream. I just jab, jab until blood pours
onto my chest. I spit out the blood, shoving his skinny body off
of me. I make my way to the bathroom to wash off the remains
of sticky blood. I walk to the front door. After looking both
ways, I cross the dark street and up the steps into my house.
Exhausted, I make it to the shower and clean up. I crawl into
my unmade bed with clothing surrounding it like a white
circle. Smoke wafts around me, and as I inhale the sweet
marshmallow clouds that leave my joint, I sleep the best I have
in ages.*

Nobody cares about dead junkies anyways.

I shook the memory from my brain; it served no
purpose right now.

If anything, it should give me even more confidence
that I could make it here; I could defend myself and
wasn't afraid to kill anyone—if it came to that.

I followed the others out of the long limo, sprawling
my hand over my cleavage as I bent to get out. The dress I
wore was long and deep purple–two slits up the sides to
my waist, exposing my round hips and lace thong straps.
The cleavage plunged a little too low for my liking, but
Alex hadn't stopped looking at my tits all night, so I felt it
was appropriate for tonight's events.

I stood, looking up at the very new, very modern house in front of me. There were three stories, the entire third floor lined with windows and a full wrap-around balcony. Party goers leaned over the railing, talking and drinking. Lights lined the steel railings, and music pumped in a steady vibration.

This entire house was a vibe, and I hoped my client tonight was the owner.

SIXTEEN

CASPER

I told her to go home. I warned her, and I told myself that was enough. I did my best to make her understand this place wasn't what it seemed on the surface.

She is stubborn, careless, and distracted.

They say that opposites attract—and she was everything I had fought against resembling since I left the military.

Raised by two women well versed in the spiritual side of life–Wicca, and astrology–didn't leave me any place to hide from the shadowy parts of my soul.

I was born a fire sign—destined for the reputation of Ares, the God of War and destruction. Short tempered, acting on impulse, and brave.

I didn't mind the latter. In fact, I liked being known for my bravery and gumption.

Celeste had no idea what it was like working side by side with vamps. I was constantly on high alert, and after hearing about two drainings on the job in the past two years, I wasn't exactly their biggest fan. I don't trust many, and I didn't trust an undead monster who thrived off blood—with a taste for a very specific blood type.

I wouldn't be surprised if she were one of them, there were already vampires clamoring after her, and I felt the desire to protect yet another woman blown in from the streets.

I may have been a little hard on her, but I couldn't get her to leave if she liked us—that was counterproductive.

I had my reservations about Moxie, but I would rather keep those cards close to my chest. If I wanted questions answered about my father's sudden doubt, I would have to investigate more.

I did a quick perimeter check around the outside of the house and the surrounding areas. My senses picked up a couple who had stolen away to the back patio; murmurs and thoughts of sex pushed up against my mind, but I ignored them and continued looking for stray vamps who hadn't paid a membership.

This would be much easier if I could hear the thoughts of vampires.

A vamps mind was like an unplugged T.V.—black and silent.

It was an easy way for me to identify who was what.

My stomach growled loudly, and I felt anxiety tingle in the back of my neck—a telltale sign that something wasn't right.

Celeste.

I jogged inside and ignored the stares of the faceless people, none of them mattered to me, and until recently, no woman did either.

A small part of me wanted to push her into my SUV

and drive away into the sunset, never looking back at this mess.

I knew she had her own mission and wouldn't stop until she had achieved it. I needed to stay close to her, but it would be difficult since I wanted to stay close to Moxie, my own mission at the back of my mind.

I grabbed a handful of almonds from the over-the-top spread, rolling my eyes as I heard someone calling my name.

"Cas! Hello there, handsome."

I turned, taking in Melody's tall, lithe body, one hand on her hip.

"Melody."

"What are *you* doing here? I don't think I've seen you at one of these since...Opique...is that her name?" She said, standing so close to me I could see the tips of her fangs.

"Opal. I guess it's been a minute."

I turned my back to her, scanning the decorated room for Celeste, taking a few steps.

She didn't get the hint, and reached out, clutching my shoulder with her right hand, and squeezing. It only took her a second to get to my ear, "Wanna know a secret?" she hissed.

She was strong, and I stayed still under her death grip.

I didn't respond since I knew she would tell me anyways. Domenico's only daughter didn't take no for an answer. She was a little scary, but I was a master at hiding my emotions.

"Domenico has a new business brewing. I'm sure he could use your *powers* to make sure he can keep a close eye on *his* girls."

New business?

I knew the day Moxie jumped into bed with Domenico and his counterparts that there was more to this 'business'.

It was rumored that he was amongst some of the oldest vampires and spent some time in Europe burning witches.

Funny how time could change circumstances.

I turned to her then, "New business? Interesting. I'll look into that,"

I shrugged out of her grip, leaving her behind me.

Turning down one of the many hallways in this place, I heard Marisela speaking low to two vamps inside a small office.

I ducked behind a cracked door and listened.

"...another Starseed, yes. I have a gift, what can I say?" she laughed, sipping a glass of champagne while the two vamps watched her.

I could hear Mar's thoughts up until about a week ago, and now it was nothing but bloodlust, and I knew exactly why.

Domenico.

I felt she had a slight obsession with him, and not just because he had a plethora of nightclubs for her to perform at.

She wanted to beat Moxie at her own game.

"Cas? There you are! Fuck sakes, I've been looking everywhere! Alex needs you; something went wrong. They're all in the back bedroom."

I swallowed, prepared to fight, gripping my tactical knife in my lower right pocket.

I had killed vamps before, and I didn't give a fuck if I had to kill more, even in their own home.

I had to protect my girls.

CHAPTER
SEVENTEEN

The house was nothing short of celebrity status. I may have grown up without nice things, but the snooty town over from me never failed to show off their high earnings to us street trash. We all went to the same school; it was hard to avoid it.

Every designer label I'd ever seen in *Vanity fair* magazine was in this great room. Floor-to-ceiling windows, covered in heavy gold silk curtains. Although it looked minimal on the outside, it was nothing short of extravagant on the inside.

I marveled at the sconces and paintings, things I had never seen before except in museums. I usually snuck into museums to smoke and fall asleep on the floor.

Every person here looked like a goddamned supermodel.

Tall, slender, and with skin that looked airbrushed. Their gowns and tuxes fit their bodies so perfectly that they had to be tailored-made to fit them.

Most of the women wore dramatic, glittering makeup of different zodiac signs. I watched them pass me by as I walked through, unaware that I myself was being watched.

Heads turned as I passed, and I swayed my hips in rhythm with the music while the long dress I wore barely clung to my curves.

"You look unbelievable, Mon cherie," his soft words whispered into my ear, while a firm hand at the small of my back had my nipples pressed against the silk of my new dress. I breathed in and closed my eyes.

Domenico shifted in front of me, his tall stature blocking my path.

"Domenico, hello. I didn't know you would be here tonight," I said, adjusting my cleavage back into place, suddenly feeling very naked in my dress.

"You look like Angèle tonight," He said, grabbing my hand and kissing it gently. I stared a little too long at his high cheekbones and blue eyes. "Of course, I am here, I was the one who purchased him the best gift there is," He continued, taking my hand and raising it above my head and twirling me in a circle.

I stopped in front of him, my head spinning and throbbing beneath my right eye.

I blinked a few times while he stared.

Me? He bought me as a birthday gift for his vampire friend.

"You, of course, *Belle fille,*" He blinked, watching my face.

I batted my eyelashes, feigning knowledge, "Of course,"

I was pretty good at faking it; I had to do it with my aunt every day of my life.

He took me by the hand and led me into a room, down a hallway off the great room.

"Wait here, and you will get the chance to meet the Leo himself. Have fun," He opened the door to the bedroom and disappeared down the hallway behind it.

I stood in the doorway of the room, noticing the massive Cali-king bed in the center. Mirrors hung on the ceilings, and crystal clear chandeliers hung in each corner of the room. A black leather swing hung in front of the window; leather straps looped down the sides, I'm guessing where your feet went. I walked over to it, wondering what it would feel like to fuck in a swing. My body would be stretched wide, so open and vulnerable.

"I see you like the swing. It was put there at first as a decoration, but it's had its fair share of uses after the sex parties began," the voice said casually, as though we hadn't just met that minute.

I stood with one hand on my hip, surveying the short, bald man before me. He wasn't exactly unattractive, if you liked older men with a dad-bod. Not me; I liked them young, rugged, and tattooed.

"Wow, Domenico does not lie. You are quite magnificent. Show me your tits."

"Damn, you *really* know how to romance a lady," I said, unlooping the dress strap from over my shoulder. Each side fell swiftly, my breasts already a heavy burden to bear under the small straps. The top of the dress fell away, exposing my pert nips to him.

My gaze remained fixed on his face while he licked his lips and rubbed his hands together, "May I...please?" he asked, stepping closer to me and lowering his head down to my chest. Caressing a wet tongue along the top of my breast, he licked his way down to the fleshy bud. Closing his mouth around it, I moaned as he pulled gently and nibbled. I hissed, looking down over this stranger so obscenely attached to my breast. A stranger; it sent a thrill through me.

Was it the thrill of power? Or was it the thrill of committing an act so vile in the opinion of my family? It didn't matter to me right now; now I was going to get a release and a high.

Don't forget about that paycheck.

I closed my eyes.

A small prick landed just above the fleshy part of my right breast. He was still lapping and sucking at them; he must have a thing for titties. The prick stung at first, but melted into a warm and calm sensation, like drinking a glass of wine.

"Ahh, the taste...it's like nothing else. Sweet nectar from the Gods," he said as he slurped from me. While alarming at first, the blood was mostly inside his mouth. And it didn't hurt *that* bad. I closed my eyes and let them drift to someone else that I wished would suckle me. I pulled at my mind for a face, conjuring Casper and his brown eyes.

Leo-vamp– whose name I didn't have yet, and maybe that was for a reason–was kissing up my neck now, giving me goosebumps along my shoulders and neck.

I tensed slightly under his cold kisses but did as he pleased. I didn't need a contract to tell me how to be a good escort. I'd seen enough of them in movies.

His body against mine moved me to the bed, where it didn't take long for him to unzip his pants and further hike up my dress. His dick was on the smaller side, but that was fine with me; all the easier this would be. He hiked my right leg up and thrust inside me without warning, causing me to flinch. My head throbbed, and so did my pussy, and I decided to make the best out of this situation. Scootching up and relieving myself of him, I sat up and pulled him to me. "Come here, big guy," I said, rolling him onto his back and climbing on top.

"Oh, you're dominant, I like that. Go ahead, take control, baby," he said, leaning back and placing his hands on my hips. While he did suck my blood, he looked less than terrifying and nothing like I had imagined.

Maybe just a little cold.

He smiled, and I observed his fangs, almost reaching out to touch one. He must have sensed my curiosity because he said, "Go ahead, *touch it*."

I reached out my finger, delicately grazing one of them and pricked the end with the side of my thumb.

He smiled, clearly amused, "A vamp-virgin, even better. This will be one of the best nights of the century, little one."

I tried to hide my annoyance at his cockiness, but clearly, my face said it all.

So far, I don't think it's very spectacular.

"Come here, let me have more of that sweet, Starseed blood," He wrapped his hand around the back of my neck and pulled me down onto him while my heart started beating out of my chest.

There was that word again...

A titty was ok, but my neck?

I cringed as his lips contacted my chords and felt the expected sting of what came next. Two small stabs, and I instantly felt the liquid warmth creep down my veins, my eyes slightly rolling back. I thought of Casper's eyes again, on me and hot now, his face flushed from his thrusting. I spread my legs wider, inviting him deeper inside me. My walls clutched around him while his mouth worked on my neck. I began a circular motion with my hips, arching my back and pulling away from his face.

"You taste so fucking good, princess. Can I keep you? Will you come back to Miami with me?" He asked, moaning and rolling his eyes back.

I continued to dip and roll my hips over him, his dick not quite filling me the way I needed. I lifted my hips, finding the spot that I needed to be pushed. I bounced my ass on his cock until I felt myself coil into a siphon of pleasure. I sat back on my heels, pumping my legs up and down until I felt like the cup full then overflowing until I cried out with orgasm. My body shook above him, and I whined as I came down, my entire body on fire. If he touched me right now, I would come undone again. I steadied myself and looked down over him, his body still and his blank eyes pointed to the ceiling.

Fuck.

Who would have thought this son-of-a-bitching curse also could take out a vampire. I scrubbed my hands over my face, guilty that my head felt better and that I just came thinking about my hunky, silent bodyguard.

I jumped down from his lap and the bed, unsure what to do next.

Casper wasn't here...shit.

My only hope was one of the Crystals or Alex was outside waiting for me; I hoped for the former.

Slowly opening the door, I peered down the hall in search of anyone familiar that I could spot. Then I saw Alex's long, brown ringlets pass the hall.

"*Alex!*" I shout-whispered, and his head instantly whipped to the doorway where I stood. I waved him over, and he casually strutted down the hall with his hands tucked into his pockets. I stepped back into the bedroom and glanced toward the bed, "I don't know what happened...I looked down and he was just..."

"Dead," Alex said, looking down over his unmoving form, dick still hanging out of his pants.

"I killed him, didn't I?" I said, backing up and pointing at his rumpled body. Alex kicked his body with a leather loafer, and the body remained still, his head bent back, and his mouth slacked.

"He's definitely dead,"

"He...he...fed off of me," I reached up to my neck and felt the sore holes, "is that what did it? He just fucking died...right there... on the bed,"

Ruby entered the bedroom nest, snickering and chewing loudly on a piece of gum. "Wow, fire crotch, I didn't think you had it in you," she walked past me and straight to Alex, surveying the vampire's lifeless body, "these things are hard to kill. How'd you do it? *Why did you do it?* That was Domenico's friend, ya know."

Alex rubbed his hands over his face and made a sound in between a growl and a moan, "We need to distract them. Ruby, go tell Marisela to find Domenico and the other two. Tell her to take them to the balcony.

Ruby rolled her eyes, "Why should I help *her?*"

"Because this is a fucking family, Ruby, and we take care of our own. Go!" Alex yelled, sending a shiver through me, and tiny butterflies at his dominance and unquestioning at the mess I'd made.

"I didn't mean to...I...I don't know what the fuck happened. This is too weird...this can't be real...I must be imagining this.," I sat on the bed, raised on a dais. I felt everyone's eyes on me, head in my hands and back heaving. My chest felt tight, but my body felt good, refreshed. The throbbing in my head was gone; it felt like I could run a marathon. And the weirdest part? I was suddenly starving.

Ruby stalked from the room in her platform boots, clearly irritated with the situation I had put them in.

Why are they even messing around with these vampires anyways? Why did they go into business with them?

"We have to burn it. There's no other way to get rid of a vampire's body," Alex looked toward the long, rounded windows and then to Casper, who appeared out of thin air beside him.

I watched him look over my neck and shoulders from the corner of my eye but immediately walked to Alex to help him lift the body.

"Celeste, open the window," Alex ordered in a low growl.

I walked robotically to the window, trying to figure out how the stupid thing opened. Lifting the two latches at the bottom, I pulled the window open as wide as possible.

Good thing we're on the first floor.

I hugged myself as I watched the pair carry his body out the window and down the lit driveway. How could no one notice two tall, burly men dressed in suits loading a body into a car? They would never get away with it.

I stood at the window overlooking the driveway and hesitated, looking over my shoulder and noticing Ruby was back inside the room again.

This is fucking crazy.

But I *thrived* in crazy; I needed the chaos, a forever tortured life who felt its absence in the presence of peace.

Almost like this was the perfect job for me, like it was hand selected.

I really needed to get to Etienna.

"Are you just going to stand there, looking into space all night? Come *on*," Ruby's rough voice was in my ear, and I told myself to get it under control, just like I always did.

Go, go...get out, dumb ass!

Somehow, the door to the bedroom was slammed shut, leaving me looking back at Ruby, the only one left in there, who was directly behind me, getting ready to climb out the window.

She noticed my questioning look, saying, "Just go," As she pushed me out the window.

I lifted my leg over the low sill, Ruby nearly pushing me out ass over tea kettle. I stood up, straightening my dress and giving her an evil glare, "I don't know what the fuck your problem is, but I didn't *ask* for any of this. All I wanted was to get the fuck out of Cali," I charged away from her, heading to the waiting limo.

Domenico was going to be pissed.

"I don't have a problem. I have a group of friends that mean more to me than family, that I'm trying to protect," she met my pace as she spoke.

"Protect? From me?" I stopped at the limo, Casper wearing his shades even though it was goddamned ten-thirty at night. I had to stifle a laugh for a few reasons.

"I don't know you. No one else knows you. So you just- what...appeared for no reason? I'm not buying it. I may be a lot of things, but stupid isn't one of them," Ruby hissed.

She looked me dead in the eye for the first time since I met her. Her irises were almost lavender, reminding me of a flower and I softened.

"Well, you're not wrong. I guess if I was in your heels, I would feel the same. I *do* feel that way, it's just hard to explain it," I let my eyes fall to her feet, then back to her crossed arms and narrowed eyes. I smiled.

Her brows loosened, and she also looked to my feet in surrender.

"Intuition, maybe? Anyways. I get it,"

Suddenly, the door to the limo opened. Alex rearing his head, "Get. In. The. Fucking. Car!"

We both jumped at the same time, scurrying to the safety of the black vehicle.

The driver hit the gas before we could even get seated; our arms and legs tangled around one another in a pile. We laughed, but Alex elbowed me in the ribs, smacking his lips in disapproval.

"Now what, El Chapo?" Casper chided, slipping his sunglasses onto his shirt.

Alex rubbed his jaw and closed his eyes, "I need to tell Moxie. You get rid of the body."

"I'm not exactly in the mood for a bonfire, I'd rather go talk to *Medusa*," Casper returned.

In frustration, Alex kicked the back of the seat, and the driver lurched the wheel, sending us flying again as I screamed, falling onto Ruby's lap.

I giggled to myself. *What a night....*

CHAPTER

EIGHTEEN

"You're not staying at the hotel, you'll be staying at the Crystal's loft, where I can keep an eye on you," Casper said as the limo turned into The Scorpion's Stinger.

I debated arguing with him, but I decided not to because I was so damn tired. Cortisol can do a number on your body.

The limo came to a stop, and everyone exited the car. I sleepily lifted my head from Sapph's shoulder so she could get out. Once she was gone, it was just Casper and me.

After my full body high, the crash that followed had me nodding off in the backseat.

"Do you need help upstairs?" he asked, entirely serious.

My body felt weak, and I cursed myself for agreeing to let a vamp feed from me, "I feel...weak. Like I can't move my limbs."

"That's what happens when they get a taste of Starseed blood. They take *too much*."

I was too tired to ask him what that meant, but it wasn't the first time I had heard them use the same nickname my mother used for me.

His kindness gave me butterflies, and I held back a small smile, mumbling something as my eyes fluttered shut.

Casper stepped out, opening the back where I still sat, and lifted me into his arms before I could even get one of my heels off.

Being so close to him, I caught his scent–it was sweeter than peppery–and laced my hands behind his head and buried my head into his neck, inhaling him.

"Are you, *smelling me*?" he asked, a slight tone of humor in his voice.

"Don't be stupid," I said into his chest, closing my eyes and pretending this was my life. being carried around by this scary teddy bear.

I opened one eye while we walked through the club to the stairs, I wanted to see the look on the strippers faces while Casper carried me.

Eat your heart out, ladies.

I smiled as we ascended the stairs.

Casper set me down abruptly, and I struggled to catch my footing. I hated heels sometimes.

I slinked over to the sectional couch, flopping down on my belly.

"Oh no, you need a bath. Get up," Sapph smacked my butt a few times, then pulled on my outstretched arm. I sat up by myself, blinking at her in disgust, "Come on, it's been a long night,"

Her only response was to hand me a fluffy white towel and point to the tub in the middle of the room in front of the balcony.

It was already full of bubbles, and steamed up the glass sliding doors with condensation..

I glanced at Casper, seated in the corner of the sectional, with his head back and his sunglasses on.

He's bluffing me with those sunglasses, and I loved a good gamble.

I walked to the tub, stepped up onto the raised dais, and let my dress fall to my feet in a pool around me. I struggled not to look back at him, but I hoped he was watching. I stepped into the tub, groaning at how good the hot water felt around my body. I moved to the opposite side and stretched my arms out, arching my back enough so that my nipples appeared through the surface of the soapy water. I closed my eyes.

I felt myself drift...

"It's not safe to sleep in a tub. Wake up."

I snapped open my eyes, feeling his hot breath in my ear. He lingered there as I surveyed the now empty room. Only one small lamp is still on behind the white couch.

I could smell Casper's sweet cologne, and my breath hitched as I felt his breath on my neck once again, "Be a good girl, and sit still."

I shivered as his pillowy lips kissed my neck. The pressure was light but deepened when he reached the marks the vampire left.

"If you keep calling me a good girl like that, I might start to like you," I whispered.

He wiped a silky cream over it and bandaged the wound.

"Get some rest and take the bandage off before you leave. One of the girls will show you how to cover the marks," he stood to leave, but I grabbed his thick arm and pulled him back down. We were cheek to cheek, and because he was standing behind me, his chest was pressed to my back, and I pulled his hand under the water as he kneeled.

He kissed my neck once again, but as he did, his fingers tickled down my belly and played with my cleft. My body jerked at the contact, and I spread my legs wider for him. He moaned softly as he cupped my pussy, teasing my entrance with his middle finger. He plunged one, then two, fingers inside me, their thickness stretching me. I gasped as he reached the spot inside my core where I needed it. I felt him smile against my neck, thumping the spot repeatedly as he thrust in and out. I bucked my hips, and he whispered, "Good girl,"

The pad of his thumb made contact with my clit, and I tipped over into orgasm as I rode his hand under the water.

Gasping for breath, his hand was gone too soon as I watched him walk around the other side of the pedestal and step down, disappearing into the dark living room and exiting to the stairs.

Fucking around with two brothers? Auntie would be so proud.

NINETEEN

CASPER

Fucking weak.

That's what I was, for giving into her. There was nothing that pissed me off more than when I folded.

If she was going to be one of the four, I had to protect and take care of her too. All it took was her sage-scented skin to bring me to my knees.

I had no intention of placing a light kiss on her neck. I was only going to bandage her up and make sure she got out of the tub and into bed safely.

But fuck, did it feel good to touch the soft skin of a woman again.

I was slipping, and it was all because of her green eyes and thick thighs.

I needed space from her because right now, my cock throbbed, and all I wanted to do was watch her full lips wrapped around it.

Desperately.

I walked through the Scorpion's Stinger, shut down and quiet.

I knew I couldn't go far I needed to keep an eye on the Crystals. Since Opal went missing, I rarely slept.

I resisted the urge to grab a bottle of whiskey from behind the bar; I didn't want to send a year of sobriety down the drain just because my cock felt alive again.

I shoved my hand in my pocket, grabbed my keys, and unlocked the Escalade.

The parking lot was empty, and I needed a release before I could go back up there.

I wouldn't be able to resist fucking the life out of her —and I know she would like that–so my hand would have to do.

I reclined back, silently thankful for my custom tints.

Closing my eyes, I imagined what kind of tricks she would use on my cock with her tongue. I knew she liked using her mouth, and I let myself imagine what it would feel like to grip her by the hair and stuff my fat cock inside while she gagged.

I stroked the tip of the head with my thumb, working my hand up and down the shaft lightly.

I wanted it to be her mouth, and it wouldn't feel this dry—it would be wet and wild.

I spit on my right hand, the wetness gliding with ease up and down.

She was scared, and she hid it so well. I wanted to question her about her past, but it would only make me look interested, and I didn't want that.

I thought about the way she tangled her fingers in my hair like she needed my hands more than I did it. Her soft moans as she came have me fucking into my hand with my hips. My balls tightened, and I loosened my grip, leaning over and spitting on the head again. I felt my orgasm building, but it wasn't my hand now; it was her tight mouth.

I spilled over my fist, wishing I could watch her swallowing it all.

Like a good little slut. My little slut.

I slumped onto the steering wheel with my forehead pressed against it. My chest rose and fell, my body singing from the release.

I pulled my T-shirt off over my head, wiping the mess clean.

This was why I needed to resist her. I wasn't the playboy Alex was, and my heart wasn't able to fuck just anyone. Feelings always came with the sex, and that's why I couldn't let myself indulge any more with her.

She would hurt me, she would get bored with me, and I would be left broken-hearted—once again.

My mother always told me I needed a girl who could match my passion but also someone who could understand what deep commitment was.

It was hard to find girls like that in an environment like this.

No, I had to remain stoic and unfeeling on the outside, while my heart thrummed solitary but yearning on the inside.

A knock on my window made me jump, and I tossed the shirt to the floor when I was finished.

I rolled down the window a little and was surprised to see Alex, looking disheveled, smoking a cigarette.

"What's up?" I asked, trying to hide my heavy breathing.

"You sleeping in your SUV tonight? I can stay with the girls, if you want," he flicked his cigarette to the ground, exhaling the smoke.

Alex and I had an interesting relationship, but we both had one thing in common: a fierce protective nature.

I pushed against his mind, watching his brown eyes.

He was feeling guilty about something, and I knew it was over a chick, as always. I just wished he could put things right with Ruby. She followed him all the way out here from New York, and he owed her a million apologies.

"You should go to her, you know she won't kick you out of bed," I said, grinning at him.

He looked at the ground, shuffling his expensive loafers around the dirt, but didn't respond.

"I really wish you wouldn't do that, man. You know I don't like it."

I nodded, holding my hands up in surrender.

The silence was stiff between us, and I silently hoped Alex would redeem himself. He deserved to be happy, and so did Ruby.

"I'll head up now, you go home and get some rest—you look like shit and you smell like a bar."

He nodded, swinging his blazer over his shoulder and walking toward the waiting limo.

That is what happens to spoiled people—they take everything and everyone for granted.

After my water sports with Casper last night, I had pulled myself together and wobbled to Sapph's bedroom, climbing into bed with her.

I stretched as I woke, the sun beaming through the small window beside her bed.

The room was small but cozy and decorated like a Genie's bottle: tapestries, plush blankets, and pillows.

Sapph yawned behind me, and I looked back at her smiling, sleep still in my eyes.

"You had some crazy ass dreams last night, babe," she said, her voice thick.

"I did? How would you know that? Was I tossing and turning?" I asked, knowing full well I had nightmares almost every single night.

"No. Every time our bodies made contact. It was like I was having a peaceful sleep and then my thoughts would glitch, like a radio interruption."

She sat beside me, careful not to touch me, "Who's Anise?"

I sighed; I should have known I couldn't keep this shit

hidden from these girls. Or the Alvarez men, for that matter, "my mother,"

She nodded in understanding, but her face was filled with worry.

"What is it, tell me," I said.

She paused briefly, looking down at her hands in her lap. She was petite and thin, making her look much younger than she was.

"Well, she's the one that's responsible for this mess. Someone is very angry with her. I can feel their anger — it's feels downright malicious." She said, raising her eyebrows in sympathy.

I shook my head, "Pretty big waste of time hating a dead person," I laughed, but my cheeks felt hot.

"Do you know who it could be?" she asked, leaning in towards me a little. It was the same words that the tarot reader had used.

Do you know anyone...

Aside from Jane, all I had was my brother and Aunt. I didn't have any distant relatives who could help me or anyone I could reach out to for support or even answers. The only person I could think of was someone I knew little to nothing about, Etienna.

How was it that I didn't know anything about the woman who had taken in my mother from when she ran away from home until she met my father? Did her practice of witchcraft simply keep me in the dark because her family didn't agree with it?

"That's the whole reason I'm here. I need to find a witch in Louisiana," It felt good to get it out finally and into the open. I didn't feel like I would be judged by Sapph. If anything, maybe she could shed some light on the belief I'd always felt close to: witchcraft.

"Get dressed...were going ritual shopping,"

When Sapph said shopping, I assumed it was for a few silly things. I'm not sure why that was my first assumption, but it was.

Instead, she took me to a small shop on the strip, the door decorated with a crystal ball, bells and some sort of gray, mossy herb that hung from a string.

As I walked into the shop, the bells chiming behind me, I was brought into what felt like a warm embrace.

I shut my eyes and inhaled deeply the familiar scent of lavender and incense.

I watched my mother practice witchcraft behind closed doors and in private. My father didn't approve, and there was always tension between the two. My aunt, however, had no problem telling my mother she was evil, and without her wits.

My father had a wandering eye, and I believed his hateful words only made my mother cling to her practice even more.

My stomach clenched at the thought of their explosive fights when he would catch her.

"Okay, you need a black candle, salt, anointing oil, and red pepper flakes. We are going to do a return to sender spell tonight and a protection jar," Sapph said, bending down to look at a collection of white crystals in various shapes and sizes, "Amethyst is a great protector, carry it around with you in your purse and charge it under the moon every now a then," She stood, handing me a small bar etched with the cycle of the moon.

As soon as Sapph set it in my hands, I felt its life. I felt the vibration run through my fingertips, vibrating to my toes. I clutched it to my chest and held it there, closing my eyes.

I can feel it.

"How is it going to protect me?" I asked, following her to another wooden stand lined with tinctures of oils.

I thought of the box in my bag and the crystal that was painful to wear at times because it made me think of my mother. This explained why my mother promised me protection if I wore it.

She laughed lightly, "You have so much to learn, and you have so much potential! I'm excited just thinking of it," She clapped her hands together, eyes still trained on the shelf.

Why me? Why was everyone I met so eager to discover what I was made of? There was absolutely no way any of them knew my secret. The only person I told was Marisela, and even then, I didn't share the details. Shit, I didn't even know what was going on. I needed to get to Etienna before anyone found out, and I was hauled off to jail for the rest of my life. I had no idea how long this crew would continue to protect me before they figured out I was just as much a monster as the vampires.

I thought back to when I first stepped into The Scorpion's Stinger, and Alex bombarded me. Only, I had convinced myself that it was because I was a hot piece of ass. He just had no idea that was a literal statement.

Or did he?

"So, is this the plan for the evening? Witchcraft 101?" I smiled, grabbing a small glass jar and a small, tied pouch of herbs.

"We sure are, we just need to stop and grab some red wine,"

*****

When we made it back to the loft, it was almost dark. The Vegas light caused excitement to bubble up in my belly every time and the feeling never got old.

Sapph set her two cloth bags on the island in the middle of the kitchen–black, glittered quartz countertops lined with tall glass jars full of fruit, candy, and mini-muffins. The space felt safe, especially with Casper always planted in the corner of the living room.

He sat on the sectional couch, head back and legs parted. He wore his dark sunglasses, faking sleep, I was certain. I had a feeling he watched all of us more than we knew.

I unloaded my bag of witchy goodies, but my eyes stayed on Casper's forearms, the thick tendons moving beneath the black tribal tattoos. I bit my lip as I remembered how his hand disappeared under the water last night, while his forearm worked me.

"Celeste...hello...the black candle," Sapph's snapping

fingers broke me from my illicit memory, and I smiled over at her.

Jade and Ruby loudly entered the loft from the stairs, carrying bags of food. They both stopped laughing when they saw me, Ruby setting down the bags beside the island, "You're *still* here? I thought after what happened last night you would be long gone."

I stiffened at her remark and her tone, loading up my arsenal of sassy remarks and witty come-back, "Nope, still here."

"I'm going to bed. No parties this weekend, and no clients. Which means I can do whatever the fuck I want to...absolutely nothing." she turned for the hallway, tossing her long black hair behind her, "No one bother me or I'll cut you."

The bedroom door slammed behind her, and I looked towards Jade, who only shrugged and sat next to Casper on the couch.

"What a sweet girl!" I laughed, and Sapph joined me, only she hampered her laugh, darting her eyes to Jade.

Sapph had already prepared the black candle, carving sigils of protection and filling a steel plate with salt. I added the red pepper flakes and did as she told me, "You have to imagine the person you believe did this to you. The one who wished you unrest or bad luck.... or worse."

I closed my eyes and lit the candle. The only person whose face came to view was my aunt, and I knew damned well she wouldn't be able to perform a curse this strong.

I sighed, "I really don't know, Sapph...but I would guess someone from her hometown. I know there are many who practice dark magic in Louisiana."

She shrugged, "Let's do it anyways,"

Sapph made snacks while I watched the candle dwindle, the flame burned at a normal pace, just like any candle I had ever lit in my life. I wasn't sure what this would accomplish, but I trusted these girls already, more than anyone from my past. I felt at home here, welcomed, accepted.

Ruby was the only person who treated me like a stranger.

"Guys—I..."

As if the thought had conjured her, I lifted my head from my hands, taking in Ruby's wet hair on top of her head.

Sapph circled the counter from the other side, walking to Ruby and taking her hands, "What did you see?"

"I saw her...Opal...she was weak and sweating...crying out...she was in so much pain...." Ruby's eyes were puffy, and she rubbed at them while Sapph put her arms around her.

"We'll find her. This isn't the first time you've had a vision of her. She must be alive," Sapph pulled Ruby to the couch, sitting beside her.

"You don't understand...she wasn't fine...she was in labor,"

Everyone went silent, looking at one another, waiting for someone to say something.

"Don't tell Casper," Sapph quietly said into Ruby's hair, "He'll go nuts."

CHAPTER
TWENTY-ONE

Shocked isn't the word for what I felt when I saw Ruby emotionally distraught. She never showed any vulnerability since I'd arrived, and this felt like watching a car crash; I just couldn't quite look away.

Jade, Sapph, and Ruby were huddled together on the couch, comforting one another. I felt a little out of place and thought about hiding in Sapph's room, but I stayed and joined them on the couch.

I was shit at friends, and I was shit at family.

I never knew what it felt like to be wholly accepted and loved. I wanted to feel sympathy for them and the missing girl, but all I could think about was how I would get to Louisiana without taking off in the middle of the night.

And what would that accomplish? I would have frayed another loose end, another mess I left behind, only adding to the problems that already haunted me. I sighed, taking Sapph's hand into mine.

I may not be the best at love and affection, but I could learn, and Sapph had shown me nothing but kindness.

As soon as our fingers tangled, her head jerked toward me, and she gasped—standing from the couch and breaking the link.

Did I want to know what she saw when she touched me? From the look of her face- I'd say probably not.

"A circle...we can cast a circle with Celeste."

I looked at Sapph, now biting at her nails and watching the other's faces.

"What? She doesn't know jack shit about opening circles or casting magic. She barely had that black candle flickering," Ruby protested, chewing her lip.

Sapph looked at Jade, who remained silent, but still had a protective arm around Ruby. Her long, coffin-shaped black nails dug into Ruby's shoulder as we met eyes, "Let's do it...if Sapph thinks it will work, then I believe her,"

"I'll turn on the tub and get the ingredients."

I had absolutely no idea what I was doing or why Sapphire even believed in me. No one knows what I'm capable of here, but maybe on some level, Sapph already knows. If she believed I was cursed, then maybe she believed I was magical.

The thought made me smile.

I watched as Ruby closed all the glass sliding doors, the traffic below sounding far away, but the cool end of summer air kissed my skin briefly before it was sealed out.

Each girl stripped down to nothing and stood around the raised tub. I still sat on the couch, unsure about following them; follower wasn't exactly in my vocabulary.

"Come," Sapph motioned to me, her small tits jiggling.

Something pulled me toward them. Suppose you wanted to call it true north, fate, destiny–whatever. I felt the pull to be close to them, united with them on their mission to find their lost friend.

I stood, strode toward the three naked human-pillars, and pulled my tank top over my head. Once I reached the dais, I was completely naked.

Each girl had her toes to the edge, evenly parted around it in a circle. I looked at each of their bodies, noting that I was far curvier than the rest, but it didn't bother me.

Jade sprinkled salt around the exterior of the tub, mouthing words that I couldn't make out except the words *protect* and *bless.*

The tub stirred and bubbled, the steam so thick it resembled smoke. Instinctively, I swatted the air around me, dispelling it from my face. Sapph took my hand and smiled. I felt Ruby, to my right, grab my other hand.

Each girl linked hands and closed their eyes, but I watched.

After a moment of silence, each girl opened their eyes and lowered themselves into the tub, one by one, hands still linked.

I followed, looking to Sapph for instructions, but her eyes were fixed on the steam. I studied each girl's face, watching the steam at the center. Again, I followed their lead and stared into the swirls and wisps of white matter.

If I squinted, I could make out a face, then maybe a butterfly. I felt myself drift inside of it, like my soul-leaving my body but I could still feel my fingertip—

"I see her!" Sapph's screech broke my trance, and I followed her gaze inside the steam but saw nothing. I continued to concentrate on the center of the tub, stealing glances at her stone face. To the naked eye, she was simply staring at Jade, seated opposite. No, she was lost somewhere inside the thick fog that plumed around us, her eyes completely rolled back and twitching. I glanced outside at the full moon, noting its bizarre placement high above the buildings, looking almost like a disco ball above the Las Vegas party.

Sapph's head lolled back, but she hiccuped and steadied her head, opening her eyes.

"I lost her...but I saw her," Sapph said, her breathing shallow and her face ghostly white.

"AND!?" Ruby said, lifting her hands from under the bubbles.

"She looked fine...but I didn't recognize anything around her," Sapph's eyes were closing again, and her manicured nails were in a fist against her forehead.

"Try harder, Sapph," Ruby barked, and I almost told her to back off. I felt for Sapph; she seemed like the kind of person who looked out for everyone around her but was never returned the favor.

"There was an ugly painting that I know I've seen before. It was obscure. I can't remember what the word—"

163

"Abstract," Ruby said, pulling herself up and out of the tub in one motion. Her body was lean and tight, and I felt a small pang of jealousy at her fit physique.

"Where are you going?" Jade asked, watching Ruby grab her towel and dry off.

"To see Alex," Ruby replied, turning her back to us and walking down the hallway to her room.

"We didn't close the circle!" Sapph yelled, hitting the water with her palms.

I widened my eyes at her outburst, shocked to hear her raise her voice. I reached over and patted her on the shoulder and squeezed.

"What happens if we don't close the circle?" I asked, remembering my mother saying something similar, saying something about cleansing your energy before and after.

"It just means we're no longer protected; *anything* can get in now. Ruby knows better," Sapph lifted herself from the water, grabbing a thick bundle of sage and lighting it.

"Do you recognize the painting? Do you know where she might be?" I asked softly using a gentler approach with Sapph, I made a mental note to ask for her sign, so I could figure her out a little better.

"No, but it seems like Ruby does," she said, walking through the loft with the burning bundle, and opening the balcony doors again.

"Why is she going straight to Alex?" I asked, noting that I had asked too many questions already; I lifted myself out of the tub and grabbed a towel.

She rolled her eyes, "They have a situation-ship. Just don't tell anyone I told you that. I hope she tells Alex if she knows, it's already been a month. And the police told us the chances of finding her after seventy-two hours were even lower. If she is alive, then we need to do something now."

"Did you guys ever think that maybe she doesn't *want* to be found?" I said, thinking about my situation.

"Maybe... she was always the life of the party. I guess that's a trait of fire signs—loud, fun and extra. I could see someone wanting to take her, keep her," she said, playing with a long blonde strand of wet hair.

Something about the way she described her hit home for me. I felt even more invested in finding her, even if it was just to meet her. I know Casper seemed to have a soft spot for this missing girl—I kind of wanted to know what all the fuss was about.

"I'm so tired, C. I'm going to bed; you should rest too...drink some water. My bed is open if you need," Sapph kissed me on the cheek, making me smile.

"I think I'm going to crash on the couch tonight, but thanks," I said, following her out of the tub and picking up a white towel with a gold *A* on it.

Not at all hoping to cross paths with Casper and his meaty arms again.

As I toweled off, I thought about staying here and what it would be like.

Could I trust these girls with my secrets? Could they help me shed this shadow that followed me like a dark cloud? Something deep down told me that my journey didn't end here. I needed to find Etienna and make sense of my mother's life before she became my mother, and why I was kept from something that felt so much like home to me.

CHAPTER
TWENTY-TWO

The next morning, I woke up to the blinding Nevada sun beaming in through the glass windows. I pulled the teal hoodie I borrowed from Sapph over my head and tried to go back to sleep. I heard a door faintly open down the hall- it had to be five or six am, and most of us went to bed not much before midnight.

Heavy footsteps made their way to the living room, and I turned my head toward the door to see who it was. I could see a long set of legs in jeans, carrying what looked like a jacket and some expensive leather loafers.

I only recognized him when he made it to the door, seeing his long, brown ringlets.

Alex.

I shut my eyes as he opened the door, making a clean, quiet exit.

Walk of shame, and I had a feeling I knew exactly whose bed he'd been sleeping in, and it wasn't Sapph's.

Once I realized there was no way I was falling back to sleep, I decided to get up and make everyone coffee. A little token of appreciation for accepting me into their little group. I guess the better name would be coven.

Sapph was up first, wearing a silky, lavender robe with a sleep mask on her head.

"Good morning, Goddess," I said, pushing a mug toward her and offering her the French press full of coffee-bean goodness.

"Morning," She yawned, sitting at the bar in the middle of the kitchen, taking the mug that said *death before decaf*.

"You guys are like a little coven. A coven of crystals," I laughed, sipping at my mug of black coffee.

Sapph's eyes lit up, "We are! I love that! Coven of Crystals. We should get a tattoo," she yawned, stirring her creamer into her coffee.

"It's kind of weird that you all have the names of crystals. Is Sapphire your real name?" I asked, hoping I wouldn't offend her if that were her real name.

"No. We all changed our names when we came here. Ya know, typical runaway shit," she said, blowing casually on her coffee.

So, they were all runaways; ironic that one of the runaways ran away again. I smirked to myself, I guess that eliminated the small talk about what her mom and dad thought about her vampire-escort gig.

"What's on the agenda today? Because I need to talk to Moxie as soon as possible," I said, turning and setting my mug in the sink.

"Well, it's Sunday, so no one works. It's Musing Day," she said eyeing me over the mug.

"Musing Day? Fill me in Sapph, this operation is confusing as hell," I laughed, pulling on a pair of ripped jeans I'd left on the floor last night.

"Well, to put it lightly, it's a viewing, and if they like you, they are free to have you. Right there," she said, blinking at me over her mug, still blowing on it.

Dammit, I needed to reread that contract and not just skim over it.

"Oh. Vampires, or just regular people?" I asked, taking a seat beside her.

"Both. And because you aren't claimed yet, they will be clamoring to get a taste of you," she said and sipped.

A mental image of me sprawled beneath hands and mouths, feeding from me like animals, sent a shiver through me.

"And if I don't want to be fed on?" I said, leaning in closer to her.

"You don't have to. If anything, it will just make them want you more. Although, Edward didn't even make it out of the room with you to brag."

Edward? The vamp I slew with a few undulations of my hips. Oh yeah, I remembered him.

Would I have to pay for my crime? Did anyone even know he was dead yet? My guess was yes, but I also wasn't sure how far the Alvarez family would go to protect their own.

I bit my thumbnail, and she grabbed my hand, pulling her face close to mine, "You need an outfit for tonight that says, *don't fuck with me*, and some claws to match."

When we arrived at Moxie's mansion on the outskirts of Vegas, I looked the best I have since my parents' funeral.

The coven hooked me up with fresh nails and a blowout; I wore a black, long-sleeved lace shirt with a leather, buckled corset. Leather leggings and platform boots with chains to match. Even my nails were pointy and red at the tips; it made me want to wave my hands and chant magical spells.

Casper took my hand as I exited the Escalade, and as I stepped beside him, he removed his sunglasses and swallowed, "Wow."

I turned so he could get a good view of my ass.

We all walked side by side, down the driveway and through the parked Teslas and Audis.

The house was Adobe style, with tan, clay walls, and low ceilings. Wood beams were exposed on all sides of the house, and soft blue globes lit the walkway.

Casper opened the door, taking one last glance over each girl's faces as if he was trying to read each one. As I passed him, I met his eyes and winked and he grinned in response.

Damn, I think that's the biggest public display of emotions he's given since I got here. The way he watched over each girl pulled a little at my heart, wishing I had someone to always cover my back.

"Qúe bonitas! Vamanos! Get in here!" Marisela greeted us at the door in a tight red dress that looked more like a bikini with how many cut-out pieces it had. I hugged her eagerly, her smell comforting me with its familiar vanilla undertones.

The five of us must have been a sight to see as we stood in the entryway, all eyes turned on us. It felt intrusive at first, a pretty menu of beauty and blood. I expected more people, although I'm unsure why I was comparing The Musing to a party, maybe that wasn't what this was at all. Mostly, men, a few were seated amongst the sofa and chairs in a sitting room to the right, and a few others, women included, were seated at the long kitchen bar. y A smooth, R&B song by *Miguel overtook their murmurs*. Glass jars of candles and jewels lined the kitchen counters and decorative tables were set up in the living room. I smiled awkwardly.

"Don't mind them, these are new patrons, just here to observe. Come, let's get to the VIP," Marisela whispered, grabbing my hand and pulling us to the wide staircase between the two rooms.

Our heels clicked up the stairs, a tiny army of witches, and I felt a rush of excitement float to my head. It was the first time I had felt this way since Jane—the nostalgia of our friendship blanketing me as I smiled at the memory.

Marisela stopped in front of a set of tall, wooden doors, yanking them open dramatically. The suspense of what lay behind that door was killing me.

As the doors flew open the large room was revealed, my eyes instantly traveled to the four beds in the middle of the room.

It was dimly lit, and I had to squint my eyes to see what was going on fully Little white lights dripped down the walls, with multi-colored tapestries of Tarot Cards hanging like hammocks across the ceiling. The entire room was a dark red but accented with black and gold.

Overstuffed lounge chairs and differently decorated beds were neatly placed at the center, surrounding a large stone statue of a nude woman with a snake wrapped around her shoulders.

Marisela must have noticed my awe because she tugged me into the room by my hand and sat me on the largest bed, the bed in front of the throne where Moxie sat.

It was hard to believe that I was looking at the same woman who offered me a job in her office a few days ago. She wore a long, blonde wig with red lipstick and dramatic false eyelashes. A small, gold turban adorned her head, but it reminded me of the caps my aunt used to wear after she got out of the shower.

I cringed a little.

The most shocking part was that she was topless, wearing only two star-shaped pasties on her very ample and perky breasts.

"Don't stare, she hates that," Marisela said into my ear, grabbing two champagne glasses off a tray carried by a woman dressed in nothing but leaves and pink flowers.

As we approached the chair, I was puzzled by its large size. It was a deep black velvet with white swirls. It could easily seat three, but the way she was sprawled out gave little room for anyone else to join. A young, attractive girl sat naked at her feet, massaging her red-tipped toes. The scene before me was intimate and erotic, and the smell of vanilla wafted heavily throughout the room. I inhaled deeply and closed my eyes:

I liked it here. I could see myself living like this.

My head fluttered as I took in the luxuriating bodies around the room. Most were engaged in hushed conversations, while others kissed deeply in the shadowed corners.

Marisela squeezed my hand, my head owling around the room and stopping at her brown, sparkling eyes.

Wow, she looked gorgeous tonight.

"Your skin looks amazing…and so does your makeup," I said, reaching out to touch her cheek, but she slapped my hand away from her face.

"Mama, you remember Celeste."

I stood in front of the curvy, Hispanic woman that exuded dominance just through her icy stare. I rarely felt intimidated by anyone, but this woman was unlike any matriarch I'd had in my life.

"How could I forget a stunner like her? Please, Marisela, I may be *older*, but I am of sound mind and body," She smirked, outstretching her hand to me.

I took it awkwardly, and she squeezed.

"That's a lovely necklace, it is Rose Quartz, a very common tool in opening and healing the heart chakra. Are you familiar?" Moxie asked, stroking the fur blanket that she lay on.

I suddenly felt very on display, as if I was being judged before a royal court of some kind. Only this is America, and we don't have kings and queens; all we had were powerful politicians with deep pockets and selfish intentions.

"I've heard of them. My mother gave this to me when I was a little girl," I said, rolling the necklace between my fingers.

"It's boring really, vibrations and all of that," She smiled, and it was infectious enough to make me smile back.

I liked her.

"Celeste wants a reading mama, share with her your *conocimiento de la astrologia,*" Marisela shoved me forward, sending me tripping over the naked girl.

Moxie sat up quickly, patting the spot beside her. I took the seat, adjusting my tight corset, forcing me to sit stick straight. I pushed my hair back over my shoulder and tried to look as comfortable as possible in this very unique situation.

"Bruno, bring me the file I asked for earlier."

I watched as Bruno retrieved the file from a small table behind him, and as Moxie opened it, I noticed it had my name on it.

So, they have an entire file on me... she really does have connections.

Moxie pulled out a thick piece of paper with a large wheel cut into twelve sections.

My birth chart.

My mother taught me about birth charts at a very young age. The main focus is the planets in the sky and where they were at the exact time you were born. It sounded interesting to a five-year-old little girl, so I always listened intently as she read off each planet and sign from the day I was born. She told me what effect each sign had on different aspects of my personality but I listened because I loved to listen to her talk.

I significantly remembered —my Venus was Scorpio, and it was a deeply passionate and loyal placement if loved correctly.

It isn't very hard to calculate a birth chart these days, especially with all the new phone apps.

"How did you get my birthplace and time?" I blurted as she handed me the paper, all the signs and sigils floating throughout.

"I'm very well connected, *amor,* that is something you will learn about me soon enough,"

I stared at the familiar chart that I had already stored on my new phone. I had googled my placements but became bored with the reading quite quickly.

"First, let me say this—if you can conquer your weaknesses, and shine light on your darkest places you will become stronger than ever. Your chart is a complicated one, and one that indicates family trauma. Eighth house moon–you may have received an inheritance because of all of this but one thing remains true—you must learn how to be a warrior and battle through the darkness and uncertainty,"

I sat and stared, unblinking at her for a moment. I felt as though I might cry but swallowed the feeling down whole.

I waited for her to continue, but she smiled and took my hand.

I swallowed again, fearful I may, in fact, cry right here in front of a room full of people getting it on.

She continued, "You, are a special kind of person, *amor.* Not one to be taken for granted," She brushed my cheek, and I felt dizzy as a wave of memories washed over me.

"Okay, mama, I think that's enough. It's time for Celeste to have some fun," Marisela was pulling me up and out of the chair, her aggressive nature forcing a giggle from me as I stood. I always had fun with Mar no matter what we were doing, and I was thankful for having her here.

"...and Celeste, if you need anything at all...really anything, just ask me." Moxie said to my back, and I turned to see her blowing me a kiss. I smiled again, but Mar and I were already on our way to the door.

"Where are we going now?" I asked as she whisked me down the hallway and to the stairs. Damn, she was fast, and I was almost out of breath trying to keep up with her.

My stomach growled as we descended the staircase and the smell of food from the kitchen hit my nose. The small group of people seated around the living room before were now crowded around the long counter.

Mar swung her hips over to the girls, all seated together on another black velvet piece of overstuffed furniture. I was hungry, and I was not about to sit down without eating. I could go for a piece of pizza, but I had a feeling that was wishful thinking at a fancy place like this.

I weaved through the bodies, perfume and cologne mixing with the smell of cooked spices.

The spread was massive, with glass bowls of caviar and tiny spoons, shrimp cocktail, and skewered meat with cooked veggies—all of which I had never seen in real life, only in the movies.

I grabbed a small glass plate, and a tall man sidling up next to me and grabbing for the same egg-roll that I was. I pulled back my hand, and he laughed lightly. I circled to the other side of the bar, eyeing the glass flutes filled with a red, syrupy liquid. At first, I thought maybe it was a dessert glass, but I realized what it was when the couple beside me grabbed two of them and sipped.

The room suddenly became smaller, and I was very aware of the jugular vein beating within my neck.

A petite blonde with perfect ringlets emerged beside

me, and I couldn't help but stare are her perky breast that spilled out of her corset.

"Don't forget, Charles, *that* kind of blood," she chided, nodding in my direction, "is only allowed to be sampled by someone *centuries* old." She winked at the tall man as she walked past us and took a seat next to another beautiful blonde in a corset that matched hers.

Charles, the handsome man from the egg-roll plate, found his way beside me again, only this time he worked up the courage to speak to me, "First time here? I don't think I've seen you before."

I was eagerly chewing on a bite of a slider with barbecue sauce—my favorite. I grabbed a small napkin and wiped the corner of my mouth, giving him the best doe eyes I could.

"Yes, it is my first time," I said, realizing how vulnerable I had made myself just by saying those words.

"I must say, I can't say I've ever seen someone quite like you, but I can't really put a finger on it. Something tells me that you are a friend of Marisela's," he drawled in what sounded like a high-garden southern accent. I watched a lot of old movies when I was a kid.

His accent made me smile, it sent tingles over my skin with each drawl, and I took notice of his sharp suit and perfectly placed hair.

"I am, yeah, I guess. I've only known her for a week but, her and I have a lot in common," I said, licking a small drop of ketchup from the corner of my mouth.

"Have you ever been to Savannah? Guarantee you will never see a place more beautiful," he said, smiling, drawing a bit closer to me and gently stroking the crystal that hung between my breasts.

The thought of being paid to *entertain* these *creatures*

was more than intriguing to me. I wanted to be in on the secrets, and I wanted to be a part of the power structure. I had barely enough money to eat, and if I ever wanted to live freely, I needed more. I had never set foot inside a place like this, not even in my wildest dreams. This was a pinch-myself-moment, and I wanted this tall drink of lemonade to be the one to pinch me.

"Can I ensure I will see you again soon?" He said, taking my hand and kissing it.

The edge of my mouth slid into a sly grin, and just as I was about to say yes, I caught Casper out of the corner of my eye.

I turned my head toward him, and he smiled at me from across the room, taking a sip from his water.

I took a deep breath, smiling at him, and he grinned.

I would never make it as an Escort if I was too busy falling in love with a stranger.

CHAPTER

TWENTY-THREE

"It was a pleasure meeting you, Celeste, I'll speak with Moxie soon," He gave me a wink and walked away to the formal seating area.

I smiled to myself. Not only did he drip with wealth, but he was charming and handsome. I bit my lip and realized electricity had begun to spark through me, igniting the nerve endings in my body. Ever since the night Alex came to my room, I could feel the sexual tension inside me brewing, the heat between my legs pulsing.

I looked over my shoulder at the four girls deep in conversation, Mar motioning emphatically with her hands. Ruby studied her nails while Sapph listened intently. I already felt like I knew these girls and wanted to know more. I crept up the stairs while no one was watching, eager to find a release before I started a literal fire. I laughed at myself, thinking about the number of vibrators I had burned up.

I peeped inside the door to Moxie's elaborate Musing room. It was still dimly lit inside, only now it looked darker, and the shadows had all come to life. I watched bodies twisting and cresting, soft moans and cries carrying throughout the room. Slaps of skin made my nipples stand erect, and I shifted on my heels, my pussy throbbing between my legs. I watched as three women mounted each other in a chain, each of their faces buried in a mound, their moans carrying my legs closer to them. Once inside the door, I leaned up against the wall nearest to them and ripped off the corset, tossing it to the floor and sinking beside them, watching.

The blonde t closest to me, receiving only, noticed me, and we locked eyes. Her eyes closed sharply as the other girl made a sucking sound, forcing her to cry out. I closed my eyes and found the waistband of my leggings.

Masturbation was a comfort for me, something I learned to do to ease my migraines. I'm sure I could come quietly here and ease the ache deep inside my core. I wasted no time sinking two wet fingers inside me, and I gasped as I slowly worked my fingers in and out. I rubbed my palm against my clit and felt myself tensing, my toes curling. I ground my hips into my palm, whining for orgasm. A shadow crossed over me, and I stilled my hand, holding my breath as I looked up.

It was Casper.

He leaned against the wall beside me, and I didn't move. I had no idea what his reaction would bc, but a big part of me wanted to continue, despite him.

I breathed heavily, my clit still pressed against my palm, and I dared myself to move against it, to feel just a jolt of pleasure while he stood beside me. But I couldn't do it.

"Please continue. Don't stop on my account," he said over me, low, daring me to continue.

Well, I was never one to back down from a dare.

I withdrew my fingers and focused on the fire-hot ball of nerves. I dragged my finger over it, bowing my back for easier access and making small circles around it. I watched my hand work beneath my leggings and began to pant, feeling the orgasm build from the arches of my feet. I pulled my head back, keeping my eyes open so I could see him watching me.

His eyes were bereft of his sunglasses and completely fixed on me. He watched my lips part, and I kept my eyes locked with his while I rubbed myself into a tight orgasm that had me jerking until I halted my rubbing. I slammed my eyes shut, letting the wave of pleasure roll through me.

By the time I opened my eyes he was gone, and I was left feeling empty and alone.

I hooked my corset around my waist outside of the double doors where it sounded like the little swaré was collectively coming to a climax, making me remember that I needed to find a bathroom to clean up.

I walked quietly down the second floor hallways, assuming one of the doors had to be a guest bath, or at least a bedroom with one unoccupied.

I stopped in front of a door that looked more like a normal door and not a fancy one—and opened.

The open door revealed a panting Alex, leaning back

on his palms, and a random stripper's mouth around his angry and erect cock.

Alex didn't move, only kept his eyes fixated on the big, busted brunette at his waist.

I slammed the door shut before he could see me, slamming my back into the wall beside it. I smashed the backs of my fists against it in rage, gritting my teeth together so I wouldn't scream.

This shouldn't bother me. I knew exactly what he was, his own sister gave me that insight.

After I had messed around with Casper—I felt *something*. With Alex, that something was only attraction. I mean, was I really looking for something serious with that strip-club-owning player?

Abso-fucking-lutely not.

Thinking of Casper made my head spin; it had been a minute since I smoked, and after last night's ritual, I was beat.

Once again, I'd fucked up. I tripped and fell over my own feet and showed my ass. I was better than all of this. I didn't need Alex and his fuck boy energy. I had bad-witch energy, and there weren't many men who deserved *that.*

Pull yourself together. Dust it off and move on.

I pulled my head high, walking down the narrow, low-lit hallway with purpose. A purpose that led me straight into Ruby at the edge of the stairs, "What the fuck's up your ass?"

This bitch.

I stopped, crossing my arms in front of me and squaring off with her. The hallway resembled a movie theatre runway with its dark red carpeting.

We were about the same height, but her stature was

squarer than mine. She crossed her arms in reciprocation, and I suddenly felt exhausted.

I prepared myself to let her have it—give her the old two, three curse word punch, with a pointed finger in her face for good measure. Only I didn't, I just looked at the ceiling and started to laugh.

"What's up my ass? Ruby wants to know what's up my ass—well lets see..." I started counting off on my naked fingertips, "One: Alex is in the other room getting a knobber from some random after kissing me. Two: This entire strip club is hiding a secret about the existence of a medieval myth—"

"What did you say? Alex is in that room, right there? With a random girl?" she pushed past me, not even a bit interested in my list of *what's wrong with this place.*

She opened the door, kicking it in for good measure, and my mouth dropped. Ruby pulled the girl off him and out of the room in one fluid motion that had Alex running after them. She banged busty-brunette's head against the wall, spitting on her, and stormed downstairs. Alex gripped his pants in one hand and jacket in the other. He shook his head as he passed me and chased after Ruby.

I assumed now was the time for me to go. I couldn't deny that running away had become my specialty since I left my aunt's house at fifteen. I needed to get back to the real purpose of this trip—Louisiana.

Casper jogged up the stairs, waving me over to him. My cheeks burned, but I acted as if it was the first time I was seeing him since we arrived.

"Time to go," was all he said.

I would call Moxie tomorrow and tell her I needed to leave. She would understand. From what I saw tonight, it was safe to say she was open-minded.

I could always just leave, tonight. Sneak out and go, but something told me she had eyes everywhere, and it didn't seem to take much effort for her to find my license and birth information.

Probably safer to just be upfront and let her know.

CHAPTER
TWENTY-FOUR
CASPER

The things I wanted to say to her were downright disgusting. She made all my walls crumble and shattered every boundary I had carefully crafted.

I already felt a selfish possession toward her, and we had only shared a brief moment of lust together.

I watched as she ducked into the Musing Party's VIP area.

I despised these parties and hadn't been to one since the night I found Opal and Alex together.

When I followed her inside, I didn't know what I was expecting to see—or do, if she was with someone. My temper often got the better of me, no matter how many deep breaths I took or mantras I recited to myself.

She felt like a drug and was more intoxicating than a stiff drink; I desperately wanted just one more taste.

I silently made my way into the dark room full of sighs and moans, scanning the faces and searching for her blazing red hair and fat-ass. I felt my cock hardened at the thought of her ass and how badly I wanted to feel it pillow against my thighs while I was buried deep inside.

The night after Opal's first job, I stayed up with her and held her all night. She was young and didn't have anyone. I let her tell me about her small-town life in California and how she had run away from her father—an abuser. I had to control my anger the next morning. It took every fiber of me not to drive out there and silently execute the man that had brought her so much pain. Enough pain to make her run.

Celeste's story couldn't be much different; most of the women who ended up here were simply lost. I knew I couldn't fix them all, but this girl was different. She was hiding something, and I was a master at finding out what was going on.

My knees almost bucked when I saw her crouched against the wall, with her hand deep inside her panties.

I let myself watch her, encouraging her to continue.

I doubted any other woman would have continued, but she possessed a competitive nature and fearless attitude, and that she did.

I didn't know how much longer I could resist her. *I wanted to be the one to make her come, make her scream. To be the one to make her pussy dripping wet.*

I watched her finish and forced myself out of the room, knowing I wouldn't be able to control myself this time.

I jogged downstairs, stepping outside and breathing in the night's cool air.

I wanted a drink, and I wanted to get some sleep.

My phone chimed, and I looked at the screen; it was Moxie:

Take Celeste back to the penthouse and keep an eye on her. I don't want to lose another one.

Moxie treated these girls like family, but I knew they were more like investments. She was ambitious, and not much kept her from getting what she wanted. I had learned the hard way that Moxie never loses—I knew that because I had watched my father die under her care.

I walked back into her house, silently praying that Celeste wasn't still in the Musing room. I took the stairs by three and was met by Celeste at the top.

Her cheeks were flushed, and she looked a little sleepy. I wished I could take her in my arms and kiss her hair. I wanted to take away her pain and harbor it as my own, so she didn't need to carry it by herself any longer.

I took her hand, pulling her along behind me.

She snapped her hand back, as I knew she would, but she continued to follow me down the stairs and to the front door.

"Stop. Casper, stop!" she shouted at my back.

I did as she asked, turning to her. She looked small from my angle, and I noticed she was rubbing the spot between her thumb and forefinger, a pressure point for headaches.

I softened, "Why?"

"You are the most confusing man I've ever met. First, you tell me to leave, and then you give me one of the best orgasms I've ever had in my life. Now you're back to ignoring me. Why do you hate me so much?" Her words came quickly, and she blinked her green eyes hard as she spoke.

It was cute how much she cared about what I thought.

I sighed, "I don't hate you, Celeste."

"Prove it, then."

I looked around the room, searching for familiar faces, but didn't see any. I grabbed her small hand again and pulled her toward Alex's bedroom.

"Where are we going?"

"Just be quiet, for once." I said, pulling her inside.

Alex was never here, and I knew his bed was a California king, carefully taken care of by Moxie's array of help.

I sat on the edge of the bed, pulling her to me.

She fit nicely between my legs, and I reached up to her face, cupping it with my right hand. I moved it down around her neck and pulled her face down to mine.

I nipped at her bottom lip and kissed her lips softly. She closed her eyes and opened to me, sliding her tongue along mine. I pulled back, feeling dizzy, and smiled.

"Take off your pants."

She backed up a little, looking to the slightly ajar door.

Doing as I asked, she slowly unzipped them and slid them down, kicking off her boots.

Her thighs kissed each other, leaving only a glimpse of her bare slit. I licked my lips and ordered, "I want you to ride my face until you come."

She stood there for a moment, and I pressed against her thoughts but receded. I wanted this to feel natural, nothing forced.

I laid back, waiting for her to climb on top of me, only she didn't.

I looked down over my body, and her eyes were wide. I resisted prodding her thoughts again, and she finally crawled her body above mine.

I could smell her musk, salivated at the thought of having her pussy in my mouth.

"I...I'm afraid that I'm going to suffocate you. I have large thighs."

I grinned, "Trust me, you won't, and even if you did—I would die a happy man."

She hovered above my lips, and I outstretched my tongue, licking the air until her cleft was level with my mouth.

She was wet, and I kissed her lips eagerly.

She groaned above me, and I wrapped my hands around her thighs, drawing her closer.

"Ride me." I commanded against her cunt, and I felt her hips press harder and eagerly rubbed against my face,

Burying my face between her thighs, I moaned at her taste. Salty and sweet, and I couldn't wait for more.

I sunk my tongue inside as far as I could reach, working my tongue between her folds.

I found the tight bud with my lips and sucked.

She cried out, and I held her close, not letting her move away from my suction.

Working my tongue in small circles around that sweet spot, I felt her juices drip down my chin.

Pulling my head back slightly, I added my finger to the mix. She sighed, pushing down onto the firm digit.

"Yes, please...more."

I swirled small circles with my tongue around her clit while I worked her core with my finger.

I felt her tighten around me, clenching and releasing.

While she squirmed, I breathed, "Is that nice? You still think I hate you?"

She moaned again, grinding herself against my face.

I let her fuck my nose and lips until she cried out, her pussy spasming around my fingers.

As she fell back on her elbows, I watched her hole spasming through her orgasm.

I pulled her to me with both hands, and wrapped my arms around her, whispering into her ear, "I like you. I like you *a lot.*"

CHAPTER
TWENTY-FIVE

"The party was amazing. Your house was stunning... and I had fun," I said into the iPhone, pacing back and forth at the penthouse. "The thing is—I need to go to Louisiana, and I'm not sure how long I will be gone for."

There was silence on the other end of the line for a few moments, but finally, she said, "I believed you have signed a contract, no? I had a small inclination of your run-away tendencies because of your Sagittarius sun. Lots of cardinal energy as well, a true leader. Am I wrong?" She spoke her words in a measured way, even over the phone. I was focused on every single word that left her mouth, like an incantation.

She intimidated me, and I didn't even know why. She was probably a vampire, too. She fit the bill.

"I would appreciate it if you would understand, please," now, I was biting at my cuticles again, but it was hard to do with these fake nails on.

"I already have a few patrons asking about you. Marisela has explained your business in New Orleans to me already, and it fits in. Domenico has a home in New Orleans. See, everything happens for a reason, fiery one...candente,"

I couldn't really disagree there.

Moxie echoed the information Marisela gave me, but I didn't mention it.

"You signed a contract to work for me, well...our family. One year at the least. Although, I have a feeling you will stay once you get a taste of the *finer* side."

"I'll come back when I'm finished. I promise," if you knew me, you would have known this was my fake 'trust-me' voice that I'd used on my aunt a million times. Stern, slightly high-pitched.

"Of course, you will. You will stay at Domenico's home, and Casper will accompany you. You can think of him as your bodyguard. He will help you and take care of you. You are precious cargo. Do what you need and then return," She clicked off without saying goodbye, and my flesh prickled.

All seemed prime and perfect on the surface. Moxie was giving me a high-paying job and letting me take a mini vacation to New Orleans. She barely knew me, but it seemed like she wanted me to stay.

I couldn't help but shake the feeling that there was more to this than I could see, and traveling with Casper meant there was no escape now.

Smoking the last of what Alex gifted me, I'd hoped I would be able to get more from him when I got back. Even though he was a man-whore, he was still a plug.

I let the smoke waft around me as I sunk into a relaxed state. I closed my eyes and allowed myself to dream about everything I wanted: A house, a new car, and a closet the size of my bedroom back home. I would have friends to get lunch with and a family who always had my back. I surprised myself at how well I was adjusting to something so permanent, but things were still unclear, and I had a witch to confront.

A heavy knock on the door woke me from my marijuana-soaked nap, and as I opened the door, Casper stood in front of me, looking less than amused.

Someone must not like to travel.

"Let's get one thing straight—I don't want to be here. Everything I have seen from you is action without thought, a very dangerous thing that could get us both killed. P*lease*, promise me you will *listen to me*," he said, placing his firm hands on either side of my shoulders.

"You think my little display for you last night was done without thought? Because I beg to differ," I said, wiggling away from his grasp and closing the door behind me.

"Celeste," he growled.

I rolled my eyes, remembering riding his face last night and leaving myself open and vulnerable to him. I was secretly excited that he would be with me. I was eager to learn more about him, "Okay."

He sat on the couch beside the fireplace and began scrolling through his phone. "Please. Hurry up."

I sat next to him, giving kindness a try this time, "Ya know, this could be a fun road trip if you would just pull that stick out of your ass. We could have *fun* together...do some sight-seeing..." I waggled my brows, and my arm stretched across the back of the couch behind him.

He clicked off his phone and turned to me, his thick eyelashes blinking a few times before he said, "This isn't going to be *fun* for me. I have other things I need to focus on besides being your *babysitter*, but unfortunately for me, I'm Moxie's lapdog."

I scrunched up my nose at the word *lapdog*.

"Then why don't you just tell Moxie to fuck off,"

"It's not that easy."

Both our heads jerked to the door at the same time, as the lock clicked and the door opened.

"Hola my darlings!! Guess who's crashing the road trip!!" Mar barged inside the room with two *Louie Vuitton* leisure bags strung over her shoulders. She double-fisted a bottle of tequila and a container of OJ.

"Hey Mar," I said, relief washing over me to have a buffer between me and grumpy pants.

"Fantastic. Three fire signs, stuck in a car together. Should be a nice, bumpy ride," Casper said under his breath.

"Mi hermano...por favor—why do you despise me so much? We used to have such fun together when we were kids. C—we used to ride our bikes to the theatre together and watch black and white movies," Mar moved to sit beside Casper and put her arm around him as he winced and pulled away. "He used to cry whenever the guy got the girl," She finished, kissing him on the cheek and leaving a big red lipstick mark.

Casper put his shades on and leaned his head back against the couch, ignoring her.

Marisela shrugged, unfazed.

Maybe she was used to his quietness.

"Wanna help me pack?" I said, grabbing the one large bag I owned.

She laughed, "That should be easy. Now hurry up, so we can start drinking!"

At the parking lot, I walked to Moe and opened the trunk, placing mine and Mar's bags inside.

"What are you doing?" Casper said behind me, putting a hand on the roof, keeping me from opening the driver's side door.

"Leaving...for New Orleans...remember," I said, huffing and crossing my arms over my chest.

"No...I'm driving. WE are all leaving, in the Escalade," He commanded, walking to the back of the car and closing the trunk.

He walked to the Escalade parked a few spots over, and I followed.

I stood with both hands on my hips, moments from stomping my foot. Just to prove a point, I inserted myself between Casper and the driver's side door of the Escalade.

"Move," His rough hand was on my upper arm, gripping it tightly. I looked down at his white knuckles and glared.

"Fuck you, I don't have to *obey* you," I spit, turning from him, determined to get my way and use my car.

"Action without thought, *again,* get in the fucking car, Celeste." He growled, grabbing my arms and pulling me to him. His face was close to mine, I could see the sprinkle of freckles on the bridge of his nose. He had one small scar above his lip, and I found myself staring at it, wondering how it happened.

"What? What is it? What do you want to know? I can see those wheels turning, just waiting to ask me *something*." he said, locking eyes with mine. He didn't seem like one who enjoyed being questioned and was most likely mad that I wasn't doing as I was told.

If I wanted someone to love me for me, I had to be myself. But I also wanted to be better—do better, and it seemed like Casper was the smartest one of them all. I could learn from him and wanted to show him that I could be calculated—cunning.

His eyes darted down to the Hot pink knuckles I had at my belt, "Just like a curious fucking cat," He pulled me in closer, tighter. We were chest to chest, with my neck craned because of his height.

I smiled, as stretched and mischievous as I could manage. "You just want to fuck me, and it's driving you *crazy*."

He released me from his hold, an incredulous smile plastered on his face, "Do you know how many *times*, I could have *fucked you?*"

I balked at this, I didn't want him to let me go, and I craved the closeness of his body to mine.

I looked down, knowing he was absolutely right.

He placed one finger under my chin, tilting It back to meet his eyes.

"I know." I said quietly.

"*Good girl.* You're already learning."

I stayed with him for a few beats too long, and Marisela interrupted us.

"Um, are you two...like...having a moment or something? Because the sooner we get to New Orleans, the faster Celeste can get rid of this curse," she said, smacking her gum.

Casper's face snapped to Mar's, then back to mine, "Curse?"

"Damnit, Mar!" I huffed, stomping my foot.

"Care to elaborate, so I know what I'm getting myself into?" Casper said softly; his eyes fixed on my parted lips.

"Not really, I thought it might...freak you out." I mumbled.

He chuckled, "It takes *a lot* to scare me, *pequeña.*"

"Ain't that the truth—Casper was willing to fight any vampire that came in between him and Opal...now *that's* brave." Mar said as she walked around to the passenger side of the Escalade.

"Did you *love* her? Is that why you're always so hateful and grouchy all the time?" I blurted, surprised at my outburst of blatant jealousy.

His eyes traveled to the crystal at my chest, briefly, "No, I didn't love her."

He stepped up to me, pushing his face close to mine. My skin prickled and my nipples strained against the fabric of my shirt, now firmly pressed against his. He smelled musky and a little sweaty.

"I'm a protector. I'm not one of those guys that walks around with his dick or his gun out all the time. I keep it all here," he pointed to his head with a rigid finger, his curls bouncing as he made contact, "inside, hidden away but ready to be unleashed if necessary. Especially when it comes to those closest to me," his chest heaved in frustration, but his eyes were soft.

I placed my palm against his chest, immediately

196

feeling the heat from him. He closed his eyes as I made contact, his abs beneath my fingers causing me to clench my pussy. Something not-tangible radiated between us, and I looked up at him, only to find him already staring at me. He looked emotional, water brimming his lids. He turned from me and climbed into the Escalade, pulling his shades from the visor and slipping them on.

I think I'd pushed him enough for today, so for once, I did what I was told and got into the SUV.

TWENTY-SIX

CASPER

I had never met a woman that drives me as crazy as her.

Not since Opal.

Most of my life consisted of caring for others, beginning with my mother.

"I need to stop in Mercury and stop at my house before we leave," I said into the rearview, but Marisela and Celeste were giggling hysterically over the spilled orange juice all over the backseat of my spotless SUV. I rubbed the back of my neck, anger prickling, but I took three deep breaths in and out slowly, telling myself to relax.

When I told them we were stopping, I was already pulling into the long, dirt road that led to my mother's lake house. I just needed to figure out how to distract these two knuckleheads while I speaking privately with her.

"We're already here?" Celeste asked as I put the SUV in park.

"Yes, and you two would stay put if I had a say. But I have a feeling you aren't going to list—"

"There's no way I'm passing up a chance to see the sweet Marie. She's like a second mom to me!" Marisela interrupted, climbing out.

"You say that about everyone," I said, taking off my jacket and walking toward the small house where I grew up.

Marisela was already knocking on the door when I made it to the front step. Woods surrounded her house, with a large lake in the backyard. Every childhood memory flooded back to me as soon as my mother wrapped her arms around my waist. The smell of dried flowers and her home cooking met my nose, and I smiled down at her small frame.

"Cas, my baby boy."

"Hi ma, I just needed to grab a couple of things for our trip," I pulled her into a hug, then passed by her and headed straight for the oven where a roast chicken sat in a pan. I grabbed a knife, carving it gently until the juices trickled down the sides and steam rose from the center. I eagerly took a piece and chewed it, warmth spreading through my belly.

Celeste introduced herself, and my mother studied her while she spoke.

I had never met a woman who liked to exercise her mouth as much as her. I could think of better things she could do with her thick lips and sharp tongue.

Walking to the back of the house, my bedroom was the same as it was the day I left for the military.

I grabbed a black bag and started to fill it with more clothes that I had left behind the last time I was there. I grabbed two Glocks and clips, a knife, and my sheathed machete. Fucking vampires were unpredictable; business partners or not, I didn't trust the fuckers. Men could kill, but vampires were undead-- knowledge spanning centuries to be used against us.

I threw in flint and matches, just in case.

I wanted Celeste to listen to me and just go. I warned her, and I even gave her a chance to disappear without question. She didn't listen—stubborn and full of herself.

Now though, I didn't want her to leave, which was exactly what I was afraid of.

Why anyone would *choose* this life, I didn't understand. I was born into a family business that I didn't want. After my father died, I stepped up, even though I was his bastard boy.

Moxie accepted me as one of her own, even though I only shared her husband's blood.

I always knew I had to help take care of these women in her employ once Opal joined. Although she was never mine, I swore I would protect her and had failed. Now I was just hell-bent on proving that we can't trust these vamps.

Domenico had Opal, I had a feeling, and his mansion was exactly the place he would hide her.

Surprise, motherfucker.

"Everything alright?" My mother's voice asked quietly as she appeared in the door frame. She was graying and small but still got around on her own just fine. She wore layers of crystals around her neck, and I could smell the incense she burned on her back porch. She reached for my hand, and I took it, nodding, "Fine, ma,"

"The red-haired girl...is she new? She's quite beautiful, but she does talk a lot, just like you told me," she said, sitting on my twin bed.

I sat beside her, scrubbing my face with my hands, "She is, just signed a contract."

Marie looked at her hands, turning them over, "Maybe it's time for you to move on from Op—"

"No, ma. There's no moving on because there was nothing between us. And that doesn't mean that I need to give up trying to find her," I said, standing again and moving to the dresser beside the bed.

She stood, and I watched her reflection as she linked her arm through mine. She looked slightly frail, and it made my stomach drop, the guilt of not being here to take care of her because of the work I did in the city and the eyes I wanted to keep on Moxie.

"I'm going to chat with her," she smiled, heading for the door.

I shook my head, "Of course you are."

"More tea? I just love it when I have company. Are you guys staying the night?" Marie asked, sitting at the antique table on her back porch.

I watched the lake's surface, still as glass tonight,

while the water bugs hopped around it. This was where my healing began and ended after I left the military.

"Your mother was telling us about your military career," Celeste said, grinning. I arched an eyebrow at her, pressing against her mind while I watched her. Her mind was quiet, a very unusual instance since she came here.

It drove me insane to know what she was thinking, and it was also the very thing that drew me to her.

While most people's thoughts were endless rambles of worrying and fear, her mind was solid black, like a fortress: tight black smoke and sex.

I turned my mind back, pivoting my eyes to anything other than her, and I decided to head outside to the dock. If I could stay away from her, I could save myself the torture of seeing her thoughts. I had hoped she would just leave once I warned her, but she was too brave and stubborn.

No turning back now; I was falling for another one.

The women I meet only want one thing from me— rough anonymous sex. No one stayed around long enough to find out anything about the broody bodyguard.

"Voices, huh? That's pretty heavy," Celeste's asked behind me, the wind blowing gently around us.

"She told you," I said, sitting on the dock's edge. She sat beside me, her toned calves drawing my eyes down to her perfectly pointed toes.

She turned to me and smiled, the tiniest little gap between her two front teeth. I grinned, but she noticed my stare on her mouth, and she looked away.

"No one believed you except her," she said, not requiring any explanation from me.

"When you tell people you can hear other's thoughts, everyone just assumes you're nuts. It wasn't like I could just self-isolate, I was in a troop of over fifty men," I said, looking out towards the other side of the lake, a stretch that seemed so much further when I was a kid.

"Try telling people both your parents died in a fire, but you and your brother were the only survivors," she said, wrapping her arms around her folded legs.

"Pity parties?" I offered, unsure what she meant other than sharing a small piece of her history with me.

"Sometimes...but mostly people just treated us like we were ghosts. I don't think anyone understood how we survived...almost like we should have been dead," she continued but spoke outward toward the water. Her eyes scanned the surface, and her naked face looked vulnerable as the wind gently swayed her hair. I wanted to kiss her, but I also wanted her to keep talking.

"I was made fun of a lot, always called the weird kid. Always being asked if I was gay. Sexually harassed by football players...I mean, the list goes on," she stared at her black nails, a suiting color for her aura.

I snorted, "Football players are gay, fuck those guys," I said and playfully nudged her shoulder.

She smiled again, that little gap showing, but the smile reached her eyes this time. "For the record, I don't think you're nuts. But it does scare me a little that you can hear my thoughts," she stood, but her waist barely reached above my head, to my six-foot-three seated form.

I laughed, "You have a very *large* personality for someone with such a small stature. Look at you, you're like a little peanut, pequeña," I lifted my arm and tugged on her hair.

She nudged me with her bare toe, and I grabbed it, nearly knocking her off balance. "Bastard," She whispered, with her knee bent and her toes still in my grasp. She tried to kick me off, but I held firm, locking eyes with her.

"I am, yes."

CHAPTER
TWENTY-SEVEN

"We've been driving all day and half the night, Casper! We need a shower and hot food," I groaned, leaning my head on Marisela's shoulder.

"Yeah, and a goddamned bed! My legs are killing me. We aren't used to a strict military schedule like *you*," Mar yelled, kicking his seat.

"Fine. But were leaving in the morning as soon as you two drag your asses out of bed," he said, finally pulling into a run-down motel with a fluorescent sign that blinked.

"Seriously? You drive an Escalade, and you want to rent a hotel room...*here*," I said, pointing at the outdoor entrances.

"Suck it up, buttercup," He called as he parked the SUV and got out, striding toward the broken *office* sign.

I turned to Marisela, and she shrugged, "I can't wait until I make things official with Domenico and then I will be living large! No more overprotective bothers ordering me around- Just brunches, shopping and expensive dinners," she said, tossing her hair and grabbing her bags.

I grabbed mine as well, noticing the extremely illegal tinted windows for the first time. So far, the perks of this job weren't showing, and I prayed that some food and a shower would cheer *all* of us up.

Once we had checked into our rooms and eaten some pretty tasty breakfast from the Diner across the street, it was daylight.

Casper had to reserve the rooms for two nights since, technically, we arrived in the middle of the night and would be leaving at night as well. We slept for most of the day, and Casper's heavy knock came at our door by the evening.

"Go away!" I yelled, pulling the blankets over my head. I smelled the inside of my sweatshirt and grimaced. I needed a shower anyways.

Marisela was still dead-to-the-world, so I sat up in bed and grabbed my phone.

6:48 PM

I groaned, twenty hours was too much time to be in a car, and I never wanted to do it again.

Four more hours to go.

I turned on the shower, and our hotel door opened, "Anybody naked?" Casper called, and I walked out of the bathroom, hand on my hip.

"Almost...would you like to watch?" I grinned, lifting my sweatshirt over my head, my tits bouncing free and my hair poking up in a frizzy mess.

"Cute. I'm going to hit the gym and shower. Then it's time to go," he said, playfully smacking Marisela's exposed foot.

"She hasn't moved all day; I doubt you will get her out of bed until we get into the car. The door shut before I could even finish, and he was gone.

Rude.

The shower was old and discolored, so I stripped and rinsed off as quickly as I could, careful to wash my long hair thoroughly. I towel-dried my hair, brushing it out completely for the first time since we left. The shampoo smelled like pineapple, and I decided to leave it wet and my face bare... for me...I swear.

I pulled on my Adidas hoodie and a scandalously revealing pair of booty shorts, in black.

Marisela snored loudly, and I sat on the end of my bed, looking around the dark room. My phone pinged, and I looked at it, puzzled since Mar was with me.

I glanced at the lock screen's notifications.

Oh yeah, Alex.

Alex: I know I'm an asshole, you can blame my Gemini moon.

I tossed my phone on the bed and rolled my eyes.

That sounds right.

I decided I didn't want to be alone, so I tip-toed out of the room and outside, shutting the door behind me. I looked around for any sign of a fitness center but found it hard to believe a place like this would have one. After I had circled almost the entire building, and only turned up an ice maker and a vending machine that was nearly empty.

I ended up at Casper's door and knocked softly.

I wasn't at all prepared for the sight of him answering, shirtless, wearing a pair of low-slung grey sweats.

His chest was bare and perfectly chiseled. Each arm was covered in tattoo ink, half sleeves of different, terrifying animals blended together. He wore a pair of dog tags around his neck, and drops of sweat decorated his abs.

Fuck me.

"I....um...I was looking for the fitness center, but couldn't find it," I stuttered, my eyes fixed on his chest moving in and out in a steady rhythm.

"They don't have one," he said, irritation in his tone, as he turned to walk back into the room. I followed him, the door closing behind me, leaving us alone. My skin felt hot, and I noticed a half-eaten carton of Chinese food lying on the table, along with three other unopened ones. My stomach growled.

"Help yourself. I ordered too much," he said, laying down on the floor beside the bed and continuing his workout. He tucked his hands behind his head and huffed out, folding his body from left to right, crisscrossing crunches. I sat at the table and grabbed his fork, heaping rice into my mouth while I watched.

Good thing there was food to eat here; otherwise, I might have drooled all over myself.

Guys never made me nervous or even excited. My bad luck with men started when I lost my virginity, and the first boy I ever loved rejected me.

After your first heartbreak, love doesn't come as easy. Someone must pick up the pieces and sew them back together, and I'd never met a man who wanted to fix anything. The men I knew just broke everything they touched.

Once I devoured the rice, I sat and watched Casper as he flipped onto his stomach and began to do push-ups. His grunts and exhales had me squirming in my seat, and his back worked while I watched his juicy ass flex with the movement. He was muscular but also thick. I imagined climbing on his back, perched there while he effortlessly continued his push-ups.

Once he was finished, he sat on the floor, legs crisscrossed like a kid, "Throw me that water bottle, will you."

He was winded, and I marveled at his flushed cheeks and wet temples. I threw it to him, and he caught it, his hand dwarfing it.

I swallowed; good hands were my weakness. I should probably stop staring at them.

"So, what am I thinking right now?" I smiled.

He laughed as he chugged the water, swallowing and replacing the cap, "that's not how it works. I can control it—and I don't think I want to know what you're thinking right now," he sipped his water.

I rolled my eyes, "Oh really? And why is that?"

"I've heard your thoughts before...and you're shameless," He took another sip of the water.

My cheeks reddened as I tried to recount every dirty thought around him—there were too many instances to count.

"I'm allowed to think about whatever I want. It's not my problem you're a freak."

I stood, heading towards the door.

If he was in one of his shitty moods, I didn't want to

stick around for it. I liked him better when he buried his face between my thighs.

A laugh rumbled low in his chest, "if anyone is a freak here, it's you."

"I may be a freak, but your cock gets hard whenever my ass is near," I blinked.

I grabbed the door handle, and Casper was up behind me in a flash.

He slammed the door shut with one push of his hand. I turned to him, back pressed tightly against the door, while his muscled arm stayed above me. He looked down over me, and I waited, a little excited.

He dragged his hand down the door and grabbed a fistful of my hair, jerking my face up to his. My breath hitched as the pain from my scalp shot straight to my nipples. I arched my back and turned my head slightly, breaking our eye contact.

He brought his lips close to my ear and said, "such a dirty mouth," he pulled tighter and forced me to look in his eyes. "I don't know who you think I am, but I don't tolerate brats, I punish them."

His grip was tight, and even when I struggled, I couldn't move.

"Then punish me," I whispered, the thrill of his threat searing my skin.

He flipped me around so fast I gasped, shoving my face against the door and holding my arm behind my back. He pressed his body into my mine and brought his mouth to my ear again, his breath intimately stroking my neck.

"I think you would like that too much," he growled.

He pressed his hard dick into the crook of my ass, and I moaned, "You're right."

He sighed, "I love it when you tell me I'm right."

He ground his hips into me, kissing my neck.

Wrapping his arm around my waist, he pulled me closer, and I turned my head to kiss him.

Suddenly, he released me, and I turned, "Why are you stopping?" I whined.

He squinted his eyes, wiping his forehead with the back of his arm, "If I kiss you now, I won't be able to stop."

"Then don't stop!"

I sounded like a child and bit my nail, looking at the floor.

"Go, Celeste..."

I turned the door handle, eyes still on the floor, and stepped out into the thick summer heat. Bright flashing lights in the field across the street caught my attention, followed by my screeches of delight.

"Look! There's a Carnival over there in that field. I love Carnivals!" I said, turning back to him.

He stood behind me, and I felt his eyes roaming over me, "Say please."

I smiled, "P*lease.*"

He let his eyes roam over my face and nodded.

This grumpy asshole was going to let us have some fun.

I almost clapped and jumped.

"Hell yeah! I'll go get Mar," I said, turning towards our door, but Casper grabbed my arm, pulling me possessively to him.

"Don't put on makeup. I like you this way,"

CHAPTER

TWENTY-EIGHT

"Girl, I am high as hell. I don't know how you do this every day; I'd sleeping all the time... eating tacos or some shit. Ooooh, Nachos!" Marisela pulled me along, and while I acted like I didn't want to stop- my insides were igniting at the excitement of screaming and fair food. Nachos sounded great right now. Absentmindedly, I reached into my shorts and wrapped my fingers around the joint in my pocket.

Just in case.

The weather was sticky and warm, and I could feel the humidity moving closer.

A small fortune teller booth decorated with sigils stood at the entrance, with a sign that read 'What's your future?', reminding me of the task at hand.

I wondered for a moment what I would say when I got to New Orleans.

Hey there, I'm Anise's daughter. Do you remember her?

That sounded childish in my head. Maybe I would act like someone else. Talk to her about something else entirely.

Again, you would just be making things harder that way.

I rolled my eyes at myself and let Marisela lead me up to the three-story fun house painted with clowns and zombies.

I stopped for a moment as Marisela flirted with the ticketeer and nodded me over.

My head was still buzzing from the weed, and I felt extra bold with the tequila Mar brought singing through my veins.

Casper stood by the edge of the building, arms crossed and shades on.

It didn't take me long to realize why he hid his eyes. If there weren't any eye contact, then maybe he could keep his abilities in check. Problem solved, what a clever guy.

"Come on! It will be fun!" I said as we passed Casper on the way in, and I tried to think of a way to get him to chase me through the fun house.

I circled back to him, swiftly hopping up and swiping the glasses from his face.

He grabbed for me but missed, and I laughed as I placed them on my forehead and made a run for it inside the funhouse.

The dirty metal floor was painted white, and the mirrors skewed around me like some alternate universe. I tripped over my two feet and stumbled every couple of steps.

My adrenaline kicked up, as I dodged mirrors and scooted around paintings of clowns. "Come get me!" I yelled, two kids easily making their way around me and up through to the next section of mirrors. I carefully treaded my way around each one until I ascended slowly up a ramp that was blacked out and speckled with twinkling lights, giving me a queasy feeling of floating. At the top of the ramp were more mirrors, only this time the room was half dark, with nothing but black lights and paintings. I blinked a few times and tore through the mirrors like a mad woman.

I started to feel confused and then scared all at once. Then, Death's face appeared in the mirror to my right.

I had always been afraid of small spaces but never thought a carnival attraction would send me into a full-on anxiety attack. I bounced off one mirror and then two, the second time knocking my head enough to make my ears ring. I pushed forward and crossed my forearms in front of me, closing my eyes.

SMACK.

I crashed my arms in a mirror and then another until I had squeezed myself into a tiny corner of the structure.

"Fuck!" I yelled; tears stung my eyes, and I let one fall, wiping the other with the back of my thumb and looking down at my arm. A thin line of blood trickled down from one clean slice above it.

My breaths started to come in deep heaves, and then shorter struggled ones, and I started to cough, my chest feeling tight.

I was full on hyperventilating, and Casper appeared from the dark, fluorescent room to my left, "Are you hurt?" his tall stature instantly made me feel at ease, relieved. I wasn't alone.

His sculpted forearm and a thick hand reached for me, and I took it. Instead of smacking him away and telling him to fuck off, I took it.

I shook my head no. I wasn't hurt.

Just freaking out.

I still couldn't manage any words, but breathing came slightly more steadily now.

"Wow, you're really scared," he turned one side of his mouth up, showing his dimple. I think I was in falling in love with that stupid dimple.

I didn't respond. I could only close my eyes and try to steady myself.

It was then I felt the heat of his body close to mine. I had to lift my face to meet his eyes and watched as his lips reached for mine, brushing my lower lip gently with the ball of his tongue ring.

My breath hitched, my heavy breathing returned, his firm center pressed into mine.

He kissed me tenderly at first but then wildly, stroking my jaw with his thumb.

"Cas..." I whispered, thinking about Moxie's party and how badly I had wanted him to fill me.

"You like thrills, right? Why don't you let me fuck you up against this mirror. Would that make it better?" With his hand encompassing my jaw, he pulled my mouth to his, and a low groan came from deep within his throat.

I opened my mouth to take him in deeper, the sensation of his tongue on mine sending me into a sexual frenzy. Every ridiculous thought about the circumstances in my mind evaporated with each throb deep inside me.

I smiled, secretly reveling in victory, "Oh, now you're giving in? What happened to self-control?" I laughed low in my throat and nipped at his ear.

He stopped kissing my jaw and looked at me with rage in his eyes.

I knew he was tired of fighting the pull, the unequivocal desire for something you shouldn't have. It called to him, and I had seen it in his eyes more than once.

A growl came from deep inside his chest, "More."

It surged through me and straight to my lower back,

tingling down my spine and filling my pelvis with warmth.

My hand surged into his soft curls, pulling him into my mouth with need.

I needed this. I wanted this.

It felt so fucking good to give in.

He stopped suddenly, briefly closing his eyes and then said, "I want you; I've always wanted you. From the day I first met you. Happy now?"

He rested his forehead on mine, looking down low enough to notice the trickle of blood down my arm.

He wrapped his large hand around it, raised it to his mouth, and pressed his thick tongue down over the dried blood, lapping up every trace. The ring in his tongue gently scraped my skin, making me rock my hips into him.

He's hard.

He looked down into my eyes, the first time he'd ever let me hold his gaze for more than a moment. The light brown flecked with gold, and I melted right there beneath him.

Without warning, his fingertips shot down my chest swiveling around, sinking deep into my shorts.

"What changed your mind, *papi*? I Thought you had super self-control?"

I ground my hips against his hand, lifting me against the mirror my legs wrapped around his sides. I spoke through our kisses, and breathlessly he growled, "just shut the fuck up, for once," My belly dropped, and I surrendered, dipping my head back and giving him the room he needed to devour my neck.

"I want you, right now," I said, breathless.

"Not yet," he said, taking his fingers and plunging them inside me.

He fucked me with his hand up against the mirror with my legs wrapped around his waist.

He withdrew his fingers and brought my wetness to his mouth, sucking them clean and closing his eyes. "You taste like everything I imagined. I'm going to pound into that pretty pussy and you're going to scream my name, *now*."

I yanked my shorts off, careful to place them near us.

I bit my lip while he watched my face.

He lifted me again, gripping my hips, and settling me over his cock, already sprung free and waiting.

I hovered above him, and he guided his cock to my entrance, the tip already wet with come.

I pierced myself on him, gasping at the contact. My eyes rolled back, and I clenched, forcing myself out of the moment so I wouldn't come right then and there.

We stayed still for a moment when he had filled me to the hilt. I looked deep into his eyes, as he held mine.

My back was against the mirror, and I saw him watching himself, buried inside me.

"Bounce," he commanded.

Again, he bit at his lip—but I obeyed.

I used the leverage from my back, lifting my hands above my head and grabbing the top of the mirror. I raised my ass high enough to impale myself over and over, while he held both of my ass cheeks in his hands.

I felt myself tighten around him, working my hips back and forth. I reveled in the closeness between us and watched his face contort in pleasure.

"Let go..." he groaned in between pumps.

I whimpered but kept bouncing as he commanded, watching his eyes never leave my body.

I unfurled, crying out as two wide-eyed women passed the illicit scene. I smiled to myself, the thrill of conquering him seeping through my veins.

"That's my good little slut."

That was all it took to send me over the edge. I was his. All I ever wanted was to be belong to someone...forever.

I wasn't sure if he had come, but our rhythm stopped, and I was suddenly very aware that we were in public.

He set me down slowly, grabbing his pants and looking over his shoulder.

I slid my shorts back on, and he tucked himself back in, slipping on his sunglasses.

"I hate those sunglasses, you know."

"I'm sure you do," he smiled up at me.

"Hey...we didn't use any...protection. Are you okay with that?" I asked meekly.

A little late now.

"I didn't finish. Besides, I trust you."

I was shocked by both admonishments but more surprised that this curse wasn't what I thought it was at all. Casper was still alive and breathing, and I came...a lot.

So why the others and not him?

Taking me by my hand, he led me out of the funhouse.

All I wanted now was to get back into the stupid SUV and get to Domenico's house as fast as possible so Casper could devour my body.

"Let's go now," I whispered.

"Patience, *pequeña.*"

When I returned to the hotel room to pack my things, Marisela wasn't there. I didn't think much of it until she returned quietly, without any bags or food.

"Where were you?" I asked, folding the last of my t-shirts and tucking them into the bag.

"I was just looking around." She said, not meeting my eyes. I watched her as she grabbed her bags, wiping a small bit of blood from her mouth with the back of her hand.

"Okay, well, it's time to go. Casper said so."

TWENTY-NINE

I groaned as we got back to the car and closed my eyes and let myself drift.

"*You're doing so great, little Starseed! Keep going. Yes, you got it! Look at that!*" *my mother clapped her hands and I marveled at the lighted candle in front of me on my birthday cake.* "*It's magic, mama!*" *I squealed.*

"*Yes, my love. You are magic,*"

I am jerked awake with a gasp, and a flash of light that looks like it had fallen from the sky; the outline of a woman, shrouded in white appeared in the middle of the road.

I screamed, and Casper jerked the wheel as hard as he could. Sending Marisela into me and bouncing her head off the window. The car careened out of control. When he overcorrected it back towards the road, two headlights rushed up toward the windshield, causing Casper to jerk the wheel again off the side of the road into a bank.

Then, nothing but black.

I opened my eyes slowly, pain burned behind my eyes and down my right side. I reached out to Marisela but couldn't feel her body there.

Then, I remembered that she wasn't wearing her seatbelt.

I looked over to see Marisela's body half hanging out of the passenger side window. Glass has broken all around her limp and lifeless body.

Tears built up in the back of my throat and bile touched the back. I gagged and coughed, tasting the iron of my blood on my lips.

Casper flung open my door and pulling me out and into his arms, bringing me our of my shock. I heard him say my name, but it didn't quite sound like him. It sounds like the voice that belonged to someone familiar. I lay my head on his shoulder and cried.

I didn't like letting anyone see me cry—fuck, I never cried. I didn't even cry at my parent's funeral, which was partly the reason my aunt thought I was a sociopath. I did cry, and only I did it in private, in the sacred space of my bedroom.

Maybe I wouldn't even make it to Etienna's; maybe I wasn't meant to. This could simply be my fate—death before I even reached thirty.

Maybe Casper would die, the damage done.

How many more lives would this curse claim? I felt

heat stir through my veins, heating my skin. Anger always followed any strong emotion I felt, and I started hammering my fists against Casper's chest, hot tears streaming down my face. Casper grabbed my face with one hand and said my name again, but he's nothing but a huge blur to me right now.

He picked me up in a bear hug and carried me to the mossy grass beside the SUV, telling me to take deep, slow breaths.

I dropped my head in my hands and sobbed.

I was tired, and emotionally drained.

"Listen to me, Marisela will be fine," Casper pulled on my arm, trying to get me back into the SUV. I resisted at first, but then relented. Call it intuition or defeat—I trusted him. He scooped me up in his arms, placing me in the front seat of the SUV, and as he stood, I wiped away my tears.

"Do you want to know what I came here for? To find a voodoo practitioner, because of a Tarot reading and a list of dead people that I loved because I can control fire." I blinked up at him, half expecting him to ignore me altogether.

He kneeled beside the seat, snaking his thick fingers up my exposed thigh. I noticed a steel, black ring on his middle finger for the first time.

"We'll find her. I promise," His eyes smoldered into mine, and my belly did little flip-flops.

"You don't think I'm crazy?" I sniffled.

He snorted, "Hardly. Although, I do think *all* women are a little crazy,"

I punched his arm playfully, but I smiled.

Casper stood, looking into the back seat, with a

222

shocked look on his face. I turned to the back, and Marisela's body was gone.

"What the fuck?" I said, my manicured nails gripping the back of the seat.

I turned back to Casper, and he was shoving me over into the passenger's seat while I squealed, his powerful body moving to buckle me in. He slammed his door shut and started the car, flooring it. The back window was broken.

"What are you doing? You're just going to leave her back there?" I asked, still unsure what exactly happened to her.

"Fucking vampires," Casper cussed under his breath.

What did vampires have to do with Mar?

"I need to pee," I say after only about ten minutes of driving. The road seemed to go on forever, and there was nothing but trees and endless wetlands. We pass a sign that says, 'Welcome to New Orleans.'

"Domenico's house is just up here, past these gardens. You can wait," Casper grated out.

Where was Mar? Why would he just leave her like that? His sister? And then, I remembered how funny she's acted the entire time I'd known her...

Fucking vampires.

CHAPTER
THIRTY

The morning was dawning again, and I had lost track of what day it was. I had only been in Vegas for a week and was already headed to another state.

I wondered if Marisela was hurt somewhere in the woods or worse, taken by someone. I hadn't protested because of something in Casper's voice.. As if he knew a lot more than I did about his sister.

As Casper slowed, I noticed that this part of New Orleans was all cypress and willow trees, surrounded by brightly colored flowers and greenery. I stared in awe as we pulled into a long, dirt driveway surrounded by a sprawling green field. When the house came into view, I pressed my forehead to the window and gazed up at the tall columns lined the front entryway. Iron-work lattices bracketed each door and window of the white mansion, and flowers lined the gates near the entrance.

The rising sun glowed red and orange on the horizon, creating a romantic backsplash against the pristine structure.

Casper put the SUV in park resting his head against the seat and closing his eyes.

"Are *you* okay?" I asked, trying to care about someone else's needs for once.

He looked at me without any words.

"Do you think I *want* to be here?" He asked, raising his eyebrows.

The SUV was silent, and I was suddenly very aware that we were alone. My skin began to prickle as the smell of his leather seats filled my senses. I let the stillness of the moment swallow me, and I felt him lightly brush his nose against my cheek. I turned, our faces close to one another, "will you just kiss me, already?"

He cursed under his breath but collided his mouth against my demanding incantation. Our lips slipped together, and his tongue found mine. His hand circled behind my head, fingers tangling into my hair, and I groaned. He sucked my lower lip, and I nipped at his.

A loud knock on my window broke our moment, and I jerked around to see an older woman in an old-fashioned apron and uniform.

Casper sighed and rolled his eyes, "That's Frida. The housekeeper,"

"Housekeeper? What year is it?" I laughed, opening my door.

"Welcome, welcome. Now let me take your things and we'll get ya'll all settled," she said, grabbing my shoulder bag while I tightly held onto it.

"No, thank you, I'm good," I said, taking back my bag and replacing it over my shoulder. Her face was slightly shocked, but she smiled and smoothed her apron.

Casper stepped out of the SUV, towering over us both, and he smiled at her, taking her hand.

225

"Frida, how's the family?" he asked, her eyes instantly lighting up at his words.

"Everyone is well, you know, as well as can be. Come inside, it's hotter than blue blazes out here...and bright," she looked over my black attire, my boots, and back to my deep purple lips.

No goth peeps in New Orleans?

I assumed the other girls must not have been guests at 'Domenico air B&B.'

"We have two separate rooms for you, and of course, stay as long as you'd like," She gave me a once over one more time, all the while smiling, and walked off down one of the myriads of hallways off the grand room.

My jaw nearly hit the floor.

Casper obviously knew his way around because he started to head down the hallway to our left. He stopped to look back at me staring, but I stayed in place, taking in the black and white checkered floor and the gold trim. I ran my hands over the silk couches lining the far end of the grand room by the windows.

"I have never seen anything like this in my entire life," I said up into the ceiling, Casper smirked in my direction.

"I'm so happy you love it so much, Celeste. To be honest, though, I knew you would," Jane's voice wrenched my head back towards the flowing staircase next to the entryway.

"Jane?" I said, walking toward her.

"What the fuck? Opal?" Casper dropped his bag onto the floor, the sound of it drawing my eyes to the spot where it lay, abandoned.

Casper's wide body picked her up easily, and she squealed, wrapping her arms tightly around him. He set her down gently and that was when I realized her belly was swollen and round.

"No one calls me Jane anymore, but yes, it's me," she said, her cheeks glowing with life, and a fancy bun twisted up her auburn hair.

She looked nothing like she did when we were teens.

"Is this why you've been gone? You didn't want Moxie to know? *Has he hurt you?*" Casper growled, and I furrowed my brows at his rapid-fire questions. He had never shown interest in anything but sleeping since I'd arrived.

A small part of me wanted to be jealous, but with her current state, I'd say it was a little too late for that.

"I'm fine. Please," she said, rolling her eyes and walking to me, her red and white floral dress floating behind her.

We pulled each other into a warm embrace, and although she looked and felt different, she smelled just the same.

I closed my eyes and hugged her tightly, the memories of nights at the basketball court near our houses, gossiping and scribbling in our notepads until the streetlights came on.

The strangest part about this was that we both talked about running away to Las Vegas. It wasn't just one of us who had the desire to go somewhere bigger and better, but both of us who wanted to see the city lights. Now, she was hidden away in a mansion, living amongst things that I'd only seen on a TV screen. She had everything I had ever wanted.

But how? When?

"I'm sure you have a lot of questions, the both of you," She took both of our hands in hers and placed them on her belly, "this is *the next generation*. This right here, is a blessing and a promise of all the things to come."

I blinked a few times; the feeling of her pregnant belly was alien-like, and I jerked my hand back. My palms tingled, and I looked down at my fingertips, wiggling them a little while she watched.

Winking at me, she said, "See? *Magic,*" she grinned.

"I...I can't believe you are here. Are you happy? Is that...Domenico's?" I asked, looking down at her belly again.

She nodded, cradling it with both hands, "Mhhm. I'm starving, and I'm sure you both are as well. I'll go get us some food."

Casper and I watched as she walked past the stairs and disappeared into the hallway behind it.

Casper looked at me, then at my hands.

"Do you think anyone else knows?" I asked, remembering how upset the coven was when Ruby had her vision. I shouldn't be surprised at this.

"I don't know what to believe anymore," he said, picking up his bag off the floor.

My body tingled, and I was eager to shower, but a part of me wanted to follow Ja—Opal and ask her more questions.

Maybe I should just look around a little and see what other skeletons are in these closets.

My curiosity took over, and before I knew it, I had found my way into a storage room where they kept the extra food. I raked a hand through my hair, blowing out a rush of air in frustration, and turned around.

"Celeste. I see you're making yourself at home,"

"Domenico, oh, hey. I didn't know you would actually *be* here. Sorry, I was just look—"

"For food. Certainly, I can't blame you for that, although I wouldn't understand the feeling of *hunger* per se. Perhaps thirst..." He grinned, both hands clasped behind his back.

I laughed awkwardly, looking for an escape around him.

"Here, while I have you," He reached into his suit, pulled out a large check, and handed it to me.

I took it, unfolding it to see the amount, and nearly choked.

I've never seen this many zeros in my life.

I smiled and thanked him, trying not to scream like a little girl.

"Allow me to escort you back to your room," he said, crooking his arm and inviting me to take it.

I smiled, following him through the hallways and richly decorated sitting rooms, of which he explained each room's purpose as we strolled.

Once we returned to the guest rooms, I was eager to say goodbye. I didn't want to be anyone's midnight snack. *Except maybe Casper.*

"Will you join me for dinner tomorrow night? I think I may have some information that you've been looking for," he said, crooking an eyebrow and bowing slowly.

"Ok, sure," I called, his back disappearing into the monstrous house.

Etienna? Did this guy know who she was?

CHAPTER
THIRTY-ONE

I decided to make my way into the kitchen, hoping to find Opal so we could talk.

The kitchen was modern, with small accents of different types of flowers painted onto the backsplash behind every kitchen appliance you could dream of. This mansion fits the bill of modern meets country.

I watched Opal's back at the stove, making what looked like an omelet with cheese and peppers. It smelled delicious.

"I feel like a place like this would have a private chef, I'm surprised to see you cooking Ja—Opal." I said, leaning against the marble countertop behind me.

She let out a little giggle, bringing me back to when we were children; I smiled at the thought.

"We do, but I'm still not used to it. I've only been here for a year."

A year? That means she got pregnant damn quick.

I moved around to the other side of the counter, sitting at the bar in one of the wooden, straight-back chairs. I stared at the back of her mousy brown hair that looked curlier than the last time I had seen her.

I struggled to find the words to say—why did she just disappear like that? Why couldn't she have told me; I was her best friend and one of the only people that she had trusted.

"Why didn't you tell me? I wouldn't have said anything—"

"Save it," she said sternly, switching the stove nob off with a sharp click.

She plated the eggs, grabbed hot sauce from the fridge and walked to the bar to sit beside me.

"It's a little more detailed than just *telling you* where I was going." She shook the hot sauce, covering the omelet.

"So, tell me, because there's quite a lot of information I've obtained in the past few days. Not much will shock me at this point. So *why?*" I placed my hand over hers, and she stopped eating, glancing at our contact.

She chewed, slowly, but hesitated, thinking over her response carefully.

She took a deep breath, sighing, "I hitched a ride to Vegas, and ended up a seedy strip club, desperate for a job. That's where I met Marisela."

She stopped, waiting for my reaction, but considering how many places Marisela made her way around too, I wasn't surprised. Mar liked to collect lost souls.

"She got me out of there fast—and I was thankful because if she didn't, I never would have met Domenico." She said, her smile reaching her eyes as she said his name.

My stomach dropped; I still had doubts about that dude, but his paychecks made it pretty easy to overlook his faults.

"What does this mean?" I motioned at her belly, "Vampires can't reproduce, any idiot knows that."

Her smile was still plastered to her face, "I'm *special*. He told me so."

Something about her euphoric attitude didn't fit with how I remembered Jane. She was different, of that, I was sure.

What made her so special that she could breed with a vampire?

It looked like she had everything she had ever dreamed of, but at what cost?

"How, Opal? Tell me. Please,"

She hesitated slightly, but after hopping off her chair and peeking around the kitchen's door frame, she scurried back to her seat.

"Do you remember that crazy night when I miscarried, and I was hemorrhaging?"

How could I forget that? She had gotten pregnant and decided to keep it—even though we both knew her family would force her to give it up for adoption. The night she started bleeding, I was the one who made sure she made it to the hospital and stayed with her all night.

I nodded, waiting for her to continue.

"You had to have your blood drawn to see if you were a match, in case I needed your blood."

I nodded again, remembering how terrified I was that my friend might die, and I lied and told them we were sisters.

"Well, we were a match, and although I didn't *need* it, I still took home the paperwork just in case I would ever need you again. Have you heard of RH negative blood?" she asked her hand on top of mine.

"No, what does that mean?"

She raised her eyebrows, leaning in closer to me, "It's the blood type that is considered a *mutation*...and Celeste, the rabbit hole I went down after looking up our *rare* blood type—would blow your mind."

I sat there puzzled, knowing I had a rare blood type— but what did that have to do with the vampires?

"Ok, so what's *your* theory?" I asked, one eyebrow cocked.

"Alien blood. An interrupted line of humans who were developed from alien breeding."

I almost laughed out loud, but I loved my friend too much to laugh at her outlandish claim. I mean, I believed in witchcraft and now I know there are vampires. Why not aliens, too?

"So, you're saying that's what makes us so special to Vampires? Are we, like, a rare *delicacy* or something?" I laughed, sounding a little manic as I asked.

She nodded, still smiling; it was starting to weird me out.

I stood from the bar, yet again trying to give myself time to process this new information.

Is this why I was sought after by Domenico? Was Marisela sniffing out these women with a rare, alien-blood type? How?

I raked my hands through my hair and groaned, "I think I need a nap."

She stood, placing her hand on my lower back, "Yes, definitely. You should rest, you travelled a long way."

I hugged her tightly, feeling her belly in between us, and wondering what kind of a creature she carried inside of her.

I felt dizzy.

The bedroom I was put in was directly across from

Casper's, but the room was empty each time I peeked inside. My flips-flops smacked against the pristine floors, and I plopped down on the couch in the grand room with a dramatic sigh.

I thought this would be far more exciting than it is.

I heard a dull thud, then another and another. It sounded like someone was hammering or hitting something nearby. I looked around the massive, empty room, and noticed a heavy door off the back wall.

I stood, walked over to it and pushed my ear against the door, furrowing my brow, trying to figure out just what I was hearing. Thud, then a deep male grunt. Another succession of thuds and more grunting.

Was Casper having sex?!

Jealousy ripped through me, and I imagined him working over her body, her pregnant belly between them. I pushed in the door roughly, shocked as I took in Casper's sweat-soaked chest and hands at his sides with boxing gloves on.

"The fuck? Jesus, Celeste. You're so damn nosey. Are you here to work out too?" he grunted, chest heaving. He wiped his forehead with the back of the glove and stared at me. His pupils dilated and angry, and then I noticed his drenched hair, droplets of sweat dripping from his black curls.

Part of me wanted to slam the door in his face for yelling at me, but my stubbornness dug in its heels. I crossed my arms over my chest, narrowing my eyes at him. He's angry, but I am not the cause.

He watched me as I approached him, fury on his face.

"Why are you so goddamn angry all the time?" I challenged, almost touching him now, craning my neck to meet his eyes. I may not be tall for a woman, but that

234

didn't bother me. I was a fiery spirit with a sharp tongue.

He pushed me hard against the punching bag in one aggressive motion, a breath of air escaping my chest. He pinned me firmly with his fist against my chest, his face now inches from mine, "Why do you ask so many *annoying* questions?"

I sneered, my body tingled, pushing my chest against his hand, "Survival skill."

He stepped back from me, annoyed. Ripping off both gloves with his teeth and tossing them to the floor, he grabbed a bottle of water and loudly drank.

"It's Opal, isn't it? You *do* love her,"

Crushing the water bottle with one hand, he threw it to the ground and pushed me against the bag again. The leather stuck to my back, and his bare hand was on my waist.

"You're wrong," He growled, holding my eyes with his.

The anger I held toward men—any man who didn't show me the respect I deserved—came from my father. His wandering eye and screaming matches with my mother were the only memories I had of him. A six or seven-year-old should never have to comfort their mother's broken heart at the hands of their father. It left a scar on my soul that could never be erased.

My instinct was to push back, to fight him, and explode. I had a reputation at home for trying to fight men, and the only place it ever got me was on my ass in a parking lot.

I chose a different approach this time.

I placed my palms against his wet chest and down the length of his abs. He clenched them in response, and I circled my hands around to the back, pulling him toward me.

I was surprised at how easily he followed my pull, his body flush against mine.

Only because *I* wanted them to be.

His hands came to the bag, his arms rested above me, but his face was close to mine. His breath tickled my top lip, and I could think of nothing more than to press my lips to his.

Before I could make a move, his mouth crashed onto mine with a ferocity that mimicked anger. Anger that quickly turned into hunger.

I surged my hand into his curls, something that was quickly becoming my favorite thing to do. He scooped me up by my legs, hooking my knees around his hips, kissing me deeply, and then gently. He kissed the sides of my mouth in urgency, stopping to curse under his breath every now and then.

"That mouth gets you into a lot of trouble, doesn't it?" he said panting, the bass of his voice sending a pulse straight to my core.

I rolled my hips against him, moaning softly, "I don't like bullshit. My big mouth usually keeps the wrong people away from me."

He kissed down my neck, carrying me to the weight bench.

I loved the way he carried me around like it was effortless; thick thighs and a big ass were all fun and games until the guy wasn't strong enough to throw you around a little.

He laid me on my back, and our bodies were still pressed together. My thighs gripped his waist tightly, and I felt his hard length against my thigh.

He pulled back, admiring my splayed body and lifting my t-shirt, exposing my breasts. He moved down to the end of the bench, licking his lips. My nipples stood out, tight, and my body flushed with heat. I was suddenly aware of how charged I felt over every inch of my body.

I squeezed my eyes shut, trying to block out the image of the dead vampire at the Leo party under me, his face screwed up in terrified shock. The image of Kyle came behind it. The same shocked expression, the same lifeless body.

Was this because of the curse? Or was there simply something wrong with me? I needed answers, and I wasn't sure if Etienna would be able to save me from myself—or at all.

I opened my eyes again, forcing myself to focus on the here and now—my life's mantra. And when I focused my eyes back on the present moment, he was already watching me, heating my skin under his gaze.

"Tell me what happened,"

Shit.

He kneeled at the end of the bench, still between my legs. I sat up so that our faces were level.

Stupid mind-reading prick.

"I heard that," he said, level.

I rolled my eyes, wondering how I would lie my way out of this one.

"I don't know. I might think about sex a lot but that doesn't mean I sleep around. I'm selective about who I let enter my body," I said, raising one eyebrow. His eyes looked soft and understanding, a complete three-sixty from how he looked earlier.

"I never said you slept around," he moved his wide hands up my thighs on each side, sending goosebumps to the apex above them.

"Two people have died after I had sex with them. That's the story. I don't know how else I can explain it to you," I shrugged.

I really didn't want to have this conversation; I'd rather be getting my back blown out on a piece of gym equipment.

He laughed, watching my expression.

I laughed, too.

"Sounds to me like two very un-lucky men. I don't know if I would call you the cause, though," He said, leaning in to kiss my jaw, "I'm not scared."

I reddened, both at his kisses and his response.

"I want you," I demanded, wrapping my hand around the back of his neck and pulling his face to mine.

He looked down over my leggings and then at my eyes, licking his lips.

He stood, untangling my arms from his neck and grabbed a towel, wiping himself off.

I wanted to pout my lips and demand, but I seemed to get my way more with him when I was sweet and kind. He frustrated me more each day, and I couldn't tell if it was the sexual chemistry or my need to feel loved.

I stood, prepared to stomp away in a fury—but then he spoke to my back.

"I think you need to practice self-control. It would do you well," he said as I stopped at the heavy door.

I turned, choosing to accept his challenge, "I agree."

I smiled, even though deep down I was pissed and wound tighter than a spool of thread.

If I needed to practice self-control, I would just have to lock myself in my room until I found Etienna.

I could avoid him for a couple of days, right?

THIRTY-TWO

The wooden door to my room clicked as I opened and closed it; my feelings hurt, and my pussy was neglected. Two things that pissed me off to no end.

Control myself.

Did he want me to back off? It looked and felt like he wanted it just as bad as I did. Or maybe he was talking about more. He was a mind reader after all.

I piled my hair on top of my head and snickered to myself, scanning the bedroom I would be sleeping in for our time here.

The room looked oddly suited to my taste. I noticed it this morning but fell into a blissful sleep in the deep reds and dark blacks of the linens.

A long table lined the bay window that overlooked the backyard gardens. The table was draped with a dark floral tablecloth with tassels on the ends, and candles of all different colors and sizes were assembled in the middle. A single wine glass sat beside a crystal tumbler filled with a dark, amber liquid. Rose petals and different colored crystals sat in a neatly placed circle around the candles.

I stared at the arrangement, feeling a pull toward the candles, concentrating on the feeling of rejection that Casper left stinging on my skin. It only worked when I really *tried*, and I promised myself I would stop trying after that night and only use it if I *had* to.

Casper *did* say self-control. Not to control myself. I got that backward because I was so enraged. Maybe he's right. If I *tried* to control it, while I wielded it.

My father's voice echoed in my head...*see...this is what happens. It's the curse. We are all fucking cursed.*

I gritted my teeth and clenched my fists, feeling the heat radiating from me. The angrier I got, the more power it gained.

I slammed my eyes shut and tried to think of something. Anything happy. I thought of tacos and pizza, but then my mind traveled to Casper's mouth. I could stare at it for hours, and kiss him for days. I felt myself getting turned on and steered my thoughts back to something that would flood me with dopamine besides sex.

I remembered the first night that I met Mar, and how much it felt like she needed me. She never made me feel left out or odd but quite the opposite. She had stuck up for me and welcomed me. I smiled, feeling the heat leaving my body, just as a cool breeze from the window brushed back my hair.

I was in control, and that was why I decided to come here in the first place.

I sat on the winged back chair beside a built-in bookshelf that lined the far wall. A heavy, knitted throw hung over the arm of the chair, and I pulled it over me and tucked my legs under me. The wing made for a surprisingly nice headrest, and my eyes began to feel heavy as I leaned on it.

The cool breeze made me shiver, and my body felt like I had just run laps around this mansion. The window was open wide, dusk settling over the property. I wanted to close the window; I just felt so sleepy.

A small, rapid knock came at the door, and I croaked out a "come in" after Casper had already opened the door.

He stood in front of me, dressed in a casual collared shirt, that opened at the chest. Grinning, he walked to where I was seated, a tray of food in his hands. I almost laughed at him, but I was too tired.

"I'm sorry for earlier. I could have said it, *kinder.*"

I sat up, smelling the food–grilled shrimp on top of thin noodles nestled in a buttery sauce that made my mouth water. I grabbed for the fork and stabbed a spicy shrimp, kneeling beside the seteé the tray sat on.

"I like watching you eat. The look on your face of satisfaction—I could get used to that." He smiled.

Would he still feel the same if he knew about all the things I have done? Would he still want me if he knew I carried magic inside of me so lethal, that it could kill?

As if he already knew, Casper headed to the window, closing both sides, and locking them in with two clicks.

I shoveled the food into my mouth while Casper looked on, smugly.

He sat behind me, in the now empty chair—where I planned to return once I was done eating this bite.

"I wasn't trying to insult you; I just think you need to try harder—with your abilities," he said softly, kindly.

I picked up the tray and turned toward him, sitting on

the seteè and placing the tray on my lap. I stabbed another shrimp and chewed, "Continue."

He placed his hand on my knee, "whatever it is that you think you can do...or maybe I should say—what you're capable of doing—needs to be controlled. Regardless of what it is," he leaned forward, still taller than me, even seated.

Although he rarely spoke, he was careful with his words. I was captivated each time he blessed me with his spoken word, and I took what he said and held it tight but kept the words I usually spilled so freely to myself this time.

He was right. I needed to try harder.

THIRTY-THREE

CASPER

S he thought she was being coy, but at least she was listening to me. She filled me with more heat than I already had inside of me; something Opal liked to remind me of often. I had a temper, and she had seen it the night Alex broke her heart. My rage got the better of me and Alex was in the hospital for a week.

I wanted to take her, make her obey me in a way she never had before. Giving herself and her trust to me in full, but I had a feeling I would need to demand it.

"You think you know what's best for me, huh?" she grinned, putting down the fork and picking up a noodle with her fingers.

The pasta tasted amazing, Domenico's chef always outdid himself, the knowledge of an immortal creature had no end, and that wasn't even half the reason the fuckers were intimidating.

I wanted to lick the butter from her fingertips, take them into my mouth and suckle each one. I reached over and tossed the tray off her lap, grabbing her by the throat, her sharp intake of breath let me know just how much I had taken her by surprise.

I liked that.

"I think I know what every human needs, special or not—and you need to be understood," I kissed her jaw, right next to where my thumb is pressed, "and cared for," I trailed down her neck with kisses, and she sighed. I am purposefully light and gentle while she squirmed against me in need.

"You sure like to take your time, don't you? I don't like to be teased," she said, standing, practically shoving me off her. She took her natural, defensive pose of crossing her arms in front of her and jutting out one hip.

I stood, grabbing her wrist, drawing her to me. She resisted at first, but I stroked her hair lightly, and she relented. Resting her head against my chest, I slowed my breath, inhaling deeply and out with measure.

Soon, she did the same, breathing in sync with me. I palmed the back of her head, feeling the connection to her mind drawing me in like a river. I closed my eyes, the innate need to give in to the feeling that felt so natural to me.

The black smoke was gone now, and a smoldering fire filled her mind.. When the screams of children filled my senses, I turned away as if I was turning my back on her. The pain hit me like a punch in the gut, and I ripped open my eyes, staring down over her tear-stained face.

"I'm sorry," was all I could manage; I felt a choke at the back of my throat, and her green eyes looked up into mine. She raised her eyebrows, and her cheeks were wet with absolution. I kissed her forehead.

"Don't go into my mind again without asking, fucker," she said, sniffling. Pushing me playfully away, I growled, grabbing her by her red hair and tugging. Her jaw dropped, and her head is pulled tight, craning up at me.

"Listen, I may be kind and caring, but I'm also cautious," I said low, with the bass from my chest.

She smiled, "kiss me."

I wrapped more of her hair around my hand and pulled, "So bossy. I'm in charge right now."

She hesitated for a moment but finally said, "Ok."

"Go to the bed and lay down," I ordered, and she obeyed.

First, she sat, trying to skate around what I told her to do.

Although I wanted to punish her mouth, making her do as I demanded, I wanted her to take something from this. Even if I never saw her again, I wanted her to learn about the power she held in her spectacular mind.

"Strip. And lay down, like I asked."

I could see the excitement in her eyes, goose flesh running over her skin as she took off the t-shirt. Her nipples were tight with need.

I stood over her, completely naked and vulnerable to me. There was something exciting about seeing her submit. I had watched her act without a thought over and over, going into every situation blind. She liked to act like she knew things, but she didn't know the kinds of things I did.

Her pink pussy matched her nipples, and her curved hips smushed against the bed, made my hands tingle.

I walked to the edge of where she lay, leaning down to grab her ankles, and sinking to the floor in front of her. I placed each foot on my shoulders, and she gasped, looking down over her body, "Yes, lick it."

I looked up at her, irritation on my face, and smacked her pussy in succession twice. Her hips jerked, and her pretty mouth dropped open again.

I was really enjoying the shocked looks she gave me, my cock rigid against my thigh.

I wanted to toss her around, but this bed didn't give me much room. I also wanted her to understand that sex didn't have to be about the finish but the journey.

I stood, frustrated by her cockiness, "get on all fours, and don't say *anything*."

She watched my face and did as I said.

I gripped her ass cheek in my palm, jiggling it lightly and ending my grope with a swat. Her hair was draped to one side over her shoulder and her pink pussy was spread slightly; I brought my hand down to cup her heat.

She sighed, and I could feel her wetness on my fingers as I slipped one gently inside. She cried out, and I followed it with another, curling my fingers up and down her walls. She pushed back against my hand, and I swatted her ass harder this time.

"Please," she begged, biting her lip.

"Just because you want something badly, doesn't mean you will always have it," I said with a voice full of authority.

I undid the buttons on my pants and pulled out my cock. It throbbed with need as I fisted it in my hand, rubbing the head of it over her wet slit.

Women constantly complained of my large size, and there was nothing that turned me on more than a woman who could take it all.

"I'm going to slide my cock deep inside you, and you're not going to cry out. Control it. Do you understand?" I said, pushing against her tight entrance.

She nodded, but her ass shimmied against me, and my balls tightened at the thought of claiming her body once again.

I eased in slowly, watching her take me inch by inch. She did exactly as I said and remained silent, but her hands gripped the edges of the bed tightly.

I slammed my cock home, nearly doubling over at how tight she was, gripping me like a vice.

I pulled out slowly and heard her whine while she wiggled her ass against me.

I panted but thrust inside her again; this time, she did cry out, "Are you trying to get off, *pequeña*? Does that fat cock feel good inside you?"

I didn't relent; instead I assaulted her with deep thrusts, using her hips as leverage. "Fuck! Oh Gods, it's too big! Please, go easy–"

I groaned, almost losing my orgasm to her right there, but I used the control I had learned over the years.

"You feel so good. *So fucking good,*" I urged, pumping into her deliciously slow.

"Yes..." she groaned, reaching between her legs. I bent over her, halting my thrust, and grabbed her hand.

"Don't. Good girls get to come, brats have to wait," I growled, assaulting her body harder as she cried out, her body falling forward so her ass was higher in the air.

I moved with her, mounting her with one knee bent on the bed.

"Yes...take me," she cried as I continued.

"Are you sure about that?" I ground out as I pumped, "I can be very possessive over what's mine."

Flesh slapping against skin filled my ears as her perfect words coaxed my orgasm., "Then possess me."

I couldn't hold on any longer, the fire inside this

woman's veins brought life to me, and when she gave me those vulnerable words, I exploded.

I pulled out, ropes of come dressing her back and ass as I fist myself to completion. I hovered above her, bracing myself by wrapping my arm around her waist and resting my sweat-covered face on her back.

"Good girl," I whispered into her neck, "I knew you could do it."

CHAPTER
THIRTY-FOUR

My core throbbed at the intense relief. My breathing came in heavy droves, and when I felt him collapse on my back, I felt victorious.

I'm not sure if it was because of the amount of control I had to harness *not* to come or if I was scared I would kill him.

I was proud of myself for not taking what I wanted so damn badly. I was happy that I could please this man who barely spoke a word to anybody. That he had trusted me enough to let me see him crumble at my hands, well, pussy.

Once he was finished, I moved to a seated position, uncaring of the bulges at my waist.

He sat beside me, placing a wide hand on my knee and squeezing.

"As much as I love playing with you like this out in the open, what I really want to do is take you back to my house and enjoy every inch of you...privately."

I smiled, giving him a rough kiss, and stood,

outstretching my hand. He took it, gathering my clothes off the floor.

"I think that's the best idea you've have had all week,"

After stepping back into my clothes, I stood in the hallway, and we walked to the kitchen together.

I tiptoed behind Casper, but he stopped me with his hand. Two shadows crossed the floor of the great room, heading toward the kitchen. A man and a woman's voices echoed off the walls, one of them was clearly upset.

Casper glanced at his phone, the time shining brightly in the dark. It was nearly midnight.

I followed behind him as he creeped through the room, side-stepping couches, and a piano to make it to the corner near the kitchen. It was thrilling sneaking around, and I just never thought I would be doing it with him. As the couple came into view, I recognized Marisela and her wild, long hair. She looked fine, with a few bruises on her right arm that were very faded.

Kind of like she never got into an accident at all.

She was swinging her hands emphatically, and I caught the words 'crazy' and 'selfish' flying between her expletives.

When the man circled her to the bar on the other side of the room, I noticed who it was.

Domenico.

He poured himself a drink, looking bored while Marisela yelled in his direction. Her tight red dress was bunched up at the bottom, and it looked like she'd been crying.

I moved closer so I could hear, but Casper stayed behind me.

"Why is she here, Dom? Everyone thought she was missing—gone! But no, she is staying here at chateau Domenico! Is it yours?!"

"I have already told you, what you have done has destroyed your chance at sitting beside me and carrying on my line. I told you I would not turn you for a reason,"

"It was the contract, wasn't it? She waited it out here until it was over, now she is yours,"

Domenico nodded at her subtly, and Marisela shouted, both her hands on top of her head while she turned in circles.

I watched as she threw a temper tantrum like a child.

I looked back at Casper, and he shook his head but pointed at his room door. I nodded at him and turned around, heading back toward the guest bedrooms. Following me, we rushed into the room, Casper gently closing the door behind him.

"Holy fuck! She's turned, isn't she? Is that why she took off unharmed?" I asked as quietly as I could.

Casper sat on the edge of the bed, his head in his hands.

"Counting Opal, Mar is the third woman Domenico has tried to get to join his 'harem.' I think Mar mistook that role as being a vampire queen, but in reality—that's not the case.

"What is it then?" I asked, standing beside him and

shivering. I hated being cold. And it was dark and freezing in this house.

"It's your blood type. I'm sure of it. It's the only thing that makes sense to me now that she's a vamp...well... she's dead inside. Get it?" Casper reached inside his pocket and pulled out a knife, twirling it in his hand.

"Using women with our blood type like a damn breeding factory." I said and sat beside him.

Now I know why I should always trust my gut. Sure, Domenico was a vampire, but taking these 'special' women and breeding them? That sounded like making a deal with the devil.

'It's too late for me, I signed a deal with El Diablo.'

Those were the exact words Marisela had said.

If Domenico refused to turn her, I could absolutely see her going behind his back and doing it anyways.

"I guess so. I'm not even sure if Opal is the first."

I shivered again, reaching over to take his hand, "Do we have to talk about this right now? I don't feel like I can take in anymore. My brain capacity for the paranormal is about full," I smiled at hi.

"What we really need to figure out is if we should kill that blood-sucking-fuck," he withdrew his hand from mine, opening and closing the knife. Casper stood, and walked to the bed, searching for a gun he pulled out from the mattress.

I *cared* about Mar, but not to the point where I wanted to kill.

What I wanted right now was to climb into his bed, safely sleeping beside him while he held me.

Call it childish, but I wanted to submerse myself in him, and give myself to him.

How could he not understand the whiplash this was

causing me? I needed to recover—from it all. The Leo party, the séance, the traveling. ...It was nearly midnight, and all he could think about was killing? I couldn't take anymore, and if he didn't want to comfort me, I would just go to bed.

Self-control...

I ignored the thought and stormed from his room, slamming his door behind me and whipping mine open. I slammed my door shut and climbed into bed, exhausted.

I didn't take rejection very well, and all I wanted was to be understood.

My eyes stung, and I sat up, wiping away my tears.

I would just go to Etienna's on my own, and I didn't need anyone's protection. I had my crystal and my cat knuckles. First, I just needed some sleep.

I pulled back the covers, my body aching and my eyes heavy.

A soft knock came on the door a few minutes later, and I rolled my eyes, "I'm tired. Go away."

Casper's curly hair poked inside, and I rolled my eyes. I pulled the covers over my head, but my belly was full of butterflies. I'd never had a man chase me the way he did.

He wanted me enough to not take no for an answer, andsI loved that about him.

"I'm sorry. I shouldn't have said that. I *know* you're not a killer like me. I've seen it, and I've *felt* it," He casually laid his long body at the foot of my bed, looking up at me under thick black lashes. He was blindingly handsome, and as I pulled the cover below my eyes, I could barely pull myself to look away-he was way too cute to be mad at when he looked at me that way.

I scooted a little towards him and watched his bowed lips. I waited for him to say more; I *always* wanted more.

"Stand up," He commanded.

I obeyed, my body responding to him instantly, chasing the high of being dominated by such a perfect man.

He stared up at me from where he was laying, and I looked down at him, awaiting further instructions.

"I want you to take all of that pent up orgasm, and the urge you had to slap me just now—and bottle it up but focus on those candles over there while you do it," he stood, taking his place behind me. He placed his hands on my hips, and I closed my eyes at his touch. I could see the fire building behind my lids, and when I opened them again, the table lined with candles erupted into orange light. Each wick ignited with ease by a flame that swayed in the heat. My eyes grew wide, and my body tingled. I felt Casper's hand graze my lower back, and I began to shake. Every ounce of pain and frustration funneled into one kinetic moment of fire.

"Holy shit," I said under my breath and allowed myself to fall back onto the bed, taking him with me. I felt exhausted, and it was late. Casper kissed me on my neck, and I turned my head toward him, eager to feel his lips on mine.

"Stay with me," I whispered into his lips.

THIRTY-FIVE

Waking up in the morning next to Casper had me smiling like a fool as I stretched. The sunlight streamed through the window, the small pots of flowers reaching up toward the hot rays.

I turned to his still sleeping form, his face looking peaceful and a little puffy. I felt a sudden urge to sprinkle his face with kisses, but I held back. He didn't need to think I was *that* needy.

I rolled over and grabbed my phone, groaning. It was already one in the afternoon; we had slept for most of the day.

I guess today wasn't the best day to drive around looking for my witch.

I stood from the bed, not remembering falling asleep naked, and walked to the attached bathroom.

"Celeste?" Casper called from the bedroom, and I poked my head around the doorway.

"Good morning, *Papi*," I cooed.

"Hey," he said with a grin, stretching his arms and scratching his torso.

"It's already one, and I'm going to dinner with Domenico tonight. I need a shower," I called, walking to the glass-standing two-piece jacuzzi tub.

As I stepped into the steam, Casper's frame appeared, leaning against the doorway, arms crossed, "Dinner with Domenico? I thought we were taking a trip to the French quarter?"

I let the shower spray my face, finding it adorable how protective he was over me. Something I could get used to.

"Yes, *Papi*. It's just dinner—besides, I think he might know where Etienna is," I said, lathering my hair with soap.

He didn't respond, and I assumed he was gone, but then, "I'm coming with you."

I grinned and turned my head to rinse under the water, "You're not coming Casper, he might not tell me if you're there."

"So, then I'll stand by the door, like your *bodyguard*," he mocked me as he stepped into the shower behind me.

I smiled, his arms wrapping around me and pulling me close, "*Fine.*"

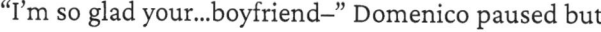

"I'm so glad your...boyfriend–" Domenico paused but

continued when I didn't respond, "–allowed you to join me this evening,"

"He's not my boyfriend," I blurted, taking a sip of my water that left a wet ring on the fancy, white tablecloth.

I instantly felt guilty saying it, especially after the conversation we had last night. It wasn't like we were official—he was a quiet and stubborn asshole most of the time.

"Perfect," he took a slow sip of the red wine he ordered for our table.

I didn't like to drink wine because of the headache that always followed. I sniffed my wine glass but set it back down on the table with a grimace.

"I wanted to bring you here tonight to address a few things with you. One thing being *Moxie's business*. The second is a bit more...complicated," His suit was pressed, the creases in the grey color casting shadows on his sculpted arms. His salt and pepper hair was neatly trimmed, and his high bone structure giving him a nefarious gaze.

I wondered what the complicated part of the conversation was going to be. I only came here tonight because he alluded to knowing something about my witch.

The waitress was dressed in black and white, her apron covering her legs like a skirt. Her hair was in a tight bun, but her makeup was done like a runway model. I had to look twice at her as she set down a plate of clams, and I scrunched up my nose.

Domenico laughed lightly, tickling me behind my ears. His laugh was lilting and almost sounded familiar. I brought my eyes to his stormy ones, and he smiled.

He was charming and always finely pressed, from hair

to manicured fingertips. I would be lying if I said the smell of power that rolled off him didn't entice me.

Our table was private and dimly lit by candles in tall, red glass holders at the back of the restaurant,.

"I hope you are finding your way around The Crystals. They tend to be a bit...intimidating. This lifestyle isn't exactly for everyone," he said, placing a linen napkin on his lap.

I wasn't sure if I should be offended or thank him for the opportunity. Knowing about vampires and magic in our world only gave me nightmares, not comfort, after all —the punishment for letting the cat out of the bag was death.

And I was sitting right in front of the final-level big boss.

"I really like the girls. I think that's a part of the reason I want to stay," I said, picking up my water again and sipping, trying to mask the nervousness in my voice.

"I'm pleased to hear that. Marisela speaks so *highly* of you. It's sweet, really," he leaned back slightly, allowing the posh waitress to set a very bloodied steak in front of him.

"While I would love to sit here and talk about *business,* I'd rather talk about what you know about Etienna. I mean, you're old, right? You must know everyone in New Orleans," I said, picking at my salad with a fork.

He grinned while looking down at his plate, carefully picking up the fork on his right and the knife on his left. He cut the steak and bit, the blood coating his lips as he chewed.

I swallowed, wondering if maybe he was truly evil, like most horror films I had seen. I shivered and absent-mindedly clutched the crystal around my neck.

I felt his eyes on me, his stare heavy, and I blinked a few times before I made eye contact with him again.

"Smart girl. Yes, I've been around for a while. That does not translate to knowing *everyone*. Why are you looking for a witch, anyhow?" he said, his tone dripping with authority.

I took a deep breath, preparing to lay it all on the line. How strange could a curse and a hocus pocus-pussy sound to a *vampire*? I didn't care at this point.

"I need a curse lifted...or maybe an exorcism," I trailed off.

Domenico wiped the corner of his lips gently and chuckled, "Perhaps a gift and a curse to watch the love of your life incarnate, time after time. Clueless to what power they hold. You do *not* need an exorcism, l'amour."

The blood drained from my face.

Incarnate?

Standing, he pulled his chair closer to mine, and his close proximity spread goosebumps down my arms.

I knew a few basic things about Vampires; they couldn't be exposed to the sun, they fed off blood, and they've been around for a very, very long time.

Who was he talking about? A past love that he knew centuries ago? Decades ago? I was young and virile, certainly not from centuries ago.

"Tell me, do you practice magic with the coven?" he leaned his arm on the table beside me, bringing his face close to mine.

I wore a strapless mini dress that was black and red, with small spikes on the waist and hips. I was hyper-aware of my exposed neck and chest and could feel the blood beating in my neck. My cheeks reddened, and I leaned in on my elbows so that we were nearly touching.

I was calling his bluff, and I wanted to see what kind of move he would make next, "Yes."

He sneered, but his half grin was sexy, and I kept eye contact with him. Eye contact often asserted dominance, and I wanted him to understand that I was a strong woman who couldn't be pushed around.

Holding eye contact with me, he leaned down and kissed my shoulder; his lips were soft.

"Magical *and* a Starseed...I'm willing to wager that you taste divine,"

Could Starseed be referring to my blood type? It was the only connection I could make.

While entranced by his harmonious speaking pattern, my mind only registered the sexual portion of his comment, and I smiled wide.

"Indeed," I said, eyeing his lips but remembering everything Casper told me last night. I *did* have power over these vampires. I was able to kill one with the swish of my hips and an orgasm. What power did they have over me? Aside from the capability of ripping out my throat and draining me, I evened the score between humans and vampires just a little. Something told me he wanted to use that to his advantage.

He reached over and took my hand, holding it tightly. I flinched at the iciness off his fingertips, my arm nearly going numb at the contact.

"Power is a very dangerous thing. You should know that," he whispered into my ear, and I looked down at the tight grip he had on my hand.

He opened his mouth just a little, revealing two pointed canines I still wasn't used to seeing. I ran my tongue over my teeth, imagining what it would feel like to wear a threat like that inside of mine.

I suddenly felt very tired, drained even. My arm throbbed, the coldness from his hand seeping through my body.

He released me, and I instantly felt a surge of energy return. Heat rushed to my limbs, to the tips of my toes. I looked at him, confused.

He returned to his side of the table, removing a piece of paper from his pocket and sliding it on the table in front of me. He snapped his fingers a few times, and the waitress reappeared, waiting for instructions.

"Wrap this up please and be sure that Miss Moore makes it back to the mansion safely. Goodnight, Celeste," He's gone in a flash, with waiters scurrying around me, picking up plates and glasses. A take-away box appeared in front of me, and I stood, looking towards the front entrance.

Casper stood by the door, waiting, sunglasses firmly in place.

I sighed and grabbed the box and piece of paper, and walked toward my ride home. I wondered if he would subject me to a punishment of silence the whole ride or if he would choke me again.

I honestly preferred the latter.

"Listen, I know you think this guy has the key to everything you've ever wanted, but he doesn't," Casper said into the rearview mirror as he drove. Headlights roved over his stone face, and I had the urge to crawl into his lap and ask him to kiss me all over, but I stayed put with a frown on my face.

"How do you know he doesn't?" I quipped, looking at him in the rearview.

He sighed loudly, gripping the steering wheel.

"We know things about Domenico that Moxie doesn't. And if she finds out—there will be war," His tone was even but wary.

Who better to forecast a war than an ex-military?

"Like, what? That Marisela is a vamp now? Domenico didn't turn her, he said someone else did it," I crossed my arms over my chest as we hit a bump and my tits jiggled.

"No. Not that..."

"Then just tell me, because I don't like secrets and I don't like lies,"

"I can't do that right now, it's too risky. If Moxie new his end game, she wouldn't want to be in business with him anymore," he put the SUV into park, "then who knows what would happen to us *mortals."*

I shivered; he had a point.

Guess that's the risk you take when you do business with the devil himself.

We were already back at the New Orleans mansion, and I wanted nothing more than to get in some comfy sweats and crawl into bed. My brain hurt.

The SUV was silent for a moment, but then Casper

opened his door and got out. He opened my door and outstretched his hand to me. I took it, weary with all the information I was given in the past three days.

He pulled me to him, so we were chest to chest, "I don't like to share."

I grinned, turning up to look into his soft brown eyes. Leaning down, he kissed me square on my nose, and I sighed. Playfully shoving him, I said, "Don't tell me what to do."

I bent down and unclasped my heels, taking them off and carrying them to the house. Casper jogged behind me to catch up and flung his heavy arm around my shoulders.

"I want to show you something," he said, tugging on my arm and leading me into the main entrance of the mansion and down the hallway into his guest room.

I plopped on his bed, rubbing my feet and blowing my hair away from my face.

He pulled out his phone and opened the photo app, pulling up something that looked like an official document. I squinted as I read, and at the top of the photographed document was Opal's full real name, birthdate, and place, along with blood type and heritage charts. I looked up at him, pretending not to know the information Opal had already shared with me.

"I found these in Dom's office. Files on every girl that Moxie's had in her Coven of Crystal's."

He swiped through more photos with names and blood types on them, "They all have the same thing: RH negative blood."

"Yeah, so," I shrugged.

"Come on, they're vampires. Blood is their sustenance and it seems they have a preference. Do you know how rare some of these blood types are? AB negative is the rarest, and that's exactly what you have," he said, pulling up the file they had on me.

"How do you even know it's rare?" I asked, testing him.

He sighed, "*Google* is pretty easy to use if you do your research."

"I'm not even having this conversation if you don't want to tell me what's really going on with him. I'm tired and I finally have what I was looking for," I held up the piece of paper Domenico gave me.

"Is that really her address?" He asked, sitting beside me and squeezing my thigh.

"I sure hope so."

THIRTY-SIX

We both reluctantly got into the SUV the following morning, thick fog rolled over the meadow in the late August weather. I wasn't used to getting up this early; it felt like I hadn't slept in a month, every event from the last two weeks was hitting me hard.

I refused to give in to the feeling of hopelessness or fear, and on this early but quiet morning, I was forced to sit alone with my thoughts. Both Casper and I readied in silence, and I didn't know what to expect when I made it to my destination.

Was he worried about going to visit a witch? I wondered briefly if he even believed in any of this—the curse included.

Although, my pyrotechnics could have been enough proof for him the other night. I looked over at his profile, seated in the driver's seat of the SUV. He was still sleepy from the night before, rubbing his eyes, but he looked softer, almost innocent. I brought my hand to his curls, unable to help myself. He turned to me and smiled, eyes shining. For the first time in my life, I felt safe. I wasn't worried about what was coming for me next and just focused on this moment, right now.

"Are you ready?" he asked, turning on the ignition.

I grabbed his hand, grasping it tightly in mine and faced forward and looked toward the end of the gated driveway, "I was born ready,"

The further south we drove, the thicker the trees and swamps became. My face was glued to the window, searching the surface of the mucky water for any signs of an alligator. Excitement bubbled under my skin, and my stomach did little fluttered.

I was here, I was finally here.

Casper glanced down at the address on the paper, raising one eyebrow and handed it back to me, "I can't read this *vamp* cursive."

I took it from him, amused, "what can't you read? I can read these numbers just fine."

"The street, smart ass. Read it please," he demanded.

I squinted a little at the hard-to-read, wispy lines, "Pointe á La Hache."

As we left the city, the houses became older and more

run down. Each one we passed was raised high on stilts, and the water kissed the edges of the banks beside the road; it felt like we would be swallowed by it with one wrong turn.

"Creepy," he said, watching the edges of the road.

I glanced over at him and squinted my eyes, "stop reading my mind."

He chuckled.

I was glad he was here to keep me from coming undone. If he weren't, I would be chain smoking like a maniac. I had tried so hard to quit since I had got to Vegas. Why exactly? I'm not even sure. *I just wanted to do better.*

We pulled into a narrow, dirt driveway covered by tall cypress trees. My throat suddenly felt tight, and I panicked, "Stop!!"

Casper slammed on the brakes, the branches of the tree scraping along the windshield, "Christ, Celeste! What is it?" he roared.

We were sitting in the middle of a stranger's driveway, someone who didn't know who the fuck I was. Not to mention she was a witch.

Was I walking straight to my death?

Casper watched my face, and I knew he was tapped into my thoughts. I could feel him pushing against my mind as though my thoughts were no longer my own—a prickling of my senses, sort of like when someone was watching you.

"I'm here," was all he said, lifting his foot off the brake and slowly continuing down the drive.

I swallowed, realizing there was no turning back now.

Casper parked the SUV, and we both exited, surveying the house and its surroundings.

268

The front lawn looked wet, and cypress trees surrounded the weathered front porch. The house sat on stilts, about two feet high, and I peeked around Casper's broad shoulders at the surrounding swamp. There was no way out of here, but through to the end of the driveway we just drove down.

Nowhere to go but straight to the alligators.

A black cat sat perched on the railing to the stairs, its black tail ticking and its wide eyes fixated on our still figures.

A screen door slammed, and I heard feet shuffle from the ripped screen, "Come on in now, wouldn't want the Rougarou snatchin' you up."

I walked to the edge of the stairs, grasping the railing and eyeing the cat, who remained where he was, eyes still focused on me.

"Etienna?" I asked, my voice sounding feeble and somewhat childish to my ears.

"I been expectin' you; I knew one day you'd come," she stood with the heavy, black-painted door opened. She wore a tight-fitted, white and purple summer dress that hugged her large chest and very round hips. Her skin was black, and her lipstick matched, a large septum piercing brushing her top lip.

My head felt light, and I blinked my eyes a few times to adjust to the darkness. The house smelled of pepper and oil, and she smiled when I reached her side.

"How? What do you mean you were expect—"

"You're Anise's girl," she said sharply, and the weight of her words landed hard on my chest, "ain't that hard to tell."

Hearing my mother's name still made my knees buckle, but I had overcome all of that.

I am stronger now.

Then why did my body suddenly feel so weak?

My stomach lurched, and the porch began to swim, spinning me until my face was level with the floor, and I heaved all over Etienna's house slippers.

"*Merde,*" she swore under her breath, helping Casper bring me to my feet again.

"I'm sorry. I don't know why." I wiped my mouth with the back of my hoodie's sleeve, trying to acclimate myself to the strange house with the pungent, unfamiliar smell.

Strings of bones hung from the windows, feathers and crystals lined the windowsills.

"The bathroom is there—help her clean up and we can have a chat. I'll make us some tea, yeah?" she shuffled to the kitchen at the back of the house, and Casper led me down a creaky hallway to the bathroom.

"It isn't safe here," he said as he closed the door behind us. I stared at the small sink that looked like it belonged in an outhouse and turned on the water. Cleaning my mouth and face, I turned to him, expecting him to tell me we should leave, "Why?" I asked.

Jars filled with herbs and spices, some with water and a few unidentified objects lined the counter. A small cone of incense burned inside of a skeleton skull. He waved his hand over the array, with a facial expression of shock, "you may have been the one to vomit, but I feel nauseous as fuck—a thing of danger, I've learned."

I rolled my eyes at him and reached for the door, "I'm doing this, and you're not going to stop me. I've been hell bent on coming here since before I met you, so either get on board or get the fuck out."

I exited the bathroom, leaving him behind me, but he stayed close to my back as we entered the sitting area.

He grabbed my hand and yanked me to him, "I'll never leave you."

I smiled at him but continued walking.

Candles were lit throughout the house. I noticed one small lamp in the corner of the room beside a stack of books. A small portion of the area had two overstuffed chairs that looked clean and new, along with a small hutch filled with china. The house looked like a hodge-podge between dark magic and a High-Garden housewife.

I sat with Casper standing beside me, arms behind his back and sunglasses in place. He looked silly, but he was *my* silly bodyguard.

"Is this your chaperone or your boyfriend?" she chuckled, her chest jiggling, and she handed me a steaming cup of tea that looked very dark and foreboding. I set it on the table next to me.

"He's..." I looked up at him, while he adjusted his stance, "my friend,"

Etienna sat beside me, a loud groan escaping her lips as she did.

She sipped her tea in an extended silence that felt like forever, but her face was grim when she met my eyes again.

The mood of the room changed entirely, and the candles around the room extinguished, one by one. Casper lifted his sunglasses off his face, smoke curling around the lifeless pillars, and he looked toward Etienna.

"Now, there's not much you can do to harm a voodoo practitioner like myself, but I've heard of your kind. Are you one of those bloodsuckers?" she chided, sipping her tea.

Casper didn't respond, only shook his head no, stoic as always.

I swallowed, speechless, for once in my life.

Where do I even start?

"I want to know about my mother," I said simply but sat forward in the chair, bringing myself closer to her.

"Ah, there it is. You wish to know about your wily mother and her tricks," she struggled, reaching under the chair and retrieving a black, leather-bound book with stars covering it and handing it to me.

I took the Grimoire; I knew exactly what it was and stroked the soft cover, opening it to a page full of my mother's handwriting. Her natal birth chart was drawn on the first page and her notes about each placement in her chart were jotted around it. I looked down over the words, so familiar yet so strange, and looked back at Etienna.

"Thank you," I said, continuing to flip through the pages.

"This comes with a price. I will tell you the story, but you may not like the truth. Am I clear, *little star*?" she leaned in close to me, our knees nearly touching.

"I didn't know we had guests! Etta, why didn't you come get me?" A greying, white woman stood in the hallway, her hands clasped together at her chest. She wore a collard sweater and khakis, with pearls adorned her ears and neck.

"This is not your concern, Alice. Please leave us," Etienna waved her hand at the woman, but she continued making her way to us.

"Non-sense! Is this the runaway girl? We have been

best friends for years! I know all your secrets," she teased, walking over to us and her expensive perfume was like a breath of fresh—albeit flowery—air.

"Go wait outside, woman! You can have her when I'm finished," Etienna said firmly, and the woman waved her hand, turning toward the back screen door.

"I don't care what it is. I need the truth about my mother, I think someone's cursed our family," I said, grabbing her cold hand.

Etienna looked down at the contact between us but pulled back and began to sputter. She coughed loudly, and her body jerked with the motion, but it wasn't until she was slapping her leg that I realized she was laughing.

I looked at Casper, startled, but his eyes stayed fixed on her and probably on her next move.

Once she gained control of herself again, she said, "Well you came to the right place. If you want that curse reversed—I'm the only one who can do it."

Relief washed over me.

"Thank the Gods. Is it because you are powerful?" I asked, hanging on to her every word.

She laughed low, "Oh no, *Cherie*. It is because I'm the one who called upon the curse."

CHAPTER
THIRTY-SEVEN

Immediately, I sensed Casper's unease, but instead of saying anything, I thought it.

Chill. I want to hear her out. She could have already killed us both by now if she wanted to.

I tried to keep my face as still as possible, even though every emotion I ever had I wore on my face. I maintained control and said, "Tell me everything."

She nodded and reached for one of the books stacked next to the chair. She opened it carefully, and retrieved an old photo, handing it to me.

It was of her and my mother, from the same day as the photo I always carried with me. In this photo, my mother looked older, more beautiful. But there was one thing that was different about this photo, "my father, he's holding your hand..."

She nodded again.

It took me a minute to realize what exactly was happening in this photo. My father was noticeably older than my mother, and they always fought over his constant fear of her cheating and running off with someone else, "Were you two together?"

Etienna took a deep breath and closed her eyes, looking down at the floor. She shook her head gently, "John Luke and I were married, when your mother came to live here,"

What the fuck?

"So, my mother ran away with your husband...my father?" I began to feel dizzy again, wondering if maybe I should just trust Casper and get the hell out of here. A small voice inside of me insisted that I press on; this was part of my story.

"A foolish man, he was. You look a little like him. I should have known better after he left me the first time, but it didn't matter, we were never meant to be. We were unable to bring children into this world... perhaps that is why he wandered."

I sat still, reliving every memory I had of my parents. Their relationship wasn't healthy, they constantly fought, and I had survived on disassociation most days.

My mother told me that she was a runaway; that Etienna found her digging through a restaurant's trash for food and took her home. She taught her about life and magic. What it was like to have a family. I never forgot those stories.

So why would she betray someone who had shown her such understanding?

"I'm so sorry. I can't believe she would do such a—"

She held up her hand, silencing me, "And what pain have you endured because of your mother's mistakes?" she raised one eyebrow.

I looked down at my hands, the chewed cuticles, the

small tattoo of an upside-down cross on my thumb just to piss off my aunt, "Too much."

"Tell me, how did they die?" she hissed, and my eyes began to well, the sting of her words igniting the smell of smoke in my nostrils. The anger and hatred I had for him when he screamed at my mother.

"I...I...set the fucking house on fire, with my rage." I whispered.

Her laugh was maniacal, and Casper gripped me by my arm, pulling me up and out of the chair, "Let's go, Celeste. This bitch is crazy."

"Afraid of an old woman, are you?" she laughed harder now, raspy and deep. The only thought lingering in my mind was that she had the answer. She was the one who held the shadow above me all my life. I wanted it gone, once and for all. I didn't want to worry about the man that I loved dying on me.

The man I loved...shit.

"I don't want to *go*," I gritted up at him, snatching my arm away from his hold.

He rubbed his temple and shook his head, "You *never* fucking listen. I'll be in the SUV when you're finished...*waiting.* Good luck."

He stalked from the small room, slamming the screen door behind him. I suddenly felt very aware of her stare on my back, but I refused to back down now.

"Remove the curse, Etienna. I don't deserve to be punished for my mother's discretions anymore. I've suffered far enough." I stood with both hands on my hips and a wide stance. I glanced around the room, remembering how Casper taught me to funnel my heavy emotions into concentrated action. I found each wick with my eyes, concentrating on the heat building up in my spine. Every candle in the room lit with one bright flash. I smiled, proud of how far I'd come.

Etienna cursed under her breath.

Why should she even reverse the curse? Voodoo practice did not acknowledge the rule of three—the idea that any dark magic would come back to you times three. I had been doing a lot of research with my new fancy phone, and the magic I practiced was not the same as hers.

Etienna was betrayed by *my* mother. Did I deserve punishment for her actions? Absolutely not. Would she dismiss me by telling me she would help but then do nothing? I had to try anyway, for my sanity. This woe had hung above me for far too long. I wanted to put an end to this misery. Today.

"Are you working with a coven? A coven will strengthen your magic and train it like a muscle," she smiled, and I noticed for the first time that one of her canines was missing and replaced with a gold tooth.

I nodded but stayed where I was, near the door.

"I must gather the necessary items, and you will wait. It takes more than just one witch to lift a curse," She stood and began sifting through an apothecary table next to the kitchen.

While Etienna's back was turned, the other woman, Alice, poked her head through the back door and waved me to her silently. Her kind smile pulled me toward her, and I was shaking where I stood now.

I rushed out the door and onto a back deck that looked unfinished. It was the platform only, jutting out behind the house and over the swamp.

I gasped, looking over the edge.

"Sit, darlin'. Let's chit-chat," she said, sitting on the

porch swing that looked more valuable than the house itself.

I sat, smacking a mosquito on my arm but telling myself to take deep breaths while I wasn't in the presence of Etienna. She scared me down to my bones.

She patted my leg, picking up on my nervous movements, "she ain't so scary, really. She's a big ole' puppy dog in wolf's clothing."

"I just want this curse to be over. I don't want to spend another minute thinking about it. Life is too short as it is," I said, picking at the split ends of my red hair.

"She will help you; I know there is a goodness inside of her. We've been friends for a long, long time and if we never met—I'm not sure she would still be here."

"Is she sick or something?" I asked, suddenly interested more in their relationship than my bad luck.

Alice sighed, "In a way...yes. The demons, they speak to her too often, and some days are harder than others. I support her practice, but she has medicine for the voices, and if I wasn't here, she wouldn't take them. Pills don't fit into nature."

Witchcraft and insanity were too closely associated, and I knew that from a very young age. It was something you hid from people and never talked about freely for fear you would be called 'crazy.' It always confused me why most religions allowed almost the exact same practices, but once Jesus was removed from the equation—you were blasphemous, considered evil.

"Oh," Was all I could manage.

"Sometimes I come out here 'round nighttime, and I just listen to the big bullfrogs singin'. It's like a bedtime lullaby," she said, looking out over the still, murky water.

"I guess I would be worried about an alligator eating me alive if I lived out here," I laughed quietly.

"They don't bother people if you keep your distance. Nothin' but lore and tall tales 'round here," she said, adjusting her necklace.

A warm breeze blew in, moving my hair gently away from my face. A memory of my mother's soft hand brushing my cheek incurred a small sob in my throat. I held back the tears, but Alice was too close to me not to notice, and she put her arm around my shoulder and pulled me into her chest.

"Maybe I don't deserve to be happy. I'm not worthy of peace and love. It's always just chaos and fire, followed by smoke," I struggled out, treading lightly with what I said since I barely knew this kind woman.

Years of pent-up sadness suddenly came pouring out of me at this woman's words.

"But you *are* worthy, Celeste," She squeezed me, the warmth of her body pressed to my side. I allowed myself to rest my head on her shoulder and *feel*.

"Some can *see* energy and you...you can *use* energy. Most importantly, you can *sense* it. I know the power you hold inside of you; Etienna has told me of it."

Her voice was as soft as flower petals, and she kissed the center of my forehead before giving my shoulder one final squeeze.

I let two fat teardrops fall from my eyes and wiped my nose with the back of my hand.

"What is it, lovely? You can tell me, it's okay. There, there," Alice pulled me close. I needed to forgive myself for all of their deaths, "You have had a large burden to bear, Celeste. Believe me, I have heard. But take your power back and use it in a way that can help others to be open. Open to all of what life has to offer them...even magic."

I sat up, moving away from her a little but took both of her hands into mine, feeling the closest thing I have to any maternal kind of love since my mother.

Etienna may be the strong one here, but Alice was the spiritual one; that was clear.

"Well, have some sweet tea then, darlin'. That always does the trick for me. The best remedy for tears is tea," Alice struggled to get up from the swing, and I shot up quickly from the seat, helping her to stand. I pushed the nausea this house kept conjuring in me away.

I tried picturing what it would have been like to grow up here, like her.

I am always with you, little star.

I took one last look at the bayou behind me, the sun moving higher in the sky as it lined the edges of the swamp with orange and pink. The water gently moved with whatever lurked under its murky surface.

I hoped this was the last time I would ever have to worry about Death, his dark spirit hovering over me like an alligator ready to strike.

I walked numbly back inside the house, following Alice, who was speaking low to Etienna in the kitchen.

Etienna sidled up to me again, "You come back here tomorrow night, and bring your muscle man with you. You might need him."

"Are you going to help me? I need to know. If this curse was set by you, it is only right that you give me that peace of mind and maybe I can sleep tonight." I begged.

She stayed silent for a moment, but eventually she answered,

"I will. You have my word."

THIRTY-EIGHT

CASPER

I had seen some wild things in my life but witnessing Voo-doo magic wasn't one of them.

Not going to lie; that woman had me shaking in my boots.

I was proud of Celeste for holding her ground and even more excited knowing she had her powers.

I didn't need to worry about her half as much.

As we drove back to the mansion, I could only think about was the conversation Domenico and a mystery caller had the night before.

I had a bad habit of waking in the middle of the night for a snack, and my military training made it hard not to notice what was happening around me, in secret or not.

I knew where his office was, and it was conveniently located near the kitchen. I took advantage and listened silently: '...*they will die, but who cares? We can find more thanks to Marisela.*'

Mar was known for her divinity and finding other gifted people, but I had no idea she was also feeding the vampires.

I never could shake the suspicion that Domenico had Opal—I always took notice of their private talks and his sudden interest in her. I just didn't realize he would go as far as impregnating her—who would have thought a vamp could breed with a Starseed?

When I made my way back to her bedroom that night, I wondered if I should scare her with this new knowledge or just keep it to myself.

Ultimately, I realized she would figure it out on her own. She was a smart girl.

"Look—all of these are love spells! My mother was obsessed with love," she said as she traced the words with her fingers.

I didn't pay much attention as I ate the bagel and cream cheese on my plate.

She opened her mouth, and I fed her a bite, smiling at how her nose scrunched up as she chewed.

"Sounds like your mom had some pretty wild interests," I said, trying not to sound too judgmental.

She crooked an eyebrow but kept skimming the pages.

"Is there anything in there worth noting?" I asked in between bites.

"Not really, it's a lot of drawn birth charts. There is a

section of notes about vampires, but it looks like she couldn't prove anything...."

I rolled my eyes, knowing I had seen enough to believe in them.

"Put it down, you need sleep. If you want a clear head tomorrow, you should just lay your head on my chest and give in, pequeña." I smiled, and she smiled back.

She closed the book but tucked it deep inside the pillows.

"You're right, as always."

CHAPTER
THIRTY-NINE

The vibe the next night as we arrived at Etienna's, was the total opposite of the night we met the two older women for the first time.

Music played outside, floating up among the cypress trees, the greenery hanging down to the ground. An upbeat groove played and had the guests swaying to the beat.

Etienna was straight up having an outdoor party.

Casper stood beside me, his hand firmly placed on my lower back, and standing in front of him, I reached back to take his other hand in mine. I squeezed it, smiling up at his beaming face.

I slept restlessly and tossed and turned under the soft murmurs of Casper's comfort. I may have felt the turmoil from yesterday's events, but Death did not visit me while I was resting in Casper's arms that night.

He bent down and kissed my lips softly, and we walked toward Etienna hand in hand.

"Welcome, welcome. Are you ready, my dear? Did you

bring the Grimoire?" she asked with her hands on her hips and her voice stern and proud.

My stomach turned, and I gripped the book I held close to my chest with my free hand, "I have it."

I kept it close as we walked to the enormous fire that burned in the middle of a small patch of green near the shaded forest. Rocks surrounded it, sigils and symbols scrawled onto each one with coal.

Alice wore a dress that was yellow with intricate and bright patterns sewn on the breast. Her hair was almost completely white, and she waved at us with both of her hands. I instantly felt more relaxed once I made eye contact with Alice.

"I will require a payment, for this service," Etienna's voice cut my happy thought short, and I looked at her, confused.

"Payment? What kind of payment?" I asked, still holding the book to my chest; it smelled musty and old, and I loved it.

Etienna inched closer to me, eyeing Casper and not me, "I want that necklace around your *dainty* neck," She sneered, pulling her head high.

This was my mother's necklace and almost the only thing I had left of her besides the wooden box it came in. My belly began to burn with a deep hatred for this woman.

Maybe she deserved betrayal.

"This was my mother's."

"And so was that," she replied, pointing to the book I held so tightly.

Tentatively, I handed over the book to Cas, and he took it, "Thank you, Papi," I tried my best to pronounce it correctly, and he smiled.

I reached around to the back of my neck where the clasp was. I pulled the small lever out, the chain loosening and falling into my palm. I handed it to her, and her eyes were wide, focused on the pink crystal I held out in my palm.

Etienna tucked it into her dress pocket, and smiled, two teeth missing on each side of her mouth, "let's begin."

The black cat from yesterday sidled between my legs and nearly tripped me. Etienna called to him, "Come, come, Boudreaux. She means no harm."

I stopped, the cat hissing in my direction, then running off behind Etienna. Etienna reached down to grab the cat by the scruff of the neck.

I counted each woman that surrounded the fire, eight in total. Each one had a different skin color, some lighter and some dark as midnight. Most of them wore colorful turbans and wore their hair in braids with beads.

Before we left yesterday, Etienna instructed me to take a bath in salt, lemon, and pepper. When I was finished, I took a mason jar and filled it.

"Did you do what I told ya?"

I nodded, pulling the small jar out of the bag at my side.

"Drink it."

I didn't hesitate and knocked it back.

I watched Casper wince out of the corner of my eye. I coughed and gagged.

I texted Sapph last night before the bath and told her exactly what Etienna had directed me to do. She told me what the next step would be. I half expected her to say I would need to drink it. I think I was getting the hang of this witchy stuff.

All eight women stood around the fire, holding hands. Etienna still held the cat by the scruff of his neck, the cat struggling to get free.

A mirror pointed at the fire was set up against a small tree stump nearby. Herbs of hyssop and frankincense permeated the air as Etienna tossed them into the fire, chanting something so low I couldn't make it out.

With the noises of celebration all around us, my hands shook as I took in the ritual that was taking place before me. Their bodies swayed, and the chanting became a low hum, making my hair stand on end.

In one violent movement, Etienna cut the cat';s throat, spilling blood onto the ground beneath her feet. I gasped, grabbing onto Casper, who stood firmly in place, keeping his eyes on the horrific scene.

"Step into the circle, now," Etienna called to me while she poured spiced rum into the brass cup at the edge of the circle, the animal's blood along with it.

The warm breeze stroked my face, and I breathed in deeply, silently chanting my spell for protection, even though I felt naked without my mother's stone.

Grabbing the grimoire from Casper, I held it to my chest.

The thick Louisiana humidity clung to my skin, and small beads of sweat dotted my chest and forehead.

Captivated by their chants and movements, I slowly walked toward the circle next to Alice. The mirror on the other side looked as if it were alive, casting the reflection of the fire within it.

"Join me, Celeste. This must be done with your blood," Alice reached for me, and I numbly accepted her hand.

I watched as Etienna grabbed my forearm and

scratched a thin line across my skin, and I took a sharp intake of breath. My throat felt tight, and I struggled not to choke. My limbs felt heavy, and I glanced over my shoulder to ensure Casper was still with me.

Stay close. I willed myself to share with him.

The world spun around me, waves and lines blurring my vision.

The thick liquid oozed down my arm and into the cup below. The women to her left, who looked like blurry figments now, lifted a piece of paper and held it over the fire, setting it alight and dropping it into the bowl.

I watched as a figure stood, just beyond the fire, as if emerging from the mirror itself. I squinted, not trusting my wavering focus. A tall, black top hat and a face that was painted like a skull, only it wasn't paint, it was Death's face.

Goosebumps prickled my skin, and the hairs on the back of my neck stood on end.

"No fucking way," I felt my legs weaken, and the ground started to tremble.

My body went slack, and Casper wrapped his arm around my waist before I could fall. His senses prodded my mind as everything went black.

When I sat up again, the world was still spinning, but I could make out the dark figure as it walked slowly towards the circle. Shaky and skulking, he made his way to the circle of witches as they continued to chant.

Was I the only one who could see him?

I was paralyzed and unable to move; I could feel Casper's heavy breathing on my neck, "Lets, go, *now*," He growled in my ear.

I kept my eyes on the creature that had haunted my dreams for so many years as a child. An odd familiarity and a sick feeling began deep in my gut. I swallowed, sweat trickling down the small of my back. I aggressively shook my head no.

Before anyone could react, he was on top of Alice, directly beside me. She screamed as Etienna yelled obscenities. I watched as Etienna grabbed for him and her hands simply passed through his body.

"She is here! Legba, take her and not my Alice!" she howled, pointing her finger to me. Blood gushed down its painted white face and a low laugh-growl escaped from his horrifyingly open mouth.

I felt faint as if my eyes had deceived me and my brain couldn't keep up with what I was witnessing.

Not Alice...

I felt a sob rise in my throat, and Casper pulled me to my feet. I looked back at the scene, screams filling my ears, running my blood cold. The mirror that had been resting against the tree was shattered.

We ran to the SUV, and I couldn't feel my legs moving until I was scooting myself into the passenger seat of Casper's car.

Casper slammed his door shut and turned on the ignition, whipping it into drive. Tears rolled down my face, and I sobbed into my hands.

She had tricked me...she had lied to me...I should have known as soon as she took the crystal from me.

What had I done? Why did I keep pushing for these answers when I should have been trying to escape it? And now, an innocent life was taken because of it, again.

"I need a goddamned cigarette," I rifled around my bag, reaching for the pack I'd been ignoring for a week, and lit up an unfiltered American Spirit, rolling down the window and taking a long drag.

My mother's prayer ran through my mind, again and again, as if I needed to keep saying to keep myself safe from him:

Maman Brigitte, it is I who am calling you, do you see me? This smoke is for you. Maman, please give me protection.

Gentlemen of the cross, my deceased ancestors, advance for her to see

them!

Maman Brigitte is sick; she lies down on her back,

A lot of talks won't raise the dead,

Tie up your head, tie up your belly, tie up your kidneys,

They will see how they will get down on their knees.

The further we drove away from her house, the lighter I began to feel. My head wasn't throbbing, and aside from the nicotine buzz, I felt something inside of me shift.

A weight lifted from my heart.

Had that done it? Was the curse lifted because of Alice's sacrifice? I felt relief and guilt roll through me at the same time.

I flicked the butt out the window and sunk deeper into the seat. Casper reached over to rub my thigh, "I don't think I've ever said this but—holy shit that was crazy."

I looked at how his face lit up when he looked at me, and I felt warm inside. I let out a small laugh, "Yeah it was. Something neither of us will ever forget."

I placed my hand on top of his, leaning my head back against the seat and closing my eyes. I felt drowsy, and my body melted into a completely dreamless sleep.

CHAPTER
FORTY

When we returned to Domenico's house, fancy cars filled the driveway and surrounding grass. It was late and the night sky glimmered with stars.

"What the hell is going on?" I asked no one in particular as I opened my car door. My body felt heavy, and I still wore my denim cut-offs and hoodie, my hair in tangles around my shoulders. I pulled on my hood while classical music wafted from the open windows, and Casper walked with me through the door.

We were greeted by Ruby and Marisela, running down the lit walkway.

"Did she do it? Did she help you lift the curse?" Marisela asked, linking her arm through mine.

She was wearing a tight-fitting black dress with a one-shouldered white strap. Her dark hair was piled high on her head, and her makeup created sharp cheekbones and a cat-eye.

I rubbed my forehead, trying to convey my exhaustion, "I think so. Yeah. I really just want to climb into bed."

"No! You can't *just go to bed*. This party is for you! From Domenico!" she pulled me along while I rolled my eyes.

When we finally got inside, they had decorated the house in the colors of Mardi Gras; purple and green. 'Congratulations' in glittery, silver letters hung above the back balcony doors.

This felt wrong on so many levels, and I was not in the right headspace for a party. It felt downright inappropriate.

Celebrations were thrown in happiness and excitement for dreams and goals. Having a dark shadow lifted from my life by sacrificing of another. At least, it wasn't one of them.

"I don't know Mar...I don't even know anyone here."

"Que?! All the girls are here!"

I turned, and behind us was Ruby, Sapph, Jade...and Opal.

I hugged Sapph, and Ruby side-eyed me while she sipped on her champagne flute.

"My father threw parties *much* bigger than this back in New York."

I wasn't sure what she was talking about, but if I were going to participate then I would need to change.

I just want to climb into bed with Casper and never leave...preferably with a nice fat blunt.

"I really thought you would be happy. I helped him plan this," Mar gloated, looking at the decorated great room.

"So, are you two together now?"

She looked down at her heels, then lifted a champagne glass to her red lips, "It's complicated."

Casper stood beside me and reached out his hand to mine. I took it, following him back to our rooms.

Before we parted ways, he faced me and knelt.

"Um, what the fuck are you doing?"

He pulled me to him, by my waist, his head level with my chest.

"Before this shit gets even crazier. I want you to know I am yours, however you need me. I will follow you, wherever this insanity takes you...or...us. Witches, vampires, or any other monster that comes for you. I'll be right behind you."

I ran my fingers thru his curls and smiled, warmth filling me. It wasn't in the chaotic way it used to feel like.

I leaned down and kissed him, running my thumb along his full, lower lip.

"Thank you."

"I've never met a woman like you; so fierce, strong and un-giving of fucks," he laughed nervously, and I silently prayed he wasn't about to propose to me, "I...I love you."

It felt like I had been punched in the chest, and I sank to my knees with him, closing my eyes and wrapping my arms tightly around his shoulders, burying my face in his neck.

No one had ever told me they loved me besides my mother.

I let the tears fall and pressed my cheek to his, "You saved me and for that, I love you more than you will ever understand."

He stood, helping me up with him, and we looked

down the hallway together, eyes lingering on the crowd of people.

"I'm going to change," I whispered.

As I turned to my room, he yanked my arm and pulled me to him again, kissing me deeply.

"I'll be waiting, always."

I traded my tattered clothes for a little black dress.

I walked down the hallway to return to the noise of people talking and glasses clinking. I surveyed the room for Casper, but he was nowhere in sight, and his bedroom door was ajar but empty.

I had no desire to put on a happy face and mingle with *anyone*. I felt like I could sleep for days, and a new desire to stay in one place and rest came over me.

A tall, hooded figure caught my eye as I approached the dining room, littered with drinks and appetizers.

Taj?

His light eyes were uncovered; it was the first time I noticed one pointed fang at the corner of his smile. He raised his champagne glass, his long fingernails glittering beneath the lights.

Well, well. I guess that explains a lot.

As I took a step toward Taj, I felt a cool chain kiss my neck from behind, and a heavy crystal landed in the middle of my breast. I cupped it with my hand, smiling at the rich blue color.

"Your neck looked very naked without a necklace, I thought this would look most adoring in the middle of your creamy décolletage."

I turned to find Domenico's handsome face and chiseled cheeks smiling down at me.

I looked down at it again, "It's stunning."

"This stone is rare, a blue Lapis from South America. The ancient Egyptians, or Sumerians depending on who you ask, thought it came directly from the Gods of the night sky," he said, his demeanor always well-manicured and sophisticated.

"Thank you."

"Follow me, I have something to show you," he took my hand in his cold one.

My stomach fluttered, and I did as he said.

He led me down to a wine cellar just off the chef's kitchen. I looked over my shoulder before we descended, finding it strange that Casper was not on my heels.

The floors were a deep red and shined like gloss. Thousands of wine bottles lined the room, and Domenico looked back at me, marveling at the display.

"When you're as old as I am, you tend to collect things. Special things. Some of these wines date back to 1749."

I ran a finger over one label written in French, with not a speck of dust on it.

"I guess I wouldn't expect anything less from a wealthy vampire," I smiled, but crossed my arms over my chest, feeling the chill from down here. I began to shiver.

"You are very sensitive to the cold, no?" he said, circling me.

"I mean, I guess so. No one really likes to be cold."

"Ah, well, being cold is something that comes along with your blood...amongst other things," he laughed, one that sent a chill to the inside of my ears and down my spine.

"You are magnificent, and of course, almost a perfect copy of her," he circled closer to me now, pushing my hair back over my shoulder.

"I'm sorry...who?" I asked, feeling the chill creep to my fingertips.

He paused his circling, biting his lip, "Lilith."

I had no idea who he was talking about, and the only woman I had ever heard of with that name was the woman who was kicked out of the Garden of Eden for not submitting to Adam. My aunt had called me blasphemous when I asked her who she was. My mother had been the one to teach me.

"Little *Starseed...*"

I flinched at the name my mother used to call me, now I knew something wasn't right.

"H-h...how do you know that *name*? It was what my mother used to call me."

He laughed low, "I am well aware of your mother *and* her indiscretions."

I started to back away, towards the stairs, "You knew her?"

I suddenly felt dizzy.

"Of course. How do you think I knew where the Voodoo practitioner resided?" he said, stroking my face.

"I dunno...well connected," I said, the back of my heel making contact with the bottom step.

He laughed low again, making me swallow. He was

nearly toe to toe with me, and I could smell his expensive cologne.

"You see, Celeste, I've known your family for *centuries*. Of course, I had to be sure you were what I thought you were before I invested much more time. Hence the vampire you were gifted too that night,"

I blinked a few times, remembering him talking about 'a gift'.

That must have been why I never heard about the dead dude again.

"You do not even *realize* the weapon between your legs, *mon cherie*. My succubus queen with blood that tastes so sweet. We have once again been reunited," He brought his hand to my cheek again, stroking it with the back of his bony fingers.

I smacked his hand away, feeling the urgency to find Casper.

Weapon? Was he referring to the curse? Did he know about the others?

"Wait, *weapon?* That can't be true. I slept with Casper and he's not dead." I blurted.

"Ahh, I knew there was something between the two of you. The only thing I know of that can stop it, is *real* love."

My mind spun; that would mean everyone I had slept with, I never loved, even my high school sweetheart.

I loved Casper?

"I don't believe you."

"Believe it, my darling. You are mine, once again. I will always find you," he sneered.

"I'm not *yours*," I gritted.

I turned up the stairs and ran, not checking to see if he was following behind me. My heels clicked up the expensive, polished wood. When I made it to the top, I ran straight into Casper.

"Are you ok? What happened?"

I swallowed, but I smiled at him, happy to feel his warm embrace, "Nothing...nothing, I'm fine. Domenico was just showing me his wine cellar."

I'm not sure why I lied, but I wanted to get back to Vegas and my car as soon as possible.

"You are a lying, deceiving BASTARD!"

We both turned to the front door at the same time, and Moxie stood in the foyer looking like a woman possessed.

"Where is he? Where is Domenico!? That filthy blood-drinker has taken my Marisela straight to the underworld with him!"

Alex rushed to her side, taking her arm and hushing her. She ripped it away from him and cursed.

Marisela stood in the adjacent kitchen, staring.

Moxie stormed over to Mar and slapped her face, a loud smack filling the quiet room, "How could you do this to me? I never want to see you again!"

CHAPTER
FORTY-ONE

M oments after Moxie's dramatic departure, Domenico appeared in the center of the room, "Please, everyone, continue your celebrations. Everything is just fine."

I didn't know what any of this meant for me, and how did I know I could even believe what he said? A succubus? Wasn't that just a myth? Besides, the power I held was controlled now, and he mentioned nothing of the fire that ran thru my veins.

I would never be his 'Queen,' and I would run as far away from him as I needed to.

I made my way to the bathroom, needing a break from the chatter and the stares.

I sat on the toilet to pee, and no sooner did the stream begin did Marisela and Ruby were barging their way inside.

"What the fuck?! I'm trying to piss!"

Ruby sat on the edge of the jacuzzi tub, looking bored, and Mar leaned against the jack and jill, white granite countertop, "Listen Celeste, you can't go back to Vegas.

You need to come with us...with Domenico," Mar said, a seriousness in her tone.

I looked at Ruby, and she shrugged, "I want more, I want to be *wealthy* again."

I grabbed toilet paper and wiped, careful not to drop my dress in the can.

I flushed, purposely making them wait for my response. I didn't even know what I wanted to do.

"What about the others? Sapph? Jade?" I asked, caring more about what Sapph had to say about it than Jade.

They both looked at one another silently.

"They aren't sure, but I'm betting if you're on board, they will be too."

I watched Mar closely; she looked thinner and less vibrant than when I first met her. It made me a little sad for the friend she used to be. I could only imagine what that felt like as a mother.

I thought back to how he made me feel in the basement: slimy and cornered.

I wanted to be wealthy too, but that seemed like a high price if it involved Domenico. Casper would never go for it...

"I don't know."

"Ruby! Are you in there!? We need you!" Sapph shouted through the door, "Hurry up! Opal is in labor!"

All three of us ran towards the commotion. Opal was on the large couch in the great room, clutching her belly and looking terrified.

"Why do they need *you*?" I asked Ruby, realizing my tone was just a little bitchy.

"I've delivered a baby before...one of my father's housekeepers,"

Damn, there was more to Ruby than I had originally thought.

Opal was panting hard, and the dress she wore was wet, a clear sign of her water breaking.

Shit.

"Alex! Come help me!" Ruby called, immediately acting and lifting the hem of Opal's dress. Alex moved beside her, obeying.

"What do I do? I've never done anything like this before, Ru- fuck!"

Alex said, and I almost laughed at his scared expression.

"Shit! There's too much blood, something's not right."

As soon as the word *blood* left her lips, the growling began.

I looked behind us, past Casper, and watched in shock as each vampire in the room bared their fangs. A woman dressed in a navy tux licked her lips, and her eyes were large black discs of darkness.

Bloodlust.

The room erupted in shrieks and yells as the vampires

began to grab the closest, warm, beating neck they could find. Blood spilled onto the floors and Opal screamed and cried at the same time.

"Carry her outside!" I yelled, running for the back balcony doors, "Hurry!"

Mar stayed behind, the vampires charging forward and around her. She disappeared into the crowd, and I didn't stick around to see if she would follow us.

Alex scooped her up, Ruby and Sapphire following closely behind.

Casper slammed the French doors shut after we were safely outside on the patio. The doors shuttered as the vampires tried to escape.

"What do we do? There's no way that door will hold!" Sapph shrieked, panic in her voice.

"Are you in a lot of pain, Opal?" Ruby asked, inserting her hand under the dress once again. Opal shook her head yes furiously.

She was disturbingly pale.

At the end of the green backyard was a large helicopter. I looked at Casper and smiled, "Can you drive one of those?"

He followed my eyes, then looked back to me, "Probably, but we'll need the keys."

"It's not a military copter, dumbass, you don't need keys," Alex interjected.

Casper ran to the helicopter, flinging open the door and hopping inside.

I had to stall the vamps and knew there was only one way to do it.

I would have to use my fire magic.

The force of the wind as Casper fired up the copter

had hair and dresses swirling through the air, and I turned back toward the house.

I heard Casper and Ruby yelling my name, but I knew a lock wouldn't hold them in place for very long—not enough time for us to get Opal inside safely.

Moxie ran to the group from the front of the house, her makeup smeared as if she had been crying. I tried to imagine what it would feel like to lose a child, but I couldn't put myself there because I was only a child when I lost my parents.

I looked over my shoulder as they worked together to lift Opal inside while Casper watched me in terror.

I stalked to the heavy double doors, placing both hands on the handles. I could hear their feral growls, and heat ran through my veins as the doors shook.

I closed my eyes, remembering the night of the fire, the night my father struck my mother so hard that I leaped onto his back, scratching and biting at his head until he flung me to the floor.

My mother's voice screamed for me to go downstairs —lock myself in my room with Logan.

I did as she said, only my rage sparked an uncontrollable fire that would never be contained.

A powerful wind picked up around me, and all the rage, sadness, and despair unfurled from me like a storm.

When I opened my eyes, the gardens surrounding the house smoldered. I stepped back as I watched the house disappear behind a wall of flames.

I turned and ran back to the helicopter, Alex and Ruby hanging out of the side with their arms outstretched to me.

I grabbed their hands as they hoisted me inside, just as Casper eased it off the ground.

I hadn't seen Domenico since our conversation in the wine cellar, and part of me hoped that the house could be saved.

I didn't know where we were going, and I didn't know who's side I was on. If there wasn't a war between the vampires and witches yet, there would be now, and all I knew was that I needed to be with my family- the Coven of Crystals.

Book Two: **Ruins of Ruby...coming soon**

Acknowledgments

Firstly, I have to give a warm thank you to my writer wifey, H.L. Hines. You talked me through so many block-ages, and were my sounding board so many times. I adore you, and we are never ever getting divorced.

Ayden P- my other Alpha reader who always tells me where it needed to be smuttier. I couldn't have finished this book without you.

Michelle, you developmental edited your ass off on this story, and you are never getting rid of me. Thank you from the bottom of my heart.

Thank you to Teresa at Wolfsparrow pub for the cover that brought Celeste to life.

And my girl, Lo. Thank you for bringing to light all the sensitive issues there are when it comes to writing BIPOC characters. Thank you for being a guiding light for me.

And to my readers, there's so many of you that have been with me from the very beginning, and watched me grow. Thank you so much for loving my smexy albeit sometimes weird ideas.

About the Author

Savvy Rose is a self-published author of Dark Romance, Erotic thrillers and Paranormal Romance.

Her writing began in middle school and continued through High school, fueled by her love of Poetry by the likes of Poe, Bukowski and Shakespeare.

She enjoys writing about magical and complicated people, with steamy romance and thrilling adventures.

When she isn't writing, she enjoys spending time with her husband and children in New York.

Her many hobbies include: Art, Astrology, Music, Spiritual study and most of all, reading.

Most nights you can find her drinking wine and ugly crying over foreign films, cleansing her house and dancing naked under the full moon.

You can find free chapters and short stories on her website

www.savvyroseauthor.com

ALSO BY

The Beautifully Broken Series:

Tangled Garden

Twice as Twisted

Forbidden Fables:

The Wolf of the Woods

The Wicked Witch of the Woods- coming November 2022

Coven of Crystals:

Chasing Celeste

Ruins of Ruby- release date TBD